MESSAGE FROM A KILLER

Turner and I would manage, but it wouldn't be pretty. I'd hired him a couple of years ago because the restaurant had gotten so popular it was hard for only Danna and me to keep all our diners happy. Len wasn't usually available on weekdays. Adele helped out sometimes, but she was currently out of the country. I could ask Phil, who also knew the routine, but it depended on his schedule. And Abe would be at work. Turner and I had no choice but to manage.

I'd better get my beauty sleep while I could. I stuck the phone under my chin so I could clear the table with both hands. I was halfway to the door when it buzzed again. I nudged open the door with my foot. Birdy raced in ahead of me, following his operating principle of, *Whatever is on the other side of any door is always more interesting than where I am.*

Dishes on counter, door shut and locked, and cat door also secured, I frowned at the phone. No number was listed on the text, only *Private*. I opened the message. And gasped.

We know about you. Butt out of the case or you'll regret it . . .

A Country Store Mystery

Batter Off Dead

MADDIE DAY

Kensington Publishing Corp.
www.kensingtonbooks.com

For my favorite bakers: my sisters, Barbara and Janet; our mother, Marilyn; and our grandmothers, Ruth and Dorothy. These women nourished—and continue to nourish—family and friends, one cookie at a time.

ACKNOWLEDGMENTS

In the previous book in this series, *No Grater Crime*, Buck Bird mentions that his mother was murdered when he was a teenager. After John Scognamiglio, my fabulous Kensington editor, read the manuscript, he said he expected the next book would address that murder. I hadn't made Buck tell Robbie about the murder on purpose, but John's idea was a brilliant one (that's why he's the big cheese over there!). Many thanks to him and the crack crew at Kensington Publishing, including publicist Larissa Ackerman and amazing cover artist Ben Perini, for keeping this series going to book ten and beyond, and to my agent, John Talbot, for boosting my dream of the series in the beginning.

Thanks to my much taller partner, Hugh Lockhart, for acting out the attack scene with me, on my request. It's always handy to have a willing (mostly) partner in crime around the house.

Adrienne Linnell was the high bidder on naming rights to a character in this book at the Merrimack Feline Rescue Society Fur Ball auction. She asked if she could honor her late mother-in-law, Joan Warner Linnell, as well as Joan's late sister, Edna Warner, if she made a further donation to the kitties. Of course, I agreed. Adrienne told me both were avid readers of mystery fiction and had enjoyed several earlier books of mine she had given them. Thank you for supporting our wonderful no-kill shelter, Adrienne, and I hope you enjoy Joan and Edna's roles in the book.

The book features a good number of senior citizens, including Buck's father and grandmother. I've always enjoyed the company of my elders and still do, even as my age draws shockingly closer to theirs. I owe a big debt to my late friends Annie and Richard and to the blessedly still living Sam and Joan Baily, plus my uncle Richard Reinhardt. They all inspire me to live my best life.

Many thanks to my niece, Sarah Baier, for helping me with writing the Cornerstone Connections folks. She has worked with a population like theirs for many years. Gratiude, as well, to my northern Indiana sister, Barbara Bergendorf, for lending me her popular Snickerdoodle recipe. Robin Agnew let me use the name of Aunt Agatha's, the mystery bookstore she owns with her husband, Jamie, a formerly brick-and-mortar shop in Ann Arbor, Michigan. Thanks, Robin!

Once again Sherry Harris lent her eagle editor's eye to the manuscript, making Robbie a better person and helping me untangle an unnecessarily snarled skein of a story. I seriously couldn't do it without you, Sherry. She and the other Wicked Authors keep me sane (as far as that's possible), especially during the tough year-plus of the pandemic. Thank you, ladies, brilliant authors to a one: Barbara Ross, Julia Henry, Sherry Harris, Jessica Ellicott, and Cate Conte (and all their other names).

Batter Off Dead is the tenth Country Store Mystery. When Robbie opened Pans 'N Pancakes in *Flipped for Murder,* I had no idea if readers would fall in love with her and South Lick, Indiana, and I'm delighted you all have. Thank you for your enthusiasm for my fictional community, for buying the books or asking your library to, for your reviews and recommendations, and for your kind notes about how much joy my stories bring you.

CHAPTER 1

"This kind of weather could make anybody commit murder."

"Abe, don't say that." I twisted my head to stare at my husband of six weeks, seated in the camp chair next to mine in Jupiter Park, waiting for the weekly Friday night South Lick fireworks.

"I hope it doesn't, Robbie." He blotted his brow with a folded handkerchief. "But you have to admit, it's stinking hot, even now, at nine o'clock."

"I know. And hot can lead to tempers." This July had broken records for heat here in southern Indiana, and tonight, the temperature was not falling in tandem with the midsummer dusk. I patted my own forehead and neck with a turquoise bandanna. What made it worse was the humid air sitting as still as the water in the pond. Not a breath of breeze moved to alleviate the oppressive evening.

"With any luck, whoever gets mad will be too wiped by the temperature to do anything about it," Abe said.

We'd set up our chairs at the edge of the park, which gave me a good vantage point to see who was there. "It looks like Buck is helping out with weapons checking." I pointed toward the entrance, where tall, lanky Lieutenant Buck Bird in uniform stood with arms folded, shaking his head at a couple of young dudes. While it was legal for civilians to carry guns in the state, a town ordinance prohibited them from municipal gatherings like this one.

"Boggles the mind, doesn't it?" Abe asked. "The ordinance is posted right there at the gate."

I glanced at my metal water bottle, which tonight held a refreshing white wine spritzer. Alcohol was off-limits, too. I gave a little mental shrug. I was a married woman of thirty with a handsome designated driver and no intentions of getting rowdy. Judging by the relaxed appearance of other spectators holding opaque water bottles, I might not be the only wrongdoer.

Buck sauntered over. "Howdy, there, Robbie. O'Neil."

Abe stood and shook Buck's hand. "Were those guys giving you trouble?" He gestured toward the entrance, where another officer now stood guard.

"Not really. I've knowed 'em since they were snotty-nosed tykes. They didn't dare give me no lip. Say, my pop is over yonder. I wondered if y'all wanted to meet him."

I set down my bottle and rose. "I'd love to, Buck. We still have half an hour until the fireworks, don't we?"

"Yup."

"I'll stay and watch the chairs," Abe said.

I expected he might have a quick catnap, too. We were both super-early risers. After I'd closed Pans 'N Pancakes, my country store restaurant, and finished breakfast prep for tomorrow, I had grabbed a little rest this afternoon. Abe, on the other hand, had helped his teenage son, Sean, pack to spend a week camping with his grandparents. Sean, now motherless, was a great kid, and I loved having him and his black Lab, Cocoa, live with us. Still, Abe and I both looked forward to having the house to ourselves for a bit. They'd taken the large and energetic pooch with them, so we didn't have him to walk and feed.

As I left with Buck, a man's voice said, "Abe, my man." I glanced back to see Abe greet a petite man, the two exchanging a bent-elbow hand clasp. So much for Abe's nap. I thought I might have seen the guy playing at a bluegrass concert last June.

I walked with Buck toward a line of chairs holding senior citizens at the rear of the crowd. They sat in front of the woods that formed part of the park, not far from the restroom building at the back. "Does your dad live around here?" I asked.

"He surely does, over to the Jupiter Springs Assisted Living place. Just so's you know, he's blind, but it don't hold him back none. The man is adaptable as all get-out."

We reached the group.

"Evenin' there, Miz Vi," Buck said to a tiny woman who sat knitting. "Hey, Pop. This here is my friend, Robbie Jordan. Robbie, please meet Grant Bird and Vi Perkell."

Grant also held a knitting project in his lap, his fingers deftly clicking the needles through forest-green yarn. He glanced up. "Forgive me if I don't get up, Miz Jordan.

Once I drop a stitch, it's a lost cause." He was an older version of Buck, with the same long limbs but way more lines in his face and thin gray hair that might or might not have been combed before he left his residence.

"Please don't do either," I said. "I'm happy to meet you both."

Despite the heat, Vi wore a red cotton scarf wrapped around the neck of a pink-flowered blouse. She peered up at me. "Aren't you the girl who runs the best restaurant in town?" Her high voice was as birdlike as the rest of her.

"People do seem to enjoy coming in for breakfast or lunch," I said. "I'm happy you've heard good things about my place. Have you been in to eat?"

"Not yet," Vi replied.

"Breakfast is the best meal of the day, I always said, didn't I, Buckham?" Grant asked his son with a toothy smile.

"You did, Pop, and you'd be right. Jupiter Springs should oughta round up the crew of you and load up that bus of theirs, drive it over to Pans 'N Pancakes."

A thin woman sitting beyond Grant piped up. "I put in a request for a lunchtime field trip to your country store, but they turned me down." She jabbed a long needle into the elaborate needlework on her lap.

"Robbie, this is Nanette Russo," Grant said.

"Good evening, Ms. Russo," I said.

"Ms. Jordan." She picked up a blue plastic water bottle with *Jupiter Springs Assisted Living* printed on it in white letters. She took a long swig and set it down with a satisfied look.

I could smell the whiskey from where I stood. I glanced at Buck, but he only gave a *What can you do?* shrug.

"Ten minutes, South Lick," a loudspeaker blared. "Are you ready?"

A man in a wheelchair beyond Nanette began to sing in a loud voice, "I'm a Yankee Doodle dandy, a Yankee Doodle do or die, a real live—"

"Hush up, now, Horace," Nanette growled. "Independence Day was a couple weeks ago."

The man looked bewildered but stopped singing. Instead, he whistled the same tune in a beautiful warble.

"I'd better get back to my husband," I said. "Enjoy the fireworks."

"You'll come visit us at the old folks' home one day soon, won't you?" Vi asked.

"I'd love to."

"Bunch of characters, they are." Buck walked me halfway back. "Poor old Horace. There's a light on, but nobody's home upstairs." He pointed to his head. "He used to be a brilliant scientist over to the university. Dementia is a terrible thing, Robbie."

"Let's hope you and I don't end up that way, but it comes with the territory of aging for some."

"It surely does."

"See you later, Buck." I thought I might very much want to pay a visit to the old folks, as Vi put it. Including to dementia-plagued Horace, who nevertheless remembered all the words to a song he must have learned as a child.

CHAPTER 2

The *oohs* and *aahs* at the fireworks grew louder with each colorful explosion. After a multitiered celestial flower in subsequent waves of red, white, and blue sprinkled away and faded to black, I held my breath. But no more stellar explosions filled the moonless sky, letting the actual stars twinkle at us. The air was finally cooling a bit, too.

"Looks like that's it," Abe said.

I drained the last swallow of my spritzer, then tucked the bottle into my bag. "I think the last one was a leftover from the Fourth, don't you?"

"Could be." He stood, chuckling.

"They were all pretty." I covered my mouth as a yawn slipped out. "Sorry. It's past my bedtime." And it was, being at least ten o'clock by now. I would be opening my restaurant a scant nine hours from now.

"Come on, beautiful." Abe extended his hand to me. "Let's go home."

I accepted it and stood. A man and a woman not far from us were collapsing their chairs.

"Don't you want to go say good-bye to Mom?" The bald-headed man spoke in a louder voice than necessary.

"No. I need to get out of here." The woman, about my height or shorter, spoke in a high voice that reminded me of Vi's.

The two bustled away. Abe and I helped each other slide our camp chairs into their long cylindrical bags.

"Who was the dude who came up to you when I left with Buck?" I asked.

"He's a guy who plays dulcimer and accordion. He lives right here in town."

"I don't think he's ever been into the store."

"Maybe not," Abe said. "He only moved here last year from Bloomington, and he might be on a tight budget."

"Help!" A man's call rose out of the din of people talking, laughing, and packing up blankets and the detritus of picnics. "Somebody find Lieutenant Buckham Bird, please."

Nobody but Grant would call Buck by his formal given name. I whirled to peer toward the row of seniors. Because many in the crowd were now standing, I couldn't see much except Grant's head and torso as he waved his arm in the air. Buck headed toward them at a lope.

"There's trouble." I grasped Abe's arm. "Something bad has happened."

"How do you know?"

I shook my head. "I don't, really. Grant is apparently fine, but one of the other seniors must have had a serious health incident."

Some of the crowd noise quieted, as people watched. *Uh-oh.* A siren wailed to life in the distance. I couldn't see Buck's or Grant's heads anymore above the people milling about, but I kept watching.

"Is anyone a doctor?" Buck's voice rang out, urgent, anguished.

I looked with alarm at Abe, who had been a medic in the service. "Go!"

He nodded, dropping the chairs, and jogged toward Buck. After I stashed the chairs in the car, I wove my way across the park as fast as I could. Bumping a few elbows on my way, I didn't stop to apologize.

I arrived to see Buck kneeling in front of Vi, who sat bent in half in her chair. Abe squatted next to him. Vi's head lolled between her knees as if she were unconscious. Her hands dangled at the sides of her legs, the knitting project on the ground at her left hand, a lone plastic knitting needle below her right. Buck's palm pressed against the scarf covering her neck. He held two fingers of his other hand against her wrist.

Grant was on his feet, shifting his weight from one foot to the other, his breath coming fast, his fingers rubbing together. Nanette, Horace, and the rest of the seniors seemed to have already headed for the van.

"Help Pop, Robbie," Buck said in a soft voice. "Please."

I nodded, but I stared at dark drops staining the dirt under Vi's head. And wondered where the other knitting needle was.

"Mr. Bird, please sit down." I took his elbow. "Help is on the way. Your chair is right here."

He shook off my hand. "I know where the . . . chair

is." He didn't quite snarl, but he'd clearly held back an expletive. "What's happened to my Vi?"

Buck looked at me and shook his head furiously as the siren strobed closer.

"I'm not sure," I began. "She doesn't seem well."

"Buckham, tell me the truth, son. Is Vi dead?" Grant's voice quavered, no longer strong.

Buck gazed up at his father. An ambulance roared up to the park entrance. A muscular young Hoosier in a blue polo shirt with the Jupiter Springs logo on his chest hurried toward us. Two EMTs carrying red bags jumped out of their vehicle.

Buck removed his hand and stood. As he did, the scarf fell away from Vi's neck. But her skin was still red. Wet-looking, as if coated with blood.

"Yes, Pop," Buck murmured, moving to his father's side. "I'm afraid Vi has died."

But the tiny old lady had more than died. Under cover of darkness and noisy, exploding lights, it appeared someone had killed her.

CHAPTER 3

I was really dragging the next morning, between not getting enough sleep, thinking about the events of the night before, and feeling a back-burner sadness for the late Vi Perkell and for Grant. But work was work. I was a responsible business owner, and the posted Pans 'N Pancakes opening hour on Saturday mornings was seven. If my assistant chef, Danna Beedle, and I didn't open on time, hungry fans would be peering in the windows and quite possibly rapping at the door.

Danna showed up ten minutes late, rubbing her eyes. "Sorry I didn't make it in on time."

"No worries. Is there anything I can do?"

She shook her head.

"If it makes you feel better, I'm not at my best, either."

She pulled on an apron, washed her hands, and went

about her share of our opening routine with nearly robotic movements.

"We're quite the pair," I said.

Those were our last words until, at six fifty-nine, I asked, "Ready for the starving hordes?"

Of course we were ready. Sausages and bacon sizzled, biscuits waited in the warming oven, with more baking, and pancake batter and beaten eggs filled their respective pitchers awaiting orders for flapjacks and omelets.

"Just do it," she mumbled from the grill.

I did it, unlocking the door and turning the sign to *Open*. Sure enough, more than a dozen regulars and tourists eagerly poured in. I greeted them, telling them to sit anywhere. Until our newest employee, Len Perlman, showed up an hour later, I did nothing but pour coffee, relay orders to Danna, deliver food, and bus tables.

Vi's death was the topic of the morning. No surprise there. My restaurant had become the community water-cooler, so to speak. Residents gravitated here to learn gossip, to share news, and sometimes to commiserate. All of that went on this morning.

For my part, I claimed ignorance of the details. Which was mostly true. Abe and I had stayed last night until the county coroner had come. Until Detective Oscar Thompson with the Indiana State Police was summoned, South Lick being too small of a town to have its own homicide unit. Until Vi had been taken away in an ambulance with no lights flashing, no siren broadcasting urgency. And until Buck had helped his dad into the front seat of his cruiser.

The blood on Vi's neck was the only clue to how she'd been killed. It hadn't looked like a gunshot wound, and I hadn't seen a line indicating she'd been garroted. Strangling didn't produce blood, so I had to think she'd been stabbed in the neck.

Who would be brazen enough to kill a tiny older lady right there in public? Sure, it had been noisy and dark, with all attention on the fireworks. And the seniors had been sitting at the rear of the park with their backs to the woods. Still, it was an outrageous act of violence directly under the noses of half the town.

I poured coffee for two white-haired ladies who came for breakfast and a game of chess every Saturday morning. "Robbie, we heared little Vi Perkell was shot dead during the fireworks last night," the rounder of the pair said. "Is it true?"

Shot? Where had she heard that? "I'm not the one to ask, ma'am." I topped up her decaf and moved on.

I set a pancake special—three banana-walnut pancakes, a biscuit with sausage gravy, and three rashers of bacon—in front of a wiry local businessman who looked like his metabolism would have no problem handling that number of calories.

"There's talk of a strangling last night in town," he said. "Another homicide here in sleepy little South Lick?"

"I couldn't say." I smiled, loaded my arms with dirty dishes from a vacated two-top, and headed for the kitchen area. "Danna, the rumor mill is in high gear this morning." I hadn't yet had a minute to tell her what had happened last night.

"Mom said Ms. Perkell was murdered," she whispered.

Of course she knew. Her mother was Corrine Beedle, mayor of South Lick. No news slipped unnoticed past Corrine.

"It's true. Buck introduced me to his dad, Grant, before the fireworks started, and Vi Perkell, too. A whole group from Jupiter Springs had come in their van. Vi was apparently Grant's special friend."

"The poor man." Danna folded over a Western omelet, flipped three pancakes, and turned a half dozen sausages.

"I'll say. He was super upset."

"How was she killed?" Danna murmured her question.

"Not sure." I kept my voice equally quiet.

Across the room a man held up an empty mug, and a woman at the next table also waved for attention. The cowbell on the door jangled as four customers came in. The clock read seven fifty-five.

I gestured toward the room. "I'd better attend to some of these folks."

"I hope Len isn't late," Danna said. "We're nearly full."

"I hope so, too, especially with Turner away for the weekend." Our other assistant, Turner Rao, was as accomplished of a cook as Danna and a congenial Indiana University graduate with ambitions to become a chef.

"Those three orders are ready." Danna pointed.

"Thanks." I loaded up one arm and grabbed the coffeepot with the other hand. The bell jangled again, admitting Len, closely followed by Buck.

"Good timing," Danna said.

I'd hired Len two months ago to help out on weekday mornings, but his schedule had changed. Now he filled in on weekends. My friend Lou's younger brother, the tall twenty-year-old college student, was a fast learner and a great assistant, willing to do all the grunt work but slowly acquiring competence on the grill, too. This way, each of the rest of us could have the chance to take a weekend off without the others being stuck with only two working the restaurant on our busiest days.

Buck made his way to the two-top at the back, where he preferred to sit. After helping other diners, I poured the last of the coffee into Buck's mug.

"We're pretty busy," I said. "You're lucky your table was open. I'll get back over here soon to get your order, unless you're ready now, and have a little chat."

He glanced at the Specials board. "Gimme the special, plus my usual, if you please."

"You got it." I smiled to myself as I bustled away. The lieutenant's appetite was legendary. Today's special was a bacon and cheese omelet with scrapple hash. Buck's usual sides were pancakes, sausages, and biscuits with gravy. And he never gained an ounce. He tended to avoid our more exotic specials, like Turner's Indian-spiced roasted potatoes. Buck had also turned down a Greek-flavored feta omelet with Kalamata olives, as well as any of the Cali-Mex foods I sometimes dreamed up, like breakfast burritos or a Southwestern quesadilla. Buck preferred plain old Hoosier cooking. Lucky for him, we always had that fare on the menu.

I intersected with a now-aproned Len as he bussed a four-top. "Good morning. Thanks for saving our bacon, so to speak."

"It's super busy, isn't it?" He widened his pale green eyes, identical to Lou's.

"Yes." A customer hailed me. "I'll tell you why later, if I get a chance, or after we close." I headed off to scoop money off a vacated table and take four credit cards from a party of four. I managed to keep my groan to myself and not say, "Seriously?" out loud. Did they not know what I paid for each credit transaction? *Oh, well.* It was the price of doing business. I also once again delivered the news that I didn't know anything about Vi's death.

By the time Buck's order was ready, Len was swapping jobs with Danna. I liked to encourage my team to shake it up so nobody got bored, including me. I would also take a turn cooking when the moment was right.

I hefted Buck's breakfast onto both arms and headed his way. I'd apparently been too busy to see Oscar come in and sit across from Buck. Oscar and I had not really seen eye to eye on an earlier case, but he'd seemed to mellow since and become a bit more social. His engagement to Buck's cousin Wanda Bird, a detective with the Brown County Sheriff's Department, might have something to do with it.

"Good morning, Oscar."

He nodded his acknowledgment, rocking back and forth in his chair with a subtle movement.

I shifted my gaze to Buck. "How's your dad doing?"

Buck shook his head. "He's grieving something awful. The man had a deep love for Vi Perkell."

"I enjoyed meeting both of them." I laid a sympathetic hand on Buck's shoulder, knowing we were good enough friends for that. "And I'm so sorry I won't be able to get to know Vi better."

"You would have liked her," Buck said. "She was one smart cookie. Sweet as they come."

"I'm sure I would have. Oscar, can I get you coffee?"

"Please. And two over easy with white toast, bacon, and a fruit cup, please, when you can."

I hurried to hand off his order, grab the carafe, and bring it back before anyone could waylay me. I loved that my store was a gathering place for the town. Being known as a person who had helped solve more than one mystery in the past, however, could be inconvenient. Right now the restaurant looked quiet enough for me to sit for a couple of minutes and maybe learn a thing or two. I knew to grab calm moments when I could, because quiet could turn to frenetic in the blink of an eye if a tour bus pulled up or a big group burst in after an early hike.

I pulled over an unused chair and perched on it. "Can either of you tell me how Vi, uh, met her demise?" I asked, gazing from Oscar to Buck, who was demolishing the plate of pancakes. I kept my voice as low as I could and still be audible.

"Puncture wound to carotid artery," Oscar whispered, barely moving his lips.

"With?" I asked.

Oscar shook his head. "All we know is that it was something sharp."

Which meant they hadn't found the sharp thing at the scene. I pictured Vi's single knitting needle. "Did you find Vi's other knitting needle?" I gazed from Oscar to Buck.

"We have not," Oscar said.

Buck blew out a breath and actually set down his fork, a move I'd never seen him do in the nearly three years since he'd been eating here, at least not while food still sat in front of him. I realized he hadn't smiled once since he'd ambled in.

"You know my mama was murdered, Robbie," Buck began. "When I was still in school."

I nodded. He'd mentioned it once earlier in the year, and I'd been shocked. But I didn't know any more about her death than that. I didn't even know her name.

"It was exactly the same way." Buck stared at his plate, rubbing his forehead. "Right down to the fireworks."

CHAPTER 4

The lunch rush was even busier than breakfast, and my team had barely even gotten a break during the usual ten thirty lull. I'd taken a minute to brief Danna and Len about the murder, but it had been on the fly.

In addition, immediately after Buck dropped his bombshell about his mom's murder, the predicted touring van had arrived with twenty silver-haired tourists hungry for one of my famous country store breakfasts. I couldn't complain, and my bank account would be happy Monday morning. The excited ladies on the bus had also nearly cleaned out my supply of antique cookware. It was all good, as Danna liked to say.

Except I hadn't had a chance to nose out the facts with Buck and Oscar. They'd eaten and left together, and Buck hadn't come back for lunch. Maybe he was over at the assisted living place comforting Grant, who would surely be needing it.

Now, at one thirty, we actually had a few empty tables. With the weather feeling even warmer and stickier than yesterday, Danna and Len were looking pretty ragged. I was sure I was, too. Abe had helped me install a couple of window air conditioners, but they really couldn't keep up with the heat, even with the antique ceiling fans rotating on their fastest speed. Whichever of us stood at the grill had it worst.

I mustered a smile when the bell on the door jangled. It turned to a real one when Mayor Corrine and her mother, Josephine—Josie—Dunn, pushed through. I adored both of these smart, caring women and gave them a wave from the grill. Corrine, wearing a red-and-black sleeveless top and white Capris, waved back, as did her mom, a savvy businesswoman in her early seventies. During the week Corrine invariably wore dresses and blazers with high heels, tipping her height into the six-foot range, but she went stylish casual for Saturday attire.

Danna hurried up to them and delivered hugs, then led the women to a four-top. She returned with their orders. "Gazpacho for both. A grilled ham and cheese for Josie, and a cheeseburger for Mom."

"Did you ever tell me why you call her Josie and not Grandma or Nana or something?" I asked.

"I don't know. I always have." Danna washed her hands. "The mayor wants to talk with you. I'll swap in here."

"Okay, thanks." I slid out of my dirty apron and donned a fresh one before ladling out two cold soups and heading their way.

"Hey, Josie, Corrine." I sat across from Josie, which put me next to the mayor.

"Hey, Robbie." Corrine lifted her spoon and dipped into the gazpacho. "Don't this look good? I love me some spicy soup."

I laughed. "Don't get your hopes up. We are in Indiana, after all. If I made it spicy, as it rightly should be, I'd lose most of my customers. But that's why we put these bottles on the tables." Len had suggested providing optional heat for diners who wanted their cold Spanish soup to taste a bit spicier, so we'd added a bottle of hot sauce when we switched over to lunch service.

"I'll be fine with mild," Josie said. "My taste buds have aged with the rest of me, and I can't tolerate hot peppers like I could when I was younger."

For someone in her seventies, she barely showed her age. Her short hair was still mostly dark. Her figure was trim, her linen-pale face barely lined or spotted. This was a woman who took care of her skin.

Corrine's phone dinged. After she glanced at it, she blushed and set down her spoon, her thumbs flying, tapping out a text response.

Blushing didn't look like a response to official business. I glanced at Josie.

She gave a little snort. "Ms. Mayor there is all het up about a new man in her life."

"She's dating?" I whispered.

"Hey, it's no big secret," Corrine said, her cheeks still pink. "I been perusing that matchup site for a spell now. Looks like I finally reeled me in a good one."

Online dating, no less. More power to her. "I'm happy for you, Corrine," I said. "Danna said you wanted to speak with me."

She swallowed a spoonful. "Terrible news about last night, ain't it?"

"Yes." I nodded. "You weren't at the park, right?"

"I wasn't. I sat at home in the AC. Too blamed hot to be outdoors."

"It was warm," I agreed.

"I knew Vi pretty well," Josie said. "She used to own a mystery bookstore in Bloomington, and she ran a book club I was part of for quite a few years. You remember, Corrie?"

"Sure. Aunt Agatha's, wasn't it?"

"Yes," Josie said. "I always loved that clever name."

"You said 'was.' Has the store closed?" I asked.

"Two or three years ago," Josie said. "Between competition from the online giant and a big street project, they couldn't keep it going."

"Plus Vi wasn't no spring chicken," Corrine added.

"Can either of you think of any enemies she might have had? I can't get my brain around why someone would want to murder her. Or was she rich with greedy children?"

"Hmm." Josie set her chin on her fist. "She has two adult children, but I can't say Vi was rich. Comfortable, yes. And it costs a pretty penny to live at Jupiter Springs."

"What about that crafting group she was part of?" Corrine asked her mother. "I heard rumors of something fishy about that."

"What, Stitch and Bitch?" Josie asked.

"That's some name," I said.

"I know." Josie smiled. "They've been meeting for decades, with members taking turns hosting in their homes. Quilters, knitters, anybody with a needle. Not sure I know of anything fishy, but then I don't do crafts at all, so I was never in it."

My aunt Adele would know about the group, but she and her beau Samuel were off in India again. Maybe I would shoot her an email and ask. "Corrine, have you heard anything on the grapevine—or, rather, your police scanner—about the murder?" I asked.

"A little bit." She leaned closer. "It was a sharp object to the neck."

Josie shuddered and murmured, "The poor thing."

"Have they found the weapon?" I asked Corrine.

"I don't believe so."

No progress on that front, then.

Danna walked up carrying their lunch orders. "I made you a grilled ham and cheese, too, Robbie. Thought you'd be hungry when you saw these." She set down the plates.

"Thank you." I smiled up at her, way up, since she was even taller than Corrine. "That was thoughtful."

"She's a good girl." Corrine beamed.

"Don't get carried away, Mom." Danna rolled her twenty-one-year-old eyes as she picked up the empty soup bowls. "You three have Ms. Perkell's murder all solved?"

"Not exactly." I took a bite of a perfectly grilled sandwich, the outside crisp, the cheese melty, the ham salty and a little sweet, the grainy Dijon mustard adding exactly the right amount of tang.

Murder, though, had nothing perfect about it, and in fact, this one was anything but solved. Presumably Oscar and his team were already looking into Vi's past, her children, and anyone else who might have thought she'd be better off dead. I thought I might do a little digging, too.

CHAPTER 5

I followed the last two customers to the door at three.
Our posted closing time was two thirty, but we didn't
put diners in the Eject seat while they were still eating.

"Thank you for coming," I said to them. "Enjoy the
rest of your day and stay cool."

The ruddy-faced man grinned. "We're going to the
show and enjoy some free AC, aren't we, hon?"

"We surely are." His wife tucked her arm through his.
"It's not exactly free, what with the price of tickets anymore."

"Senior discount, hon." He beamed. "Never forget the
senior discount."

"Catching a movie sounds like a great idea," I said.
Saying "show" for "movies" was one of many Hoosier-
isms I'd learned in my half decade in the state.

They trotted down the steps as a beater pulled up playing *Rigoletto* at full volume. I shook my head, smiling. My friend Phil MacDonald always drove an old car hanging on by a shoestring. And he was going places as an operatic tenor, so his choice of driving music made perfect sense. We shared a love of opera, one I'd picked up from my late mother. After I'd learned a few years ago of the existence of my Italian father, Mom's devotion to arias started making a lot more sense.

But Phil was also a part-time baker and kept my restaurant supplied with brownies and cookies for our lunch desserts. Offering dozens or even hundreds of meals every day was a lot of work. Ordering in desserts made one less thing I had to worry about. I met him at the car and accepted two wide trays of cookies. Half of them had red and blue sprinkles baked on.

"Are these a reprise of the Yankerdoodles you made for the Fourth?" I asked. We had featured red, white, and blue specials for Independence Day, and Phil's yummy snickerdoodles with appropriately colored toppings had been popular.

"You don't mind, do you? I had too many sprinkles left over. I can use the red ones at Christmas, but that's months away, and blue by itself looks garish."

"I don't mind, my friend. Nothing wrong with being patriotic all year long."

He loaded up his own arms and followed me inside.

"Yo, Phil," Danna called from where she was scrubbing the grill.

"Hey, gang," Phil replied. He pointed at Len. "How's it going, man?"

Len waved the rag he was wiping down tables with. "All good."

"Who wants a beer?" I often offered my workers a

beer after we closed. "That is, those of you over twenty-one."

Len cleared his throat and pointed at his chest. "My birthday was last week. I am now of legal drinking age."

"Dude." Danna stared at him. "And you didn't tell us?"

Len blushed and looked sheepish.

"It doesn't matter, and happy birthday." I headed for the rear of the store. "I'll be right back." I let myself in to my former apartment, but my step slowed as I moved through the small living room. I lived at Abe's house now, and he'd been generous in making room for me, my cat Birdy, and the beautiful wooden furniture my cabinet-maker mom had lovingly crafted. I'd left the apartment here sparsely furnished, in case I had guests while my three B&B rooms upstairs were full. For the moment, the rooms were all empty.

I let my hand trail along the chair rail. I'd been happy during the few years I lived here, making a go of my first solo-owned business. Meeting and falling in lasting love with Abe. Finding tuxedo-cat Birdy, who had actually found me. Renovating the store's second floor into cozy rooms to rent out. And, in the beginning, actively mourning the untimely death of my mother, Jeanine Jordan— that part wasn't a happy time, at all. But the money I'd inherited from her enabled my purchase of the run-down country store, which Aunt Adele had helped me find.

I shook off my memories, happy and sad, and headed into the kitchen, where I always kept a supply of beer and white wine. The restaurant was strictly BYOB, legal under Indiana law for establishments without liquor licenses. I did keep a bottle of Four Roses bourbon in the restaurant, but it was for after-hours private consumption and lived in a locked cabinet.

"Grab a glass if you want one," I announced back in the restaurant. I grabbed an opener and flipped off the caps of four local micro-brews. "And food, if you haven't eaten."

A minute later we sat around a table. "Here's to Len joining the ranks of legit drinkers." I lifted my glass.

The others joined in. Phil took one swig and set down his bottle.

I cocked my head. "You look worried, Phil. What's going on?"

"You haven't heard from Adele?" His eyes, a blue that matched our store linens, were always a startling sight surrounded by his dark skin.

"Heard what?" I asked, suddenly on high alert. "Are they okay?" My aunt's main squeeze was Phil's grandfather, Samuel MacDonald. The couple always did their India service trips together. They'd had to skip a year when nobody was traveling. They were delighted to be back helping out at the orphanage they had helped build.

"Peepaw is sick," Phil said.

"Samuel? That's no good," I said. "Did Adele write?"

"Yes." He cocked his head. "You're copied on the email."

My eyebrows flew up. "We've been running our tails off today. I haven't even glanced at my phone." I pulled it out of the back pocket of my shorts and scanned through until I saw Adele's message. She'd written that they weren't sure what he had yet, but they'd found a good clinic. I glanced back at Phil. "She does say not to worry."

"She kind of has to, doesn't she? But Robbie, they're in the tropics, and my grandpa is eighty-three."

Danna reached over and squeezed his hand. "He's also a tough old guy, Phil. He's going to be fine."

He drummed his fingers on the table but resumed drinking the beer. I hoped Samuel would recover easily, and that Adele wouldn't catch whatever he had, if it was contagious.

"Robbie," Len began. "My sister told me you're, like, good at solving murders. What do you know about that lady who was killed last night?"

"Not much. Investigating what happened is the job of the detectives. But here's a question for all of you. Mostly maybe for you, Len, and Phil, since you spend more time in Bloomington. Vi Perkell—the victim—owned a mystery bookshop there."

"I don't read mysteries," Phil said. "I used to walk by the place, but I never went in."

Len's face lit up. "Aunt Agatha's Mystery Bookstore. I loved that place. I've been reading mysteries since I started reading chapter books. When I moved down from Lafayette to attend IU, the bookstore was still open. I hated when Aunt Agatha's closed its doors for good."

"So you knew Vi." I sipped my beer.

"I used to talk with her all the time," Len said. "That's really sad she was killed."

"It is," I said.

"She knew everything about all the different mystery genres." Len's face lit up with the memory. "She'd met a lot of famous authors, like Dennis Lehane and Louise Penny. But the guy wasn't so friendly."

"What guy?" I asked.

"Mr. Gale." Len took a drink "He was her business partner, or something like that."

"Kristopher Gale?" Danna asked.

"Maybe," Len said. "I never knew his first name."

"How do you know him, Danna?" I asked.

"I don't, but I heard my mom talk about him a few times. You can ask her. He moved to South Lick in the last few years, I think."

Phil passed me his phone. "That's him."

I gazed at the image of a man with fine features, thinning dark hair streaked with silver at the temples, and frameless glasses. He held a red accordion in front of his chest. I looked again. He was the one Abe had run into at the fireworks. What had Abe said? That he played a couple of bluegrass instruments.

"Is he a professional musician?" I asked Phil as I passed the phone to Len.

"I don't know," Phil said. "All I did was search for his name."

"That's the dude." Len stared at the photo.

Danna stood. "I don't know about you guys, but I want to get home, and this joint isn't going to clean itself."

I laughed. "No, it isn't."

"Let me help you stash the sweets," Phil said to me.

He and I carried the dessert trays into the walk-in cooler.

"Samuel's going to be okay, Phil," I said. "Adele said they had a good clinic. I mean, I know it's India, but they do have modern medicine there."

"I know. I'm going to put in a call to his men's prayer group. They have some powerful juju going on. And I might do some praying myself. That is, go outdoors and sing Gregorian chants. There isn't any more prayerful music than that, in my book."

CHAPTER 6

After I got home from doing breakfast prep yesterday afternoon, I'd had every intention of searching the internet for information about Vi, her children, and Kristopher Gale, not to mention Buck's mother. Instead, Abe had swept me away for a swim and a beach picnic on the shores of Lake Lemon, a perfect end to a long, hot, fraught day.

Now, at nine on Sunday morning, the restaurant was full of all the usuals: the early exercisers and the pre-church crowd, a big table of people who looked dressed for hours of bird-watching—a few of which might already be behind them—plus several dads with kids, who were either giving Mom a sleep-in or giving themselves a break from preparing breakfast. Three guys in camouflage had ordered hearty meals, but at least they hadn't tried to bring their guns in with them. I'd had to post my

no-weapons policy on the front door shortly after I'd
opened the store almost three years ago. Firearms were
simply something I didn't care to have in the mix in here,
and it was my right as a business owner to ban them.

So, we were busy, but the line for tables wasn't out the
door. I was well-rested and not frantic. My team was operating with a well-oiled efficiency. And a more recent
email from Adele said she thought Samuel was feeling a
bit better and was holding down a small serving of soup
for lunch. Mumbai was something like ten and a half
hours ahead of us. I wasn't surprised they'd already had a
midday meal before I woke up. It was good news no matter what the time was.

Yesterday Len had suggested crêpes for a breakfast
special today. "My dad makes them every Sunday morning, and I'm pretty good with a crêpe pan, myself."

As we already had all the ingredients on hand, I'd
given the idea an enthusiastic thumbs-up. He'd come in
early this morning to mix the batter for the thin French
pancakes and precook a stack, stockpiling them before
we opened. He even brought his own special pan. We'd
decided to offer either savory crêpes with a creamy
sautéed mushroom-and-cheese filling or a version with
sweetened local berries dusted with powdered sugar.

From all appearances, diners were loving both kinds,
because the pile in the warmer was dwindling.

"We're going to need more crêpes," I said to Len as
we met up in the kitchen area. Len deposited a load of
dirty dishes in the sink as I stuck three more orders up on
our carousel for Danna, who was handling the grill. "I'll
handle the front." Not that it was the front, per se, since
everything was wide open and the cooking area was actu-

ally at the side, but we used the conventional term for simplicity's sake.

"I'm on it." He scraped the last bit of batter from the mixing bowl into the big-handled pouring bowl and began measuring out flour.

I glanced over when the bell jangled to see Buck walk in. I nodded and pointed to his table. He'd texted me earlier asking if I could save it for him, so I'd dug out our sole *Reserved* sign. The table for eight we saved for Samuel's Friday morning men's prayer breakfast was the only other use the little placard got. I grabbed the coffee carafe and headed his way.

"Morning, Robbie," Buck said.

"How's your father?"

"He's taking it as hard as when my mama was killed."

"I'm so sorry. It's got to be hard." I filled his mug with steaming java. "I'm curious, Buck. Was he always blind?"

"No. His retinas detached 'bout a decade ago, and he lost his vision. It's a real shame. He's got the diabetes, too." He squinted at the Specials board. "What are them creeps you got up there?"

I blinked, then covered my snicker with my hand. "Those are crêpes. French pancakes. They're thin, with filling."

"French?" He scrunched up his nose. "Anyhoo, I don't need no thin anything. Don't you think I'm thin enough as it is?"

"Actually, you are." Not that anybody knew how he stayed that way.

"Can I get the usual, but maybe double up on the biscuits? I got me a hunger."

For a change. "What about information? Do you have any of that?"

He held up both palms. "Lemme eat first, okay?" He pulled out his phone and started jabbing at it with one long, bony finger.

"Of course." I headed away, emptying the carafe into diners' mugs, smiling and checking in with them as I went, as a good restaurant owner does. I stuffed two sets of tickets and cash in my pocket and loaded up my arms with dirty plates. I gave Danna Buck's order. As I loaded the dishwasher, I watched Len swirl the batter in the hot pan. He seemed to know exactly the right amount to pour in. He'd also mastered the wrist toss of a good chef, flipping the crêpe to the other side.

"If you order in buckwheat flour, we can do galettes sometime," he said. "They're the same thing as crêpes, but with buckwheat flour. They eat them in Brittany and in Quebec, and the buckwheat is nice, with a nuttier flavor."

"Sounds delish," I said. "I'll see if I can find that kind of flour." I glanced at the door when a man and a woman pushed through. I peered at them. I was pretty sure they were the couple who had been sitting near Abe and me during the fireworks. They weren't locals, I knew that much. I made my way over to them.

"Good morning. I'm Robbie Jordan, and this is my store. Welcome."

"Thank you." The man was trim, about five foot seven, and today wore a light-colored Panama hat, probably to protect that bald head from the sun.

"You'll have to wait a bit for a table," I continued. "Is this your first time here?"

The woman pressed her lips together and nodded.

"How long will it be?" she asked in the high voice I remembered from Friday night. She was slim, maybe in her forties or even fifties.

I gazed around the restaurant. "I should be able to get you seated within fifteen minutes, maybe sooner."

She gave a little shake of the head to her husband or friend or whoever he was. The one she'd called Upton.

"We'll come back another time," he said.

I watched them go. Was it something I'd said? I gave my own head a little shake. You couldn't please everyone. And I had a restaurant full of people eager to be pleased, Buck not least among them.

I bustled around, delivering food to diners and ferrying orders to Danna. By the time Buck's mammoth breakfast was up, Len had another stack of crêpes ready to go. I loaded up my arms with Buck's order.

"I need to talk with Buck for a minute or two," I said to my assistants. "You guys good?"

"Sure," Danna said.

Len nodded.

"Here you go, my friend." I set down the plates at Buck's table.

He glanced up from his phone, shaking his head. "A text from my granny just came in. She's near twice my age and is a texting maniac."

"Wow. Is she Grant's mother?"

"Nope. My mama's mama, Simone Walsh. But she adores Dad, always has. He took and called her about Vi." He forked in a way-too-big bite of biscuit, dripping sausage gravy as he went.

"Is Simone here in South Lick?" I suppressed a shudder at Buck's dining habits.

He swallowed before answering. "Nope. Lives down to Floyds Knobs, like she has her whole life."

"Now I remember you've mentioned spending summers with her there."

"Yup. She's lived in that town for an even hundred years, as a matter of fact. She's in one of them homes now, but she's as healthy as they come."

"That's wonderful. I'd like to meet her sometime."

"You should oughta pay her a call. The two of you would get on like white on rice." He slid in a big bite of pancakes, now dripping syrup instead of gravy. "Did I see them Perkell kids in here?"

I surveyed the restaurant. "We had a number of children in here this morning, but they all left before you arrived."

"Not little children, hon. I mean Vi's adult offspring."

"I don't know. Did you?" I asked.

"Might coulda. Thought I did, and then when I looked up again, they weren't here."

I nodded slowly. "A man and a woman came in but apparently thought waiting fifteen minutes for breakfast was too long." I held my hand flat near my eyebrows. "She's about this tall and has a high voice?"

"That'd be Tina Perkell, and her brother is called Upton. They must be in town making arrangements and whatnot," Buck said. "They live in Evansville, last I heard, or leastwise he does. I notified them of the death, but it was by phone. Had to look up their pictures on the internets."

I frowned. "Buck, they didn't come here after Vi's death."

"What all do you mean by that?"

"They were sitting near Abe and me at the fireworks."

I watched his jaw drop, and then wished I hadn't, since his mouth was full of food. "Buck, close your mouth, please." I glanced away until he had time to chew and swallow.

"I'm thinking old Oscar's gonna be pretty dang interested in what you seen," he said. "You're sure, now?"

"I'm sure."

Buck was now bent over his phone, jabbing at it.

"Has Oscar made any progress?" I asked. "He must be interviewing witnesses and stuff."

Buck made a stop gesture, then finished his message. "Hasn't made no progress to speak of. But he will. We will."

"You both know about Kristopher Gale?"

"The gent who owned that book outfit with Vi."

"Yes. Aunt Agatha's Mystery Bookstore. It was in Bloomington. It's been closed for a few years, but Gale was Vi's business partner, so money was involved."

Buck squinted at me. "Why are you talking about that? You heared about some fishy business with him?"

"No, but . . ." My voice trailed off. I didn't have any reason to suspect Gale.

"You got fine instincts, kiddo. I'll make sure the detective and team take a good hard look at the man."

Danna rang the ready bell three times. A customer waited to purchase a piece of cookware. A crash came from the sink, where a plate must have slipped out of Len's grasp.

"I gotta run, Buck. Text me Simone's number?"

"You bet."

CHAPTER 7

I didn't get another chance to talk with Buck before he left. I had wanted to learn more about his mother's murder and whether it had been solved. That conversation would have to wait for a quieter time. It was disturbing that he'd said Vi's murder had mimicked his mother's, but I had to shove that thought behind my mental door labeled *Later*.

Most weeks, the restaurant didn't have much of a Sunday midmorning lull. At least today's pace wasn't frantic, and the heat and humidity had eased a bit. My assistants and I had each snagged a restroom break and a quick bite to eat. Now, at a quarter to noon, every table was filled again. The first sweet corn was coming in, as well as local cucumbers and cherry tomatoes, so we'd devised a cold corn salad as a lunch special. I'd brought in a bag of basil leaves from my garden, which went perfectly with a lime juice and olive oil dressing. Simple, fresh, delicious.

I sidled up to Danna while she was cooking. "How do you feel about your mom dating?"

She raised the eyebrow with the tiny silver ring in it. "I think it's cool. She should be happy, you know? As far as I know, she didn't fall for anybody when I was little. But now I'm clearly not little." My six-foot-tall assistant laughed.

My single mom hadn't dated while I was at home, either. As far as I knew, that is. "Have you met the guy yet?"

She shook her head. "She'll introduce us when she's ready."

I was taking a turn at the grill flipping meat patties, turning hot dogs, and dishing out coleslaw and corn salad when I happened to glance at the waiting area near the door. A thin woman in a beige beret stood with a man a little shorter than she was. I looked again. That was Nanette Russo from Jupiter Springs with, if I wasn't mistaken, Kristopher Gale. And it looked like they were together and hadn't simply followed the other inside.

Len stuck two new orders on the carousel. "See that dude? He's the Kristopher Gale we were talking about yesterday."

"I've never seen him in here before. You said he hadn't been friendly to you, Len. Want to take a turn cooking? I'll go talk to them."

Looking relieved, he nodded. "Thanks."

I'd learned in the spring that Len had spent his life as a girl until recently. Maybe having met Gale when Len was living as Leah was part of why he seemed to appreciate my offer. I slid into a clean apron. "These patties are for the party of four." I pointed to the grill. "The savory crêpes are for table six, and the omelet, as well." I pointed to the carousel, then tied the apron behind my back. "There's one more I haven't started ahead of your new ones."

"I'm on it, boss."

"Cool." I headed for Nanette and Kristopher. "Good morning, Nanette, and welcome to Pans 'N Pancakes." I smiled at both of them, and added, for Kristopher's benefit, "I'm Robbie Jordan."

"Howdy, Robbie," Nanette said. "This is my friend, Kristopher Gale."

He nodded at me but didn't extend his hand to shake mine. A germophobe, maybe, or perhaps he'd gotten out of the habit during the time when even elbow bumping was risky behavior. I was immeasurably glad that period was behind us.

"Nice to meet you, Kristopher. I'm afraid you'll have a short wait for a table, but it won't be long."

Kristopher checked his watch. He was an attractive man for his age group, except he hadn't smiled once.

"May I extend my condolences to both of you?" I asked. "Kristopher, I know you worked with Vi Perkell."

"Vi and I were business partners for some time," Kristopher said. "I've moved on to other ventures."

"I see. Nanette, you must have known Vi for quite a while."

"I did." Nanette looked everywhere but at me. "But her and me weren't friends, exactly."

Neither appeared to want or need condolences, which seemed odd. A fellow longtime member of a crafting club and one of two partners in a bookstore venture? I couldn't dig into either reaction now.

"Have either of you eaten in my restaurant before?" I asked.

Kristopher, still stolid, shook his head.

"I was here, one time after you opened," Nanette said. "Had one of the best lunches I ever et. Then I moved out to the home and can't get a ride 'less they send a van. And I already told you they refused."

I assumed the *home* was the assisted living residence. I clasped my hands in front of me. "I'm glad you're both here." I needed to get back to work, despite itching to talk more with both of them about Vi Perkell.

The bell on the door jangled. Two cheery older women came in, moving slowly. The taller one, with short salt-and-pepper hair, leaned on an aluminum walker, while the other carried two handbags. I was pretty sure they weren't local. By the looks of their wide smiles, they were happy to be here.

I turned toward them. "Welcome to Pans 'N Pancakes."

"Are you the famous Robbie Jordan?" The one pushing the walker wore a cap of softly curling white hair.

I smiled. "I'm Robbie, famous or otherwise." I glanced at the walker. The back legs ended in two tiny turquoise plastic tennis shoes, which acted as skids.

"We heard about you all the way back in Connecticut," the other newcomer said. "I'm Edna Warner, and this is my baby sister, Joan Linnell."

"Nice to meet you both. But Connecticut?" I asked. "That's way back East."

"Sure is," Joan said. "We love it there, and spend a lot

of time doing genealogy on our ancestors, don't we, Edna?"

"You bet. Right back to the founding father of Hartford."

"But I have family living in these parts," Joan went on, "and they convinced me to move out West here to be closer to them. Edna was kind enough to drive us both and help me get settled in."

I laughed inwardly. Growing up as a Californian, anything east of the Rockies was "back East." To those from the other coast, Indiana apparently qualified as "out West."

"We got Joanie all moved into a lovely room over at Jupiter Springs," Edna said.

"My son and his wife have a full house over in Bloomington, what with their kids and the exchange student and the dog and all," Joan added.

"We stayed at a hotel there when we arrived, and I went back last night," Edna went on. "But I'd like to be closer by until I go home next week. Do you know of any places here in South Lick?"

"I happen to have three open B-and-B rooms right upstairs." I pointed to the ceiling. "I had a whole family cancel yesterday because of a death. You're welcome to whichever room you want."

The ladies exchanged glances. "That'd be perfect, wouldn't it, Joanie?" Edna asked.

"It would," Joan replied.

"There are stairs, I'm afraid," I said, even though Edna didn't seem to have any mobility issues. "If that's not a problem, I'll show you around after you eat."

"I live in a three-story antique home north of Hartford," Edna said. "Stairs aren't a problem, and I'm glad to be right here in town. My bag is in the car, too."

"My, it smells good in here," Joan said. "Homemade biscuits?"

"Yes. We offer them all day."

"Joanie and I have been baking our whole lives. Our mother owned a bakery in Hartford."

"You're a better baker than I, Edna."

Nanette seemed to be studiously ignoring the newcomers. Maybe she hadn't met Joan yet. Should I introduce them? As I thought about it, Danna, rag in hand, signaled to me and pointed to an empty two-top.

"Kristopher and Nanette? Your table is ready." I gestured to where Danna stood.

Kristopher headed for the table. Nanette started to follow, but Joan's gaze bore into her back.

"Nanette Russo from Jupiter Springs?" Joan asked.

Nanette's shoulder drooped. She turned. "I'm Nanette."

"We met yesterday." Joan's smile was warm and wide. "I recently moved into Two-twenty-six."

"Oh, yes. That's right." Nanette plastered on a smile. "Welcome."

"I'm Joan Linell, and this is my sister, Edna Warner."

"Nice to see you both. Excuse me, if you will." Nanette hurried off after Kristopher.

"Do you know her, Robbie?" Joan asked softly. "She didn't seem to like me much. I thought cold, reserved people were supposed to be more typical of New England than of here."

"No, I don't really know her at all. I met her Friday evening for a few minutes, and again right before you both arrived. Sorry."

Edna knit her brow and lowered her voice. "A resident of Jupiter Springs was murdered that night. Do you think it's safe for my sister to live there, or here in town at all?"

I took in a deep breath, channeling my inner Chamber of Commerce paid membership. "It is absolutely safe. You can't do better than South Lick for caring small-town residents, quiet and beautiful surroundings, and a responsible government."

Truth or not, they both seemed satisfied with the spiel. I wasn't so satisfied with Nanette's treatment of Joan, nor with Kristopher acting unfriendly. Finding a time to investigate both reactions was zooming to the top of my to-do list.

CHAPTER 8

My crew headed for home at four, what with the Sunday schedule starting and ending an hour later than on weekdays. Pans 'N Pancakes was closed on Mondays, and I usually did Tuesday prep on Monday sometime. I'd gotten Edna settled in her room earlier and made sure she knew I didn't offer breakfast on Mondays because the restaurant was closed. She'd said she didn't mind, that she was planning to eat with her sister, anyway.

I was about to pull the front door fast behind me and lock the dead bolt before I walked home when Buck trotted up the front steps. Even though I'd been eager to talk with him earlier, right now I was more eager for a hard, hilly bike ride before my date night. Abe and I always spent Sunday evenings together. And while I liked the lieutenant and was eager for news about the murder, a chat with him had not been in any plans for my immediate future.

"Hey there, Robbie." His tone was tentative, as if he knew he was intruding on my private time.

"Hi, Buck." I checked him out, but I couldn't tell whether he looked hungry or not. He always looked hungry. "I'm sorry, but you're not here to eat, right? I was about to go home."

He laughed. "No, I'm not here to bother you for no food. Would you have a couple few minutes for a small little chat, though?"

"Sure. Have a seat." I secured the door and sank onto one of the rockers on the wide covered porch, which ran all along the front of the building. I glanced down at my blue store T-shirt and navy cargo shorts, what passed for a summer uniform, and grimaced at the sight of both bearing grease splatters, despite the ever-present apron I wore at work. A washing machine would be the next to occupy this outfit. At least I'd finally felt financially secure enough to hire a laundry service for all the store aprons, napkins, and towels. I no longer had to worry about washing and drying them at home.

"What's up?" I asked Buck.

"Not too much. Oscar sends his thanks on the tip about the Perkells."

"What did they say?"

He didn't answer right away. I rocked as I waited. A lawn mower droned from not far away, bringing the summer scent of freshly cut grass. From a different corner of town, the equally summery tune of an ice cream truck drifted over on a light, cooling breeze. Buck gazed across the street at the now-empty limestone house where a couple had opened a short-lived antique store last spring.

He finally spoke. "I can't reveal that, Robbie."

"So, is that the only thing you came here to tell me?" I asked. "That Oscar appreciated the tip?"

"No, 'course not."

"How's Grant doing?"

"Not so good." He wagged his head. "He's pretty dang distraught. Rightly so, too."

"I thought I might ride out there and pay him a visit." If Buck ever got around to telling me what he'd come here for.

"He'd like that."

I thought about Friday night. "Where did your dad learn to knit?"

"Vi taught him. Kinda odd to see a gentleman knitting away with the ladies, but he loves it."

"I heard about a crafting group Nanette has been part of for a long time, and Vi was, too. You'll love this—it's called Stitch and Bitch."

Buck tilted his head. "Who'd you take and hear that from?"

"It was Josephine Dunn. Corrine's mom."

"Josie." He nodded. "She's a smart lady."

"She doesn't do crafts, but she knew about the group."

"We'll check into it." He squinted into the distance. "I seem to remember my mama saying something about a group like that. But it's a fuzzy memory. Heck of a long time ago, and I was a boy. Not into any of that kind of lady stuff." He chuckled. "Except being able to say that *B* word, of course."

"Forbidden except in the name of the group?" I asked.

"You bet. Pop woulda washed my mouth out with soap if I'da uttered it."

I laughed, too. "I remember feeling the same in high

school German class. The word *hell* means 'bright' and is a perfectly ordinary thing to say. Classmates used it in conversation—but never in school. And if I'd said it at home or when I visited Adele, I would have been in big trouble."

"Words aside, you should know Oscar hasn't found the murder weapon yet." He wagged his head. "With a group like those ladies have, a sharp object could be in anybody's bag."

"Are knitting needles sharp enough to pierce skin?"

"Oscar says no. They'd have to be sharpened up extra."

"Josie told me she'd known Vi pretty well," I said. "She was part of a book club Vi's mystery bookstore ran."

"Ah, yes. The wife loved that store."

"Your wife?"

"Yup."

I knew he was married and had adult children, but that was the extent of it. "You've never brought her in to the restaurant."

"She says I do too much business here. She likes me to be completely off-duty when I'm with her."

"I don't blame her."

A big hawk landed on the tall pine tree to the left of the empty house.

"Buck, you mentioned that your mom died in the same way as Vi. Are you willing to tell me more about that?" I almost immediately regretted asking. I wanted to know, but I also wanted to get home and into my cycling gear. I hadn't been out for a long ride in a few days, and I was feeling antsy from it.

His phone rang before he could answer. "Bird." He listened, then said, "Be right there." He jabbed at it to disconnect. "Gotta go. I'll tell you another time, all righty?"

"Sure."

He trotted down the steps and slid into his cruiser. I stood. He never had told me why he'd stopped by, which seemed odd. Very odd.

The hawk now intently watched a pile of leaves at the foundation of the limestone. In a flash the bird zoomed down, then flapped back up, a gray mouse wriggling in its talons. The poor little thing wasn't going to wriggle for long. I shuddered involuntarily. I hoped Vi hadn't suffered. I hoped she hadn't even known what had happened to her.

CHAPTER 9

I rode into the Jupiter Springs Assisted Living parking lot forty-five minutes later. It wasn't far from home, and I'd added my visit at the start of the ride so I wouldn't be too sweaty. The hill work would come afterward.

Cruising the parking lot to seek out a bike rack proved futile. People must not cycle to visit their loved ones. Instead, I spied Upton and Tina Perkell standing next to a smallish white SUV. The two seemed to be arguing. I pulled to a stop near them and unclipped one foot from the pedal, setting it on the pavement.

"Hi, there," I began. "Tina and Upton, right?" I smiled.

Tina frowned and peered at me as if I were an alien being or a unicorn. "Do we know you?"

I laughed and removed my helmet. "Robbie Jordan. You came into my restaurant this morning looking for breakfast, but the wait was too long. I hope you found somewhere else tasty to eat."

"We did, but we had to go to Nashville for it." Upton raised an eyebrow.

"South Lick is pretty short on breakfast places other than mine unless all you want is coffee and a pastry," I said. "I understand you are Vi Perkell's children. May I offer my condolences on her passing?"

Tina still stared at me. I patted my hairline. Nope, no horn growing out of it.

"Thank you," Upton said.

"You must have a lot to deal with," I blathered on. "Her room here, a funeral, and so on."

Tina nodded, then blinked and turned away. Overcome with grief? Maybe.

"We do," her brother said. "But we still need to eat. Can you recommend a good place that serves dinner around here? They offered us a meal in there, but—"

"But that food isn't worth eating." A dry-eyed Tina whirled. "I don't know how Mom could stand it."

"She didn't have much choice, did she?" Upton asked. "Thanks to you."

Tina's nostrils flared. "You didn't offer to take her into your house either, did you?"

He folded his arms.

This spat was getting interesting. I'd have loved to stick around for it, but I couldn't figure out how. I cleared my throat. "I can recommend Hoosier Hollow for an excellent dinner. A friend of mine is the chef, and the restaurant is right here in South Lick."

"Thank you," Upton said, but he still glared at his sister.

She glanced at me and locked her lips in a line.

"Well, have a nice dinner." I wouldn't be eavesdropping on this fight, much as I'd like to. I walked my bike to the facility's entrance without saying anything else. The landscaping at the place was tasteful, with plenty of trees and well-trimmed shrubs. I locked the cycle to the trunk of a sapling. It might be safe to simply leave the bike out here leaning against the wall, but it was an expensive ride. I didn't want to risk losing it, and I wasn't sure how the management would feel about me wheeling it indoors. I hung my helmet on a handlebar and headed in.

The expansive lobby included a desk at the side with no one behind it. A sideboard featured a pod coffeemaker and a platter of cookies under a glass dome, freshly baked judging from the delicious aroma in the air. A couple of easy chairs were on the opposite wall, one occupied by a woman gripping the handles of a fancy red walker, the kind with brakes, a seat, and a carrying pouch. The walker had a yellow plastic rose tied on the front. Her expression was both vacant and expectant, as if her ride would arrive any moment.

A couple in their fifties stood in the open hall beyond the lobby. Worried looks on their faces, they conferred with a blazer-clad woman wearing a badge. Arranging to have a parent lodged here, perhaps? Or trying to resolve an issue with a relative already in residence.

How would I find Grant? A fresh-faced fellow with neatly combed blond hair hurried toward the desk. He also wore a badge, his pinned to a green polo shirt with a Jupiter Springs logo.

"Can I help you, miss?"

"I'd like to visit with Grant Bird. Can you please tell me where I might find him?"

He sat at the desk, tapped on a laptop, then looked up. "I'm afraid he's indisposed this afternoon."

My breath rushed in. "Indisposed? Is he all right?"

He gave my biking togs a once-over. "Um . . . are you a relative?" His voice rose as if he couldn't imagine how I could be family.

"No." I smiled with regret. "Only a friend."

"I can't reveal information about our residents' health."

"Oh, Grant's indisposed, all right." Nanette's voice came from behind me.

What? I glanced over to see her lifting the cover on the cookies. She used the provided tongs to select a large one, oatmeal-raisin if I wasn't mistaken. What did she mean?

"Want one?" she asked.

I was about to decline when I changed my mind. In fact, I was hungry. The cookies looked good, and this gave me an excuse to talk with her for a few minutes. "I'd love a cookie, thanks."

"There you go," she said, as if she approved.

I accepted the sweet and lifted a napkin off a stack next to the dome. "Shall we sit outside for a minute?"

"Why not? Nothing else happens around here on Sundays if you don't have family visiting." She gave the young guy a fierce look.

I doubted he was in charge of programming. And he didn't notice her ire, anyway.

"Thanks for your help," I told him.

Outside, Nanette and I sank onto a bench. The Perkell offspring had either left or shifted their argument into their car. I admired the greenery all around as I nibbled on the cookie. The facility was on the outskirts of South Lick and nestled into woods, kind of like my store was on the other side of town.

"You don't have family in the area?" I asked Nanette.

"Nah." She took a big bite of cookie. "I'm from Chicago. Came down here with my husband, who turned out to be a rotten Italian SOB. We didn't have kids, but after I got rid of the hubs, I stuck around. Ended up in this worthless joint."

I only nodded. It didn't seem so worthless to me, and someone had mentioned it wasn't inexpensive to live here. I gazed at her. I hadn't noticed before how sallow her skin was, with an almost yellow tinge. She was quite thin, too. Maybe she was ill.

"I hope Grant isn't sick," I ventured.

"He's not. You were asking about Vi this morning," Nanette added. "I didn't want to say it in front of Kris, because you're not supposed to speak ill of the dead and all that, but the girl was a habitual liar."

"Oh?" Was that true? I wondered.

"Yes, indeed. Listen, we were in a crafting group together for decades. We were both founding members of Stitch and Bitch."

I tilted my head as if I hadn't already heard about the group. I wanted her to keep talking.

"But Vi was one of the latter," Nanette went on. "She could complain about anything. She'd smile at you as sweet as could be and lie through her pearly little teeth."

"I'm guessing you're not going to miss her much."

"I certainly will not."

"You must be retired," I said. "What was your career?" I popped in the rest of my cookie.

"I was an actuary." She gave me a grim smile.

"I'm not even sure what that is." I'd heard the term, but that didn't mean I understood it.

"It's all numbers, young lady. Something at which I happen to be better at than the average bear."

"Are there many women in the field?" I asked.

"There are not. And I didn't exactly get a warm welcome from the men I worked with."

"It's always the same story, isn't it? I have an engineering degree. Things are changing a bit, but old attitudes die hard." I smiled at her. "What was Grant Bird's career, do you know?"

She clamped her lips together and shook her head. We sat in silence as a cloud scudded over the sun. When it moved on, I detected movement near the ground at the edge of the lot. My breath rushed in when a fox trotted toward us. I pointed without speaking.

"Oh," Nanette murmured.

The fox froze, staring at us. Even its bushy tail didn't move. It turned, calmly trotting back the way it came.

I stood. "Thanks for the cookie."

"Sure." She stared after the animal, now disappeared into the woods. "Any time."

"If you see Grant, will you say hello to him from me?"

"Happy to." Nanette used both hands to boost herself to her feet and grimaced as she did. "But I won't see him. The man's in his room crying into his hankie about his poor lost sweetheart. Sentimental fool." She hit the automatic opener button with her elbow and disappeared through the slowly opening door without saying goodbye.

CHAPTER 10

After I showered off my ride and my day, I slipped on a black swirly miniskirt and a silky sleeveless top in magenta, one of the colors that made my Mediterranean skin glow. I brushed out my hair and left the curls loose on my shoulders. Yes, I was going to be lounging at home with Abe, but this was our first dinner together here without Sean in a while. Shorts and a T-shirt were my daily summer uniform at work, and the last thing I wanted to wear for a date-night dinner. Which I didn't even have to cook.

I moseyed barefoot into the kitchen, where Birdy slept curled up on one of the stools at the counter that divided the kitchen proper from the dining room. It, in turn, was open to the living room at the front of the house, complete with the rounded corners of the passageway original to the hundred-year-old Craftsman cottage.

Abe had modernized the kitchen before I'd met him. While not large, it was well-designed and efficient, with a near-professional-quality gas stove and a big window over the sink. My husband, standing at said stove, had a bib apron tied around the faded Hawaiian shirt he wore with old denim shorts. I slid my arms around his waist from the back and leaned into his strong back.

"Mmm," I murmured. "It's good to be home."

"I'm happy you're here, and I hope you're hungry."

My stomach rumbled in response. I pulled away and laughed. "I am, and it smells heavenly. What do you have going on in there?" I slid around to his side.

He slung his left arm over my shoulders but kept stirring. "Slow-sautéed mushrooms in an herb-wine reduction, destined to go on grilled chicken. With orzo salad and a green salad."

"Perfect."

"A perfect dinner for a perfect wife." He leaned over and kissed my temple. "Also, a bottle of pinot gris with your name on it is in the fridge." He lifted a half-full pint beer glass and took a sip.

"Perfect, I'm not, so don't get your hopes up, dear husband." I brought the bottle to the counter, where he'd left a stemless glass waiting for me, and slid onto a stool. "Thanks for the wine, though." I took a cool, refreshing sip, and then another. "What did you get up to today?" *Yikes.* I was starting to sound like a local.

"I went to the farmers' market and the regular market, too. Restrung my banjo and practiced for a while. Played with a certain black and white cat." He flashed me a grin. "And took a nap."

As I stroked Birdy, a yawn slipped out. "Don't speak to me of naps. I might fall asleep right here."

"You put in quite the day. Can I assume some sleuthing went along with it?"

"Not much." I sipped from my glass. "Abe, remember that Kristopher Gale you talked to at the fireworks?"

"Of course." He took a plate of chicken out of the fridge.

"He was in the restaurant for lunch today."

"He's a quite versatile musician. Guitar and penny whistle in addition to the accordion and dulcimer. I've never found him particularly friendly, though."

"He was co-owner of a bookstore in Bloomington for a while before it closed. Do you know what he does for work now?"

"No, but I'll ask my band buddies." Abe headed out to the patio, chicken in hand. "Somebody'll have that info. Bring the wine and join me while I grill? Everything else is out there."

I did as requested, grabbing an extra wineglass for him before I pushed through the screen door. Birdy perked up and dashed out with me. I knew it was a bit risky to let him into the yard. He'd been an outdoor cat when he adopted me, and I didn't quite have the heart to deny him fresh air and prowling. Abe's house—no, *our* house— was on a quiet street. It wasn't near any woods full of coyotes, foxes, and other predators of small felines, plus I'd had a microchip inserted in my kitty during his first vet visit. I also always made sure to get Birdy indoors before dark fell and locked his cat door to be sure he stayed there.

As one of Abe's wedding presents to me, he'd laid a flagstone patio outside the kitchen door and bought an octagonal teak table complete with red umbrella and padded chairs. Another gift had been building the frames for two raised garden beds in the sunniest part of the small yard and filling them with rich loam and screened finished compost. We'd eaten out here nearly every rain-free evening all summer. The table was already set with brightly colored place mats and cloth napkins. Forks and knives sat ready in their correct positions. Dinner plates covered a ceramic bowl and a wooden one, presumably to keep flies out of the salads.

I watched Abe lay the flattened chicken thighs on the now-hot charcoal grill.

"Spice rub?" I asked.

"Yes. I used an Italian mix this time, since that's the direction I went with the orzo."

"A dry rub is so good at keeping the juices in. I have no idea how, but it always works." I wandered over to the box holding annual and perennial herbs, where my basil plants were already trying to flower. I spent a few min-utes pinching off all the budding stalks so the plants could put their energy into producing more of the big aro-matic leaves. "Want to add some extra flavor?" I held out a handful of basil buds to Abe.

"Great idea. Toss 'em on."

I dropped them onto the coals, then sat at the table.

"Why were you asking about Gale?" Abe checked his watch, drained his beer, and sank into a chair.

"His bookstore partner was Vi."

"Aha. And you're wondering if he might have had a motive to put her out of business permanently, so to speak."

"Yes. I'm still stunned at Vi being killed in a public park."

"Sugar, the place was packed. And dark." Abe reached for the wine bottle. He topped up my glass and filled his own. "With the added distraction of bright lights bursting in air. I could have missed seeing my own son on a night like that."

"You're right."

He picked up the long tongs and rose to turn the chicken. "What else happened today?"

"I met Vi's children, who seemed more mad at each other than sad about losing their mom." I peeked under the plate over the ceramic bowl and fished out a sugar snap pea.

"Hey!" Abe said with a fond smile.

I held it up. "Guilty. Sorry, I'm starving." I popped in the sweet crunchy pod.

"Go ahead and serve orzo for both of us, if you will. The chicken has one more minute."

"Have you ever run into a Nanette Russo? She's an actuary." I flipped over both plates and doled out a big spoonful of the side dish, which looked mouthwateringly good. Halves of pitted Kalamata olives, the sugar snap peas, and diced red sweet pepper mingled with leaves of fresh oregano and rosemary in a pile of tiny pasta torpedoes glistening with olive oil. The green salad looked fabulous, as well, but we were in the habit of eating it after the main course.

Abe set a platter of cooked chicken on the table. Birdy trotted in from the back edge of the garden, eyes bright and expectant. But unlike my childhood cat, Butch, this one was polite enough to sit at my feet and wait, knowing I would give him a few morsels.

Abe and I clinked glasses and started eating.

"It's all so good, my dear," I said. "Thank you." I was

blessed in having found a man who liked to cook, since I did it for a living.

"A chef deserves time off."

"Have you heard from Sean?" I asked.

"He texted me this afternoon, in fact. They're all good. He said he caught a fish, and Grandpop taught him how to gut and clean it for dinner."

"Just like he taught you?"

"Exactly. Now, who was it you were asking me about?"

"Nanette Russo. She was sitting on the other side of Vi Friday night."

Abe narrowed his eyes, thinking, but shook his head. "Did you say she's an actuary?"

"Yes." I cut a few small pieces of meat and dropped them in front of Birdy on the flagstones.

"You know Dad's a science teacher, but he's always had a head for numbers. He was studying to be an actuary some years ago. He might know this lady, even though she's gotta be older than him."

"He didn't become one, though?" I asked.

"Nah. He didn't pass the test first time around, and didn't really care enough to pursue it." Abe gazed at me. "I can try to call him, but that campground they're at is famous for being remote. A text might not even reach him, even though Seanie's got through earlier."

"And they won't be back until next weekend."

"Which, if this Nanette is involved in the murder, will be too late, I'm guessing."

"I hope they'll have someone in custody by then." I took another bite of the perfectly cooked chicken: crisp on the outside, tender and juicy on the inside.

"I'm sure Buck and Detective Thompson hope they do, too."

The late-day sun splashed a male cardinal's plumage in a brilliant show of red. Birdy crept a few feet, then froze, coiling into himself for a dash after it. The bird flew in plenty of time. But the red only made me shiver, remembering the color of Vi's scarf—and her neck under it.

CHAPTER 11

I stretched in bed the next morning at seven. For a person who normally was up and at 'em by five thirty, this was a serious sleep-in. Abe had left for work an hour ago, but this was my day off. The ceiling fan rotated lazily above, circulating the still-cool air. We had a window AC unit for the unbearably hot evenings. Last night hadn't been one of them.

Abe and I had sat outside until it was nearly dark. Going straight to bed before either of us was too exhausted had been a perfect plan, one that was still making me smile.

I lay there for a while longer, my smile turning to more serious thoughts as I considered what I had learned yesterday. Nanette saying Vi was a longtime liar had stunned me. If it was true, would it be enough of a motive for murder? Even if I succeeded in seeing Grant today, I couldn't very well ask him about that alleged aspect of Vi's nature. He'd loved her. I didn't know Kristopher Gale well enough to quiz him about her, even though he and Vi had been business partners. The only thing to do was to turn it over to Oscar.

I still wanted to learn what had happened to Buck's mother, and the day stretched out in front of me. All I had to do at some point was a load of personal laundry here and breakfast prep for tomorrow at the restaurant. Making dinner for Abe would be nice, too. But I could fit in another ride to Jupiter Springs, with time left over for a drive down to Floyds Knobs and a chat with Simone, Buck's grandmother, and still get it all done. Friends occasionally asked why I didn't relax on my day off. My answer was always that I wasn't a sit-around kind of person. The idea of spending a day watching television and refreshing my nail polish made me itchy.

A rhythmic bumping interrupted my musing. It could only be Birdy bumping his head against the door.

"Breakfast is coming, Birdman," I called to him. I was rewarded with a plaintive wail indicating that no one ever fed him, ever. Not true, of course. I threw on a clean tee and shorts and narrowly avoided stepping in an entirely gross hair ball he'd deposited in the hall. It was one of the perils of owning a long-haired breed, and one of several reasons he wasn't allowed in the bedroom, ever. "Thanks for nothing, kitty cat."

Abe had left me a note saying coffee was in the carafe. He'd added "XXXOOO" and drawn a smiley face. Cat fed, hairball cleaned up, and steaming dark roast in hand, I slid open the sliders and ventured out to the patio. Birdy trotted out after me. Every surface was damp with dew, and the air was heavy. Today was going to be another steamer. I wouldn't be surprised if a late-day thunder-storm finished it off. It had been quite an adjustment for this mid-coast California girl to get used to Midwestern weather.

I thought of Adele in even steamier India. I'd never had much luck calling her there but thought I'd give it a try. Hearing her voice would reassure me that she and Samuel were all right. Alas, the call didn't go through this time, either. I tapped out a quick email instead, sending my love and wishes for good health for both of them.

I headed back inside. I returned with a rag to wipe off the table and a beach towel to sit on, plus graph paper on a clipboard and a sharp pencil. I felt the need to organize my thoughts about the homicide. It was too early in the case to complete a decent crossword puzzle, but listing all the elements that could turn into clues and answers always helped me find at least a bit of clarity.

With Birdy bathing on the patio next to me, I sipped the coffee and stared at the paper. Where to start? I jotted down *SUSPECTS* and drew a line under the word, then began to add names.

Tina
Upton
Nanette
Kristopher?

I erased the question mark. They were all question marks. Who else? Sometimes one read about unscrupulous—or evil—care providers who took it upon themselves to end an addled nursing home resident's life. But Vi hadn't died at Jupiter Springs, and she wasn't a bedridden, helpless patient with dementia. Unless I learned more, I doubted the killer was some semi-random nurse or orderly at the assisted living residence.

I added the heading of *MOTIVE*. And frowned at it. In the absence of actual knowledge, I listed all the usuals, with possible suspects next to each.

Greed—Upton and Tina (but only if Vi had a lot of money)

Revenge—?

Long-simmering resentment—Nanette

That was all so murky I nearly wiped out the whole column but told myself to let it stand. This was the brainstorming stage. I tapped my pencil on the page.

WEAPON was mostly obvious—something sharp that could easily be hidden. Like a knitting needle. *OPPORTUNITY*? They'd all been at the fireworks, plus whatever Jupiter Springs personnel had been helping out.

I sat back and blew out a breath. I was getting nowhere, fast. And I was hungry, but my phone rang before I could go inside to see about breakfast. *Alana?* Why was my childhood bestie calling at five in the morning, West Coast time? She was so not a morning person.

"Alana," I said. "Is everything okay?"

"More than okay!" She certainly sounded fine, and awake, too.

"What are you doing up so early?"

"What? Oh. I'm in Boston for a conference, so I'm in your time zone for a change. But Rob, I have such good news."

"You got a promotion?"

"No, silly." She paused. "I'm pregnant." Alana let out a happy squeal.

Pregnant, already? Alana, a brilliant scientist the same age as I was, had gotten married about ten months ago. "Al, I'm so happy for you. I didn't know you planned to get a family started so soon."

"Yeah. I didn't want to risk waiting until I was older. You know about my mom."

I did, but I'd mostly forgotten. Alana was an only child because her mother had been thirty-six when she was born, and all her mom's subsequent pregnancies had ended in miscarriages, with one in a stillbirth.

"That's right," I said. "Well, congratulations. How far along are you?"

"Ten weeks."

"How are you feeling?"

"Good, mostly. A bit of morning sickness. But now I wish I hadn't had all that champagne at your wedding. At the time, I didn't know."

"I'm sure the baby will be fine." Would it? I had no idea. "Does this mean I'd better get a move on starting my own family?" I scrunched up my nose. Did it? I'd been married only six weeks. I was thirty, which meant I should have plenty of time to bear a couple of healthy babies. On the other hand, I knew of women who had a lot of trouble becoming pregnant, and I knew it could become harder the older I got. Plus, how would I run the restaurant if I had an infant in tow?

Alana interrupted my thoughts. "Wouldn't that be fun if our kiddos were near the same age? They could be like cousins."

"That would totally be fun." We were both the only children in our families. Mostly. Any kid of mine wouldn't have blood-relation cousins except one little half-cousin in Italy. Abe's brother, Don, hadn't had kids, not that I'd ever heard about. And I had only my two Italian half-siblings, one of whom hadn't liked me much when I visited my father and his family in Pisa. "But I'm not promising anything."

She laughed. We chatted a few more minutes before saying our good-byes. A pair of robins had built a nest in the antique lilac bush near the fence. I watched as a speckled young robin made several tries before it flapped its way to the dogwood next to the lilac. Abe and I had also built our nest. Was it time for us to get our own family underway? We'd certainly discussed having children, or more children, in his case. But we hadn't talked about timing or numbers. And we wouldn't today, but we should sometime soon.

I stood, ready to get my child-free day in gear.

CHAPTER 12

I cycled up to the Jupiter Springs entrance at a little before ten. Knitting abandoned in his lap, Grant sat in a
chair on the front patio with his long legs stretched out in
front of him. Alone. *Good.* I wanted to be able to talk
with him without others around.

I braked to a halt and climbed off the bike. "Good
morning, Grant."

He turned his face in my direction. "Good morning,
dear."

"I'm Robbie Jordan. We met the other—"

"I remember." He held up a hand. "It's funny. Without
the benefit of sight, I pay a lot more attention to voices
and sounds that got lost in the shuffle before. Come sit
with an old man." He gestured toward the chair next to
him.

"Thank you. I'd love to." I dismounted and removed

my helmet before I sat. "I'm sorry I come empty-handed. I wanted to bring you some pastries, but Buck said you had diabetes. I figured I shouldn't tempt you."

"That's very thoughtful of you, Robbie. It sounded as if you rode here on a bicycle."

"I did. I'm a pretty devoted cyclist."

"I miss that," he said in a wistful tone. "I used to ride all over the county. There's nothing like having the wind rush by as you coast down a hill, is there? But I can't do it now."

"You need a tandem."

"And a riding partner." Grant wagged his head. "So far, I haven't met anyone in this joint who's interested."

I opened my mouth to say maybe I could help, but I shut it just in time. I would check into possibilities before getting his hopes up or committing myself to something I couldn't follow through on. "I wanted to tell you how sorry I am for the death of your friend Vi."

He clasped his hands in his lap and gazed down at them for a moment. He looked up and in my direction. "I appreciate that. Buckham has told me what a caring person you are. And a good cook, too." He cleared his throat. "But yes, I shall miss my Vi for the rest of my days. Even though I can't see, the world seems even dimmer without her in it."

We sat in silence for a moment. A blue jay sounded its metallic seesawing call. In the distance a woodpecker rapped at a tree until the annoying *wrang* of a chainsaw buzzed into life. A puff of wind blew a cloud over the sun. Another one moved it along, but the moment of relief from the breeze vanished when it did. The day was as steamy as I'd predicted earlier.

"I understand Vi owned a mystery bookstore for a while," I said.

"Yes. She knew every author, every title, and she loved schmoozing with customers about the kinds of books they liked. She still owned it when we met." His expression turned dark. "If it hadn't been for that Gale character, Aunt Agatha's might have been a thriving business today."

Oh? "What did he do?"

"Vi told me the whole sad story. When she was getting started, she needed capital. She'd met the scoundrel somewhere or other. He offered to put up the cash in exchange for half ownership. Vi was a lovely lady, Robbie, but she wasn't the most business-savvy gal out there."

I waited, but he seemed lost in his thoughts. "Why did the bookstore close, Grant?"

"Sorry for the woolgathering. We all know about the online behemoth, sapping sales from perfectly good, small, local stores. And when the town decided to rip up the road in front of the store to replace water and sewer lines, any remaining customers could barely reach the door. Foot traffic disappeared, and sales kept dropping. But the main reason was that Kristopher Gale wanted to cash out."

"He wanted his investment back?"

"Yes." Grant dragged out the word. "But I think something else was going on, too. I suspect Vi had uncovered some malfeasance in his past."

My ears perked up. Malfeasance was something I'd like to check into.

"She never gave me the details," he continued. "Either way, she couldn't afford to keep the store open."

"If I might ask, it must not be cheap to live here at Jupiter Springs. How did Vi swing it?"

"Well, you see, she owned the building the store was in and lived in an apartment upstairs. She sold it for a pretty penny, as well as all her inventory and such. Bloomington real estate has gone up considerably in recent years. She was able to pay off Gale and move here. Then her sister died. She'd never had children and left Vi a tidy chunk of cash. My sweetheart was all set—until somebody killed her." His voice sank to a whisper. He cleared his throat and picked up the knitting. Needles began to click in the same dark green yarn he'd been working with at the fireworks.

"I spoke with Nanette yesterday," I said. "She said she and Vi were founding members of a crafting group."

"Stitch and Bitch." He snorted. "They offended a few people with that name, I'll tell you. According to Vi, Nanette did more of the *b*-word than the *s*-word."

I laughed, although I noted that Nanette had said the same thing about Vi. "I've never learned to knit. What are you making there?"

"It's not much," Grant said. "Just a scarf for my grandson for Christmas. Buckham's boy."

"That's thoughtful."

"I like making gifts for folks. I used to have a full set of woodworking tools and made all manner of presents for my kin, but those days are as far behind me as a bicycle now."

"My mother was a cabinetmaker. I have a number of beautiful pieces of furniture she made."

His needles slowed. "Jeanine Jordan?" He smiled.

"Yes." I gazed at him. "Did you know her?"

"I surely did. I had a woodworking setup at home, but

I also taught it at South Lick High. She was one of my first students. Most of the girls didn't sign up for wood shop, but your mom took it in the ninth grade and never looked back. I was real proud when I heard she'd set up her own business out West."

"I'm stunned, Grant." My throat thickened, thinking of my mom as a girl right here in South Lick. I knew she'd grown up here, of course, but she'd been firmly established in Santa Barbara by the time I was born. Other than summer visits to my aunt, my life—and Mom's— had been in California. "I had no idea."

"Yep. Her and Adele are good people."

"I'm lucky to have Adele nearby." Wouldn't he have heard my mom had died? Maybe not. "My mom unfortunately passed away a few years ago."

The corners of his mouth went down. "I'm so sorry to hear that, hon."

"Thank you." I swallowed. "Buck told me his grand-mother—his mother's mother—is still alive and lives in Floyds Knobs. Is that where you grew up, too?"

"It is, and Mother is hanging in there. My bride and I moved up here when I got the teaching job. It's pretty down there by the Ohio River, but there's not much going on unless you want to move acrost the river into Louisville. Which I didn't. Neither did my Yolande." He held up the knitting. "She was big on this kind of hobby. She was one of the first members of Stitch and Bitch, too."

"So, she and Vi were friends?"

"That they were. Funny, I didn't have a hankering to learn how to do the craft myself back then."

"It sounds like you were busy with your own craft." I watched as he resumed knitting. Should I ask him about his wife's murder? I decided not to. He was grieving the loss of a second love. He didn't need to be reminded of the first. "Buck said he thought it would be all right if I paid your mother-in-law a visit. What do you think?"

"Gracious sakes, hon. Simone would love it. Her mind's as sharp as a fresh-honed knife, and she's basically healthy, but anymore she doesn't get around too well."

The front door of the facility hushed open. Joan emerged, leaning on her walker. "Hello there, Robbie."

"Good morning, Joan. Have you met Grant Bird? Grant, Joan Linnell is a new resident."

Joan made her way toward us. "Pleased to meet you, Grant."

"Likewise, Joan. Welcome to the Springs. How are you finding it?"

"So far, so good. May I offer my condolences on the loss of your good friend?"

"I thank you. The grapevine works fast, doesn't it?" He shook his head, but he smiled as he did so.

"Nanette Russo was telling me over breakfast," Joan murmured. She shot me a look that I couldn't quite interpret.

"Huh," Grant grunted. "Don't believe every word that comes out of that lady's mouth. No matter what she said, you should know that Vi was a lovely person. I'm sorry you won't be able to make her acquaintance."

"I'm sorry, too." Joan looked over as a car pulled up. "There's my sister. Edna was kind enough to drive me out here from the East Coast and help me get settled."

Edna climbed out and opened the trunk. "Morning, Joanie, Robbie."

"Come meet Mr. Bird." Joan gestured to her. She introduced the two.

Peering at the knitting, Edna asked, "That's a beautiful yarn. I knit, too. Where is it from?"

"Shetland," Grant said. "It's the finest in the world."

"Indeed, it is."

"My mother was a McNally, and she swore by it," Grant said.

"Edna, were you comfortable last night?" I asked.

"I was, very much. Thank you."

"Ready?" Joan asked.

"Certainly." Edna bobbed her head, then addressed Grant and me. "We're off for a jaunt around the county, and we have reservations for an early dinner at the Story Inn."

"That sounds perfect," I said. "We open for breakfast tomorrow at seven."

"I'll see you around, Joan," Grant said.

After Edna collapsed Joan's walker and stashed it in the trunk, the two drove off.

"I'd better get going, as well." I clipped on my helmet and stood. "I've got some hills to climb before I'm done."

"Ride a couple for me, will you, and say hello to Simone from her son-in-law. Don't be a stranger, Robbie. It's rare to see fresh, young faces around here."

"I promise." I mounted the bike, clipping my shoes onto the pedals. "Take care, Grant." As I pedaled onto the parking lot, I glanced back at the front entrance. A face stepped back from the window. A thin face that looked a lot like Nanette's.

CHAPTER 13

Having exercised and showered by one o'clock, I made a quick sandwich. I wanted to search for Yolande Bird on the internet, but that would have to wait. I hopped in my little hybrid car and headed southeast toward Simone, eating as I drove. A big antiques seller—well, "flea market" might be a better description—was on the route. My store was running way low on the *pans* part of Pans 'N Pancakes. This was as good a time as any to restock.

Big clouds were rolling in, which cooled the air a little. I lowered the windows. A true Californian, I loved driving, especially solo and out on the open road. It was even better when I could be air cooled and not air conditioned, which always made me too cold.

As I invariably did when I could, I chose the state route over the interstate. It was much prettier, if only one lane in each direction, and I wasn't in a hurry. Route 135 headed straight south from Nashville up and down over the Knobstone Escarpment. I'd asked Abe once about the name of my destination, Floyds Knobs. He'd said Davis Floyd was a colonel in the early 1800s who had been involved with the Aaron Burr plot, but later was an anti-slavery leader in Indiana Territory and a legislator in the brand-new state.

To me, learning about the Knobs part was equally as interesting. Abe explained that *knob* was a geologic term meaning "steep hill," and the Knobstone Escarpment was a rugged ridge that ran from Martinsville southeast into Louisville. It was what gave Brown County its hills, with the highest point being Weed Patch Hill in Brown County State Park.

We'd climbed Weed Patch together once. Gazing up at the fire tower that topped it, I'd laughed out loud when Abe had said that, with 1,058 feet of elevation, it was the third-highest point in the state. Where I come from, that's a cute little foothill.

Driving alone also let me think. After my ride, I'd texted Oscar that he might want to check into what Kristopher Gale did before—and after—he co-owned the bookstore. I added what Grant mentioned about malfeasance. My visit today to Simone was partly because I liked hanging around older people, and partly because I wanted to meet Buck's grandmother. But Buck mentioning that Yolande—his mother—had been murdered the same way Vi had really troubled me. I hoped centenarian Simone wouldn't mind talking to me about her daughter's death. I wouldn't bother her about it if she did.

I slowed at New Pekin when I passed Drifters Bar and Grill, a place famed for simple food, country music, and motorcycle gatherings. Monday afternoon must not be a big draw for motorcyclists. The parking lot was nearly empty. I kept my speed down, searching for the antiques mart. It was along this stretch somewhere.

My eyes lit up at the sight of a big, formerly red barn with a faded sign reading *Antiques Barn*. I turned into the lot in front of the structure, which had a low building attached on the right. Rusty walk-behind plows and hay rakes sat next to an antique buggy against the barn's front wall. The big doors stood open.

Inside to the left was a counter and an old-fashioned cash register, but no one sat behind it. I grabbed the largest shopping basket they had and prowled the aisles, finding tables and shelves full of tools, tablecloths, and toys. I passed an extensive books area and even a couple of clothes racks holding vintage velvet dresses for women and pin-striped suits for men, with a shelf of hats above.

The cookware ended up being all the way at the back, next to a section containing games and puzzles. Another set of wide doors stood open, with a woman and a tall man silhouetted against the daylight. I sorted through the large array of kitchen implements. Most were in reasonable shape. *Good*. I didn't have time to be scrubbing rust off pie pans or whisks to ready them for resale. The prices were reasonable, too, low enough to let me tack on a couple of bucks for resale. I didn't make much on cookware. Stocking it was part of my store's draw, and as long as I didn't lose money on sales, I didn't really care. The proprietor here might even give me a bulk discount if I bought enough.

I loaded a couple of sifters, a stack of nested ceramic bowls, four rotary beaters, and a set of cupcake tins into my basket. I added a well-used wooden chopping bowl and three Knott's Berry Farm pie pans. I wrinkled my nose. Knott's was a southern California establishment near Disneyland that made the best boysenberry pies in the universe. How those pans made their way to the Midwest was anybody's guess.

I hefted my basket. Not only full, it was also heavy, but I spied more I wanted to add. I grabbed a big woven market basket with a price tag on it and added a meat grinder. Around it I nestled cookie and biscuit cutters and a half-dozen pastry cutters with colored handles. I added a bunch of slotted spoons, whisks, and pancake flippers. And I still had my eye on a set of cast-iron skillets and a Dutch oven with a lid.

My hand was on a glass jar with a nut-chopping attachment in the top when the man who had been in the door approached the games section. I nodded at him. Dressed in well-worn jeans and a tan T-shirt, he appeared to be in his forties, with a weathered face to match.

"You have quite the haul." His deep voice had a soft tone to it.

"I know. It's wonderful stuff."

"Don't worry about clearing them out." He smiled with a dimple denting his cheek, cocking his thumb toward the back. "I just delivered an entire kitchen's worth from an estate sale."

"Good to know." I didn't often dwell on the provenance of the cookware I sold. Sometimes I imagined the elderly person whose children—before they died or after—cleared out the much-used and much-loved contents of a home. People who actually wanted old kitchen things were a niche market, one I was glad to serve.

The man started browsing the boxes of puzzles. He squinted at the side of one, then looked at me.

"Miss, can I bother you for a pair of younger eyes? I don't have my readers with me. How many pieces does it say this puzzle has?"

I laughed. "I'm not that young, but certainly." I peered at the box. "It says five hundred."

"Perfect. My daughter loves jigsaws, but she gets frustrated if they're too big. I thank you."

"You're welcome."

Next to the puzzles were a few decks of cards and a fat cylinder holding stacks of red, blue, and white poker chips.

The man stared at the chip caddy and frowned. "That just leads to trouble."

"Poker?"

"Yes, ma'am. When it involves gambling, that is. People who need chips are the people who back them up with money. Believe you me, nothing good comes of that." He shook his head and walked off with his puzzle.

CHAPTER 14

M y car happily full of cookware, I hung a left at
Palmyra onto Route 150, which angled southeast
toward the Ohio River. It wasn't long before I drove into
the village of Floyds Knobs and parked in a visitor's spot
at Knobstone Health and Rehabilitation. Before I'd gone
biking, I'd whipped up a batch of banana–chocolate chip
mini-muffins, which I'd brought in a flat plastic container
I didn't need returned.

Explaining I was a friend of Simone's grandson, Buck
Bird, got me a smile from the receptionist and an aide,
who walked me to a big, sunny common room looking
out onto a garden. After he pointed to a snowy-haired
woman in an armchair by the windows, I thanked him.

"Mrs. Walsh?" I smiled and spoke clearly. "I'm Robbie Jordan, a friend of Buck's in South Lick."

"Any friend of Buckham's is a friend of mine. And

you call me Simone, hear? There'll be none of this 'Mrs. Walsh' business."

"Yes, ma'am."

She pointed a knobby, quavering finger at the chair next to her. "But be sure to speak up. I'm near as deaf as Stone Head."

I sat. "Did you hear his head got stolen?" I'd passed the Stone Head on my way here, a bit before Story. It was a strange, antique, four-foot-tall monolith topped with a head carved in a *Mona Lisa* smile. His arms were crossed over his chest, pointing in opposite directions, with the mileage to several landmarks incised in the sandstone. Vandals apparently couldn't resist the dude.

"More than once, is what I heard. The youth of today." She *tsk*ed and shook her head. "But you know what, hon? We were no better in my day. And that was a very long time ago."

She wore black pants with black Mary Janes and a yellow sweater set draped with pearls, an outfit that would have been too warm if we'd been sitting outdoors. In here it perfectly matched the air-conditioned temperature. In fact, I wished I'd brought a light sweater to throw over my sundress. Simone's hair was puffy and curled, as if she'd just come from the hairdresser, and her nails were trimmed and polished in pink. When I gazed around the room, her put-together appearance contrasted with that of a number of the other residents, who perhaps weren't as fortunate to have their wits about them as Simone was.

"I made muffins this morning." I set the container on the low table between us.

"Robbie Jordan." She studied me. "You're the girl who bought the old country store, and you run a restaurant in it. Now I recall. Buckham has spoken highly of your food. I think I might have to try one of those muffins."

I opened the container and extended it to her.

Simone selected one and nibbled on it, but she narrowed her eyes at me. "You didn't drive an hour down here simply to bring muffins to an old lady. That boy's told me about your detecting abilities. I wager you have questions about Vi Perkell's murder."

I smiled at her direct approach and assumed "that boy" was Buck. "I do have a few questions, if you don't mind."

Simone popped in the rest of the muffin and pointed at me, as if indicating I should begin.

"I understand that Vi, Nanette Russo, and your daughter, Yolande, were founding members of the Stitch and Bitch group."

A shadow passed over her face at the mention of Yolande. "Yes, they were. They were all young moms. Gathering to sew or knit or whatnot gave them a time to get out of the house and do their favorite craft, too."

"Were most of them primarily at home with their children?"

"Six of one, half dozen of the other." She tapped her lips. "Let's see. Nanette worked for a turkey farm. Ginny's Gobblers. The place raised the birds, but they also prepared precooked holiday meals. The cooking was mostly what Nanette did. I can't quite figure her for chopping off turkeys' heads."

Nanette must have trained as an actuary after that time.

Simone went on. "My Yolie loved nothing more than staying home and being a mom. She volunteered at the preschool, was president of the PTA, and started a booster club for Buckham's basketball team. You name it, she did it."

"What about Vi?"

"Oh, she was such an educated bit of a thing." Simone smiled. "She worked as an editor up to Bloomington, for the IU Press."

"Thus, her interest in books later?" I asked.

"Mmm. That girl was always interested in books, and mysteries, too."

"Did Vi and Nanette both grow up here, too?"

"Vi did, but not Nanette. Yolie and her met Nanette in South Lick."

I leaned closer and lowered my voice. "Buck mentioned that his mother was murdered in the same way as Vi."

Simone exhaled. "It's a fact. Sounds to me like you're interested in what happened. I don't tell this to any old body, but to you, I will."

I sat back. "Thank you."

"The Floyds Knobs fireworks at Independence Day were a thing to behold. Still are. Back in the day, people came from all around, even from Louisville. Yolie had been living in South Lick for quite some time. Why, Buckham was a teenager by then, so it had been near on twenty years. But she invited her friends from the group down here for a girls' weekend. My husband and I were away at our farm in Kentucky, and the ladies wanted a break from their kids and husbands."

"Who all was in the group that came?"

"Vi and Nanette, plus Pat Blake. A no-nonsense gym teacher. Pat had a husband, but I don't think she cared much about him. She liked her kid okay, I guess." Simone studied her hands. "Anyway, those girls went off to the fireworks a group of four but came away only the three."

"Yolande was stabbed like Vi was?" I asked in a low voice.

"Yes. Right in the neck, under cover of darkness and exploding lights." She spoke in an equally soft voice. "I've always thought, if I had been there, maybe I could have stopped the killer." She plucked a neatly folded handkerchief from her pants pocket and dabbed both eyes.

"I'm sorry to bring up painful thoughts."

"Don't you worry. It's just that nobody ever gets over losing a child, no matter how old they were, no matter how long it's been."

"I can imagine." I wondered if they'd found the murder weapon. I didn't want to ask Simone about that. "Did the authorities ever arrest anyone?"

"They did not. It near ruined poor Grant, not to mention Buckham. The boy was only sixteen. But they had each other, and they pulled themselves up and out of the grief." She smiled quietly. "Why, Grant is like a son to me. When he said he was stepping out with Vi, I gave him my blessing. And now she's gone, too."

"I'm so sorry, Simone. About your daughter and about Vi."

She gave me a sad smile. "It's all right, dear. I imagine her and my girl having a nip of Four Roses up there in heaven. They're laughing and talking about knitting and books and everything else under God's bright sun."

I wanted to ask more about the motive behind the murder but didn't. I shouldn't be pestering a hundred-year-old woman with questions about painful memories, even though she'd encouraged me to. She closed her eyes. After a moment, I stood, thinking I should slip quietly away.

"Don't forget your muffins, Miss Robbie." Fully alert again, Simone cocked her head. "Or did you mean to leave them?"

I laughed. "They're for you."

She held out her left hand, which still bore a wedding ring with a floret of tiny diamonds. I took her hand and felt her soft, parchment-like skin, which had first seen light when automobiles were new, when white women first won the vote, when the technology we so relied on today was a science-fiction dream.

"You come back soon, hear?" Simone might have been old, but her grip was strong.

"I will."

CHAPTER 15

My hair was still damp as I stirred tomato sauce and ketchup into a mix of browned ground beef, onions, and garlic in a big pot on the restaurant's stove. Those threatening clouds had opened to deliver a pounding rainstorm as I'd reentered Brown County on my way back from visiting Simone. I drove straight to the store to get prep for tomorrow done, but the deluge soaked me on my way from the car to the front porch. The cookware remained in the back of the car. I'd need to unload and price it at some point. Just not now.

Danna had texted me with a suggestion of chili dogs for the next day's lunch special. My assistant, Turner Rao, wouldn't eat the chili, being a Hindu who wouldn't go near beef as food for himself, but he'd always maintained he didn't mind cooking and serving it to others. Now, at four o'clock, I turned off the burner and added

Worcestershire sauce, chili powder, salt, pepper, and a bit of sugar to the pot, giving it a good stir. The chili always ended up a bit too sweet for my taste. Our customers liked it that way, ladled atop a fat wiener in a bun, topped with pickle relish and grated cheese, with chopped onions optional. I could have bought big cans of chili. In fact, I had a few in reserve. But making it from scratch was a lot cheaper. Plus, I could guarantee what went into it and how it tasted.

Too bad I couldn't give Simone or Grant—or even myself—a guarantee that Vi's killer would be identified and locked up. I found it stunning that the police had never apprehended Yolande's murderer all those years ago. Had it been one of her friends? But why? And if not, who would have wanted to kill a former local girl, now a mother and wife, who was enjoying the fireworks on a ladies' getaway weekend? I hadn't heard the name Pat Blake before. A gym teacher. She would be retired by now, I expected. I'd try to do some internet sleuthing tonight if I could.

It made me uneasy that Nanette had been present at both homicides. Maybe whatever happened during Yolande's murder had come up again, and that was why Vi had been killed. But what had it been?

I gave the chili another stir. I would let it cool until right before I left, then stash it in the walk-in overnight to let the flavors meld. I'd decided on blueberry pancakes for a breakfast special. They didn't involve any additional prep. Adding the berries to batter ahead of time only turned the batter blue—not an appetizing look. We would sprinkle a dozen atop each pancake after it was ladled onto the griddle. After I mixed up the dry pancake mix, readied the biscuit dough, and completed a few other tasks, I could head for home for the night.

Thinking about my visits with Simone and Grant, it hit me that neither of them spoke like Buck did. He was always so, "Aw, shucks," with his accent and his grammar. He used colorful phrases that made him sound like he was from a lot farther south than Floyds Knobs and not the educated man that he was. But neither his father nor his grandmother talked like that. For the first time, I wondered if it was an act, a persona Buck put on for his work so he could relate more easily to everyone he came into contact with. Not that one couldn't speak colorfully and ungrammatically and still be educated. It was a lot less common, in my experience.

As a time-saver, I'd started ordering a coleslaw mix. It was a colorful combo of grated green and red cabbage and carrots. In our largest container, I mixed up our special dressing, including the secret ingredient—horse-radish—and dumped in the giant bag of veggies. As I used a big metal spoon to toss the salad, I reflected on how this stage of the investigation was kind of like that random mix of veggies. Unsorted and all mixed up. I wished I had a secret ingredient to help sort it out and solve it.

I'd measured out the whole wheat flour for pancake mix when my phone buzzed from the counter nearby. It was a text from Oscar Thompson. And the detective said he was on my store's front porch. I shook my head as I dusted off my hands. He could have knocked. The man had grown slightly less socially dysfunctional since he'd been going out with Wanda, but not entirely.

I unlocked the door. "Oscar, come in."

He opened his mouth to respond. The rain-soaked sky lit up, followed by a mighty *crack* and a rumble of giants throwing bowling balls. He winced and followed me in. I'd halfway expected to see Buck with him. I hoped the lieutenant's absence meant he was taking a day of rest. He deserved one, and homicide was Oscar's responsibility, not the SLPD's.

At the kitchen counter, I turned. Oscar stood dripping in the waiting area. The door stood open, the wind scattering a stack of store brochures onto the floor. I wasn't sure how a state police detective could have so little common sense. I pressed my eyes shut for a moment, then opened them.

"Would you pull the door shut, please?" I waited until he complied. "Thanks. I'm doing breakfast prep. You're welcome to sit and talk while I work."

He removed a red IU ball cap and shook the rain off of it, then clomped over in his signature black cowboy boots and sank onto a chair. Not the nearest one, either.

"What's up?" I asked.

"Got your text about Gale."

I measured baking powder and salt into the flour. And waited.

"Thank you," he added.

"Sure. Did you find out what he does for work?"

"Seems he's a CPA."

Another numbers person. Maybe that was why he and Nanette were friends. At least they appeared to be.

"Did anybody see anything during the fireworks?" I asked.

"As of yet, our interviews have yielded no useful information." He cleared his throat. "Would you have something else to share?"

I stirred brown sugar into my mix. "Maybe. I visited with Buck's grandmother in Floyds Knobs this afternoon."

"Where is that located?"

"Down on the Ohio River." Oscar was a Hoosier, but from the northern half of the state, I seemed to remember. Floyds Knobs was a small town. I wasn't surprised he didn't know where it was. It must not be part of his beat.

"What is the grandmother's name?"

"Simone Walsh. She's a hundred years old." I should be so lucky to be as clear as she was when I reached that age. "She's still completely there upstairs." I tapped my head. Which meant I probably now had flour in my hair. "You know about Buck's mother's murder?"

"He has told me it's an unsolved homicide. A cold case."

"Yes. It turns out Yolande Bird had gone to Floyds Knobs for a moms' getaway weekend with her friends. Vi Perkell and Nanette Russo were two of them." I stretched plastic wrap over the pancake mix bowl and turned my attention to the biscuits. Into another big mixing bowl, I measured the flour, baking powder, and salt, and began to cut butter into half-inch cubes.

"The third was Pat Blake," Oscar said. "We actually have our eyes on her."

"Why?"

"She has what you might call an interesting past."

I stared at him. "What do you mean?" I'd never heard of her until a few hours ago.

He shook his head. "What I can tell you is she still

lives in her own house. Teaches water exercise and so forth at Jupiter Springs."

"She and Nanette are the only two left of those who were at Yolande's death all those years ago. Sounds like her present is interesting, too."

Oscar bobbed his head. "Yes, doesn't it?"

CHAPTER 16

At our patio table after dinner that evening, our plates held only the remnants of the chef salads I'd assembled out of local greens, hard-boiled eggs, slivers of ham and sharp Cheddar, chunks of tomato, and homemade sourdough croutons, with an herbed vinaigrette drizzled over the ensembles. By the time I'd left the store, the storm had blown through. We'd had to sit on towels out here, because the wooden chairs were soaked, but it was worth it to have an alfresco meal.

"Alana called me this morning," I said. "It was funny. She called at around eight, and I asked her why she was up so early. But she's at a conference on the East Coast, so we're in the same time zone for once. Anyway, she told me she's pregnant."

"That's good news. I mean, isn't it?"

"Of course. She and Antonio want to have a couple of kids."

Abe set his chin in his palm and gazed at me with those big brown eyes. "And that got you thinking about our family."

"Hey, no mind reading." I reached for his other hand. "You're right, of course. We've talked about having babies—or a baby—together, but it was always a bit vague."

"I can't wait to cuddle a mini Robbie," he murmured. "Sean was an infant and a toddler a long time ago. I was a pretty young dad, but I remember how much I loved it, and how hard I worked to be the best father I could be, especially after the divorce."

"Remind me how old he was when you split with his mom."

"The kid was only three. Anyway, I want us to make a family together. But the timing is up to you, Robbie. You're the one who has to carry it. Or them."

So true. "And nurse it for the first year or whatever." I knew I wanted to breastfeed any babies I bore.

"That, too."

"Do you want more than one?" I tilted my head.

"I'm up for that, if you are. I loved having a big brother when I was little, and I'm glad Don's around now, even if we don't hang out together much."

"We'll need to play it by ear, of course. But I'd like to have two, I think. With Sean, that makes three. That's a good size for a family."

"Except he'll be off to college and out in the world for most of our kids' growing up."

"He'll still be their brother," I said. How different my life would have been—and still would be—if I'd had a big brother and a younger sibling in the same house, instead of two younger Italian half-siblings I hadn't met until a few years ago.

"Of course." Abe yawned. "I'm sorry, sugar. It's early, but I'm beat."

I squeezed his hand. "Don't worry. I'll clean up. You go relax."

"But you cooked," he protested.

"So to speak."

"The person who cooks shouldn't have to clean up."

"Seriously?" I smiled at him. "You worked overtime, and all I did today was play. Visit a few people. Do some meal prep. I'm good."

"We'll keep talking about this baby stuff." He pushed to his feet, kissed my forehead, and made his way inside as if it was hard to move his feet. He hadn't even finished his one beer.

We would keep discussing it. One of the many things I cherished about Abe was his willingness to talk things through. Even his feelings. I wasn't sure how I'd lucked out to have met and married such a perfect exemplar of the species. I knew I had plans to hang on to him through thick and thin.

CHAPTER 17

Birdy sat patiently at my feet after Abe went in at around eight. I rewarded him with a couple of forlorn morsels of ham from Abe's plate and two of cheddar from my own.

I drained the rest of my spritzer, sparkling water into which I'd mixed white wine and fresh blueberries. It was a perfect drink for a summer's night, and a perfect night for a little online hunting. The sun didn't set until nine at this time of year, and any mosquitoes appeared to have been washed away by the storm, at least for now.

Before I went hunting, though, I sent Adele an email asking how Samuel was, and how she was, too. I'd never visited the tropics and could only imagine how miserable it would be to fall ill that far away from home. At least they had each other. I ended with my love and the hope that they came home safely. Her answer to my message this morning had been only a quick, **We're fine. Love you.**

Now for Upton and Tina. I wanted to know more about both of them. Have phone, will research. I started with Upton, mostly because I figured a name like that was uncommon enough for me to be able to find him. Buck had said he lived in Evansville. It was a city nearly a hundred and fifty miles from here in the bottom left corner of the state on the Ohio River, not far from the junction of Illinois and Kentucky.

I found Upton Perkell. And his father, too. Upton was apparently a Junior. I hadn't thought about Vi's husband, the father of her children, and I hadn't asked Simone or Josie or anyone else. Had Vi been widowed, or divorced? I kept poking around. There, Upton Senior's obituary. It said he was survived by his children, Upton and Tina. It didn't mention grandchildren, and Vi was not included, so they'd probably already been divorced. Upton Senior apparently owned a leather-working business called Perkell and Son, making fine handbags and belts. Vi's son must own it now.

Huh. I sat back and thought. That work surely involved more than one sharp, piercing tool, like whatever had pierced Vi's neck. Had Upton used one on his mother? The thought made me shiver.

What about Tina? I wasn't sure if her last name was still Perkell, or if she'd taken a husband's name—if she was even married. Tina Perkell popped up earning a master's degree in library science at IU twenty-five years earlier. That would make her in her late forties, about what she looked. I couldn't find any other reference to her. I popped over to the Evansville Public Library site. Maybe she'd followed her brother to the city and gotten a job at the library. But the list of staff didn't include a Tina. I checked Bloomington's public library with identical non-results. Same with the university library. I gave up. Dozens of towns and cities sprinkled this half of the state, maybe hundreds. And each had a library. Anyway, Tina might not even be utilizing her degree at all. I drummed my fingers on the table, hoping Oscar and his special police-search resources would have better luck than I had.

I also considered this mysterious Pat Blake. Or maybe she wasn't so mysterious. I hadn't heard about her before today, though, and then two people had mentioned her. Two important people. She shouldn't be too hard to track down if she taught exercise classes at Jupiter Springs. Maybe Grant even attended. Adele didn't do things like aqua aerobics, but someone else I knew did. Who was it? Maybe Josie.

Oscar had said they had their eye on Pat Blake, but he hadn't said why. He had left shortly after that revelation. I searched for Pat Blake and got way too many hits. Adding "*instructor*" didn't help. But when I tapped "*Jupiter Springs*" into the end of the search line, it was a Bingo. The facility's site said she taught something called "Water Cardio" in the pool and a balance class in the exercise room. She had a website, so I tapped over to that. It outlined her services as a fitness trainer and wellness coach. I knew what a fitness trainer was, of course, but the site was vague on specifics about the coaching part. It did mention her experience providing strength training for older individuals. It also had a line about her experience with a palliative care and hospice agency, but it didn't include any more details than that. Did she help terminally ill patients exercise?

I clicked the *About* tab. Simone had said Pat had had a husband and a child, but she hadn't included anything of a personal nature here. Under a picture of her standing on the sidelines of a girls' soccer game, she'd listed her degree in sports physiology and a master's degree in psychology, as well as her years teaching and coaching at South Lick High. She'd even written a book on how to avoid sports injuries in high school girls. A few glowing testimonials from fitness clients finished up the page.

It all seemed straightforward. I tapped the photograph and zoomed in. She was tall and lean and dressed in what looked like a team windbreaker over sports pants with a line down each side. Despite her looking intently at the field, I could see how pretty she was. A dimple split her cheek, her features were even and proportioned, and a dark ponytail threaded through her ball cap. If she was Vi and Nanette's age, more or less, this wasn't a recent picture.

Why would Pat be on Oscar's radar? Her website had listed her full name—Patricia Yellen Blake—so I tapped that in. *Yellen* was an unusual name, always a big help in narrowing down searches.

My jaw literally dropped. Patricia Y. Blake had been arrested and tried in the murder of her husband, Frank Blake. *Whoa.* So that was what Oscar had meant about her "interesting past." I shut my mouth and kept reading. The jury had acquitted her. An article from a year later reported that Frank's killer was still at large. I studied the dates. This had all taken place about five years after Yolande's death.

That was kind of a bombshell, since Simone hadn't mentioned the murder or the trial. I was surprised the high school had let Pat continue to teach. Her acquittal must have let her get her job back. I peered at my phone again. If the man had died from getting his neck stabbed during a fireworks display, it would be one coincidence too many. But the article didn't include details of the homicide.

When Birdy jumped onto my lap, I set the phone on the table and didn't bother to stifle a yawn. My eyes were tired from peering at the screen, and while I hadn't worked, per se, I'd still had a long day. I didn't need to send a message to Oscar about what I'd learned. He'd been the one to alert me to Pat being of interest, not the reverse.

Instead of poking around in a murder case, my time might be better spent by heading inside and doing the promised cleanup. Then I could do what I really wanted to—slip into bed next to my husband and enjoy his company, whether asleep or awake.

I grabbed the phone, lifted Birdy to the ground, and was about to stand when a text buzzed in from Danna. She probably wanted to talk about specials for tomorrow. But when I read it, I groaned out loud.

I'm sick, Robbie. Won't make it in tomorrow. So sorry. D.

The poor thing. I was sure it was true. She wasn't the kind of employee to call in sick just so she could have a day off. I tapped back a response.

Oh, no. What do you have? Anything I can do?

Ugh. UTI. Super painful. Started meds an hour ago but won't be in shape to work tomorrow morning. Will try for lunch.

Now I really felt bad for her. A bladder infection was the worst. I knew, having had one in the past.

Yes, ugh. Drink your water and rest. Don't come back before you're ready. We'll manage.

Thx.

Turner and I would manage, but it wouldn't be pretty. I'd hired him a couple of years ago because the restaurant had gotten so popular it was hard for only Danna and me to keep all our diners happy. Len wasn't usually available on weekdays. Adele helped out sometimes, but she was out of the country. I could ask Phil, who also knew the routine, but it depended on his schedule. And Abe would be at work. Turner and I had no choice but to manage.

I'd better get my beauty sleep while I could. I stuck the phone under my chin so I could clear the table with both hands. I was halfway to the door when it buzzed again. I nudged open the door with my foot. Birdy raced in ahead of me, following his operating principle of, *Whatever is on the other side of any door is always more interesting than where I am*.

Dishes on counter, door shut and locked, and cat door also secured, I frowned at the phone. No number was listed on the text, only *Private*. I opened the message. And gasped.

We know about you. Butt out of the case or you'll regret it.

CHAPTER 18

I sat at the kitchen table, trying to quiet my racing heart, and forwarded the message to both Oscar and Buck.

I glanced at the darkness outside the sliding glass doors and shuddered. I had been threatened before, but not for a long time. It was never fun. In the reasoning part of my mind, I knew I was in a secure house with a working phone and a strong man, albeit a sleeping one. But my brain's fear center was going wild.

Oscar responded to my text first.

Probably burner phone. Want me to come by now and take your phone so we can try to trace the sender?

No, I did not want to be without my phone.

Thanks, but no.

I doubted they could track down who'd sent the threat, anyway. It wasn't like in the old movies or books, where calls were always from a landline to a landline. Buck's responding text was next.

You take care, Robbie. Lock doors and windows, pull curtains. See you in the morning.

I smiled at his caring message—so different from Oscar's—as I complied. I rued the loss of fresh night air but switched on the AC so we didn't suffocate in our sleep. After I cleaned up the kitchen, I got ready for bed, shut the bedroom windows, too, and slid in.

Spooning with Abe, I tried to quiet my busy, angst-filled mind. I listened to his slow, steady breathing. I imagined floating on the salty waters of a Greek cove on a sunny, breezy day. Still awake. I slowly tensed and relaxed every muscle in my body, from my toes to my eyebrows. Not asleep. I began counting backward from a thousand, a trick of last resort that often put me to sleep before I reached the eight hundreds.

Nothing worked. Instead of getting the restful, restorative night I'd planned on, I nearly tore up the sheets with my constant flipping as I turned over possibilities in my mind.

The message used "we," not "I." Did that mean it was from Tina and Upton? Or did one of the other persons of interest phrase it that way to throw me off track? Kristopher or Nanette? It couldn't be from Pat. She didn't even know of my existence. At least, I didn't think so.

Abe, bless his untroubled soul, didn't awaken from my restlessness. After an hour, I finally slipped out of bed, threw on a tee and shorts, disconnected my phone from the charger by the bed, and padded back to the kitchen. Working on my clues would help. So would a little Four Roses.

Settled on the couch at ten o'clock with clipboard, pencil, and two fingers of my favorite whiskey in a glass to my right, I stared at what I'd jotted down before. Had it been only this morning? So much had happened today, it felt like days had gone by in the space of only one. Birdy chirped as he jumped up and curled at my side. I gazed around the room. We rarely closed the drapes here in the back of the house. I felt closed in, but for tonight, I was in a safe cocoon. The last thing I wanted was a malicious texter staring at me from the darkness.

I started by adding Pat Blake to the *SUSPECTS* list. I stared at the *MOTIVES* list. What if Vi had seen Pat kill Yolande all those years ago and was now blackmailing her? But why wait so long to kill Vi? Or maybe Pat had intel on Vi, and the blackmail was going the other way. No, then why kill the source? Had Pat even been at the fireworks Friday?

So far, this process wasn't clearing my mind at all. I sipped the bourbon, savoring its rich flavor, ever so slightly sweet, the slight bite of the alcohol going down, the warm feeling it left me with. I focused on the paper again.

Two homicides in the past. One in the present. At a minimum, they were linked by the cast of characters at Yolande's death. Upton and Tina would have been little kids then, although they might have taken classes from Pat later at South Lick High.

I didn't know where Kristopher had been in the distant past, and I didn't know exactly how old he was. He would have been young at the time of the Floyds Knobs murder. He'd certainly had a connection with Vi in the recent past. Nanette and Pat had both been at the first fireworks killing, and now Nanette lived where Pat taught fitness.

I flipped to a fresh page. I was better with words and numbers—and food—than I was with art, and I'd started my lists this morning with a plan to create a crossword. Right now I felt this muddle needed some kind of graphical representation to sort it out.

I wrote Vi in the middle of the sheet and drew a circle around her name. At five points at the edges of the paper, I did the same with Nanette, Pat, Kristopher, Upton, and Tina. Each of them got a direct line from their circle to Vi's. I added a connecting line between Pat and Nanette, and between the siblings. I decided to assume Upton and Tina would have known Pat at high school. No, I shouldn't assume anything. Instead I drew a dotted line between each of them and Pat. If I found out it was true, I could darken it to solid.

I stared at the paper. Kristopher was left hanging out in space alone in the bottom right corner, his only connection a line to Vi. *Wait*. The Perkell children had to at least have met Kristopher. He had co-owned the bookstore with their mother. Maybe they knew useful details about him and his business dealings. I added those lines.

But . . . then what? I set down my pencil with a bit too much force, swore to myself, and cradled my drink in both hands. I simply didn't have enough information.

So, what should the logical mind do in that case? What would Nancy Drew do? Kinsey Milhone or Hercule Poirot? Armand Gamache, Gemma James, Harriet Vane? Or even Vera? Nah, not Vera. She seemed like more of an intuitive type.

Regardless, I added one more column labeled *QUES-TIONS* to my original sheet.

What do the Perkell children know about Kristopher? About Pat?

How was Pat's husband killed? By whom?

Who killed Yolande? With what?

Does Nanette have something on Pat? What does Nanette know?

Sitting back, I stroked Birdy with one hand and sipped with the other. I was sure more questions remained. I was equally certain I could not answer any of them tonight. A big yawn split my face. My list making and whatever the graphic was called—not a Venn diagram, that was something different—seemed to have done the trick. Time for this chef to hit the sack.

CHAPTER 19

B less Turner's heart, he was able to come in at six thirty the next morning instead of at his usual eight. I was infinitely glad we were offering a simple breakfast special—plopping blueberries on our usual whole-wheat pancake batter—and that I had premade the chili for the chili dogs. Between the two of us, we didn't have a moment to spare.

"I guess they missed us," I murmured as I popped three orders onto the carousel at eight thirty. "We close for only one day a week, and look how mobbed we are on a Tuesday morning."

"I don't know. Everybody's on vacation?" Turner folded over an omelet, poured out three disks of pancake batter, and sprinkled on the blue nuggets. He was a slender man in his mid-twenties, who still struggled with acne on his face. About six feet tall, his dark eyes and hair reflected his half–Southeast Asian heritage.

Besides being stressed by everybody wanting my attention at the same time, I was still a little shaky about last evening's text. And from not getting enough rest. Even after I'd gone to bed the second time, I still hadn't been able to fall into slumber until nearly midnight, late for someone who had an alarm set for five thirty. I couldn't dwell on the message now, though, or on my unanswered questions.

Buck had said he'd see me in the morning. If he didn't get in here pretty soon, though, his table would be taken. It didn't matter. I was too busy to stop and talk, anyway. I poured coffee for two men in suits and ties. I jotted down orders for omelets, bacon, pancakes, oatmeal, and a basic breakfast of two over easy with wheat toast and hash browns, no meat. I greeted Edna, who had come down from her room upstairs for breakfast, and I delivered blueberry pancakes, sausages, and biscuits with gravy to a lone woman reading the *Indianapolis Star*.

She glanced up. "Thank you. I'm from out of town, but I heard there was a murder in South Lick recently. Do you have much crime around here?"

"Not really, no." Actually? The last homicide had been in May, not that long ago. But the one before that had been six months earlier, and prior to that South Lick had gone a whole year without a single unnatural death. Turner dinged the *Ready* bell. "Enjoy your breakfast, ma'am."

I hurried back to the grill and loaded up my arms with full, warm plates.

"How did you and Danna ever do it with only two in

the restaurant?" Turner had a smudge of pancake batter on his cheek, and the ball cap he wore backward when he cooked was askew. "This is nuts. We're running low on biscuits already, and I need more blueberries."

"I can barely remember how we managed. Anyway, I'll get the berries, and I cut out two extra pans of biscuits before you got here. They're in the walk-in. Is the oven on?"

He nodded, a spatula in each hand, pushing around onions and peppers with one hand and expertly flipping pancakes with the other. I delivered the meals before heading into the cold.

When I emerged from the cooler, the bell on the front door jangled yet again. The person who came in was a tall, attractive woman with a gunmetal-gray well-cut bob and a dimple in her cheek. Her blue polo shirt was tucked into khaki Bermuda shorts, showing off toned calves. My eyes widened. I'd be willing to bet my Cannondale Ultegra bicycle I was looking at Pat Blake. I handed Turner the bag of blueberries, slid one pan of biscuits into the oven, and set the timer. Then I pointed myself toward the door.

"Good morning, ma'am." I smiled at her. "I'm Robbie Jordan, proprietor. Have you been to Pans 'N Pancakes before?"

"No." She didn't smile, but her look was not unfriendly, and she had the most remarkable eyes. Lined with still-full dark lashes, their blue was almost violet. "Name's Pat Blake. Heard you make good food here."

Bingo. The very Pat Blake who had been acquitted in her husband's murder. "You can decide for yourself." I surveyed the room. Buck's usual two-top was the only free table. "Will you be eating alone?"

She bobbed her head once, then turned away and sneezed into her elbow. "Sorry, allergies." She pulled a tissue out of her shorts pocket.

"Bless you. You can have that small table in the back." I pointed. "I'll be over shortly with coffee." Buck wasn't here, and a first-time diner—who was also linked to the current case—totally took priority. I didn't have to deliver a menu, since we'd long ago gone with our regular breakfast and lunch offerings printed on paper place mats. They made cleanup easier and provided something for children to draw on while they awaited their meals.

"Thanks." She headed toward the back, walking with an easy athletic stride, a small backpack slung over one shoulder.

Pat didn't waste words, but maybe I could get a few more out of her while she was here. Except both coffee carafes were empty. I swore to myself. I hadn't set new ones brewing. It was an easy task, with our big, prepackaged coffee packets, but the brew would be a few minutes coming. I grabbed a rag and a tray and waded into the fray, taking money, clearing tables, wiping them down, and resetting with place mats and a silverware roll at each. I hoped the rolls lasted. In a pinch, we'd deliver a clean napkin and a set of silver if we ran out of rolls.

I finally reached Pat's table. "I apologize. The coffee had to brew, but it's almost ready. Can I take your order now?"

"I'd like Canadian bacon with a Cheddar-veggie omelet, and a bowl of fruit, please."

"What kind of toast would you like?"

"No toast, no potatoes."

"Got it." I scribbled the low-carb, high-protein order

onto my notepad. "I think I heard you teach fitness and aqua classes at Jupiter Springs."

She tilted her head. "I do. Who did you hear that from?"

"Oh, I have a friend there." I kept my tone light. "It's such a tragedy about Vi Perkell being killed, isn't it? Did she take your classes?"

She raised her chin and gazed past my left arm. "No."

The bell jangled again. If I had blinked, I would have missed the brief moment when she narrowed her eyes, flaring her nostrils and pressing her lips together. I turned to see Buck amble in, followed by a couple of other parties. When I looked back at Pat, her face was once again composed.

"I'll go put that order in, then," I said.

"Thanks." She pulled out a phone but glanced at me this time. "Coffee, too."

"Right." I wove through the tables to the grill, sticking her order up on the carousel. Buck, hands in his uniform pockets, appeared at my elbow as I grabbed the full carafe.

"I'm sorry, we're full, Buck." I was sure I looked every bit as frazzled as Turner. "Grab a mug and help yourself to coffee while you wait."

"I'd surely like that, thank you. Kinda looks like y'all are shorthanded."

"We are. I'll be right back."

Pat gave a silent nod of thanks when I filled her mug. I was waylaid for refills so many times the carafe was already empty when I got back to the kitchen area. I hurried to start a fresh pot before delivering ready orders for two tables. The oven timer dinged as soon as I returned, so I pulled out the biscuits and slid them into the warmer.

"Listen, Robbie," Buck began. "I'm all thumbs with cooking, but I wash a mean dish. You want I should work on the backlog here?"

I shook my head in disbelief. "I could kiss you!" The sink was, in fact, overflowing with dishes and silverware that needed rinsing and loading into the dishwasher.

Buck took a step back. "Let's not go overboard, now, hon."

Turner laughed. "We'd appreciate the help, Buck. And we both promise not to kiss you."

"Are you off-duty?" I asked.

"No, but I have a minute or two to spare."

I quickly showed Buck the dishwasher. "Don't you want an apron?"

"Nope. Watch me. I'm so tall, I just lean myself over. Never get nothing on my clothes."

He didn't have to push up his sleeves because he wore a short-sleeved uniform shirt for the season. He took a step away from the sink and, sure enough, leaned his long arms into it. The position looked hard on his back, but he clearly knew what he was doing.

I grabbed a handful of place mats and napkin rolls for the tables I'd cleared.

"Would that be Miz Blake at my table?" Buck murmured.

"It is. Do you know her?"

"'Course I do, Robbie. Think she'd mind if I set with her?"

"Well, that's up to you. You can ask, I guess. She was more or less terse to me, but we met for the first time only a few minutes ago." From what Oscar had said, Buck might have reasons beyond being acquainted with her to have a chat with Ms. Blake. "Is she a suspect?" I whispered.

"Not yet, but the day's younger than a newborn calf."

After I cleared and set two tables, I gestured to the parties of three and four waiting patiently. When the counter and sink were empty and the dishwasher was started, Buck dried his hands, grabbed his mug, and strolled toward Pat. I was dying to be close enough to hear. Instead, I needed to deliver more food. But I watched as I moved toward my hungry customers.

Pat glanced up at Buck, then sat back in her chair. Buck had his back to me, hands clasped behind it. She shook her head, hard. He leaned a little closer. She fumbled for her pack and stood. He kept talking. She finally lowered herself back into her chair with a resigned air. Buck pulled out the chair across from her. We were apparently going to have a little police interview right here in my store.

CHAPTER 20

Buck stayed on long enough after Pat ate and left that we actually had a bit of a lull. I'd brought him a full breakfast without even taking his order, for which he'd looked grateful.

Now only three tables were occupied, and the diners were already served and eating. I would have thought Buck needed to be out and on the job. Maybe not. He seemed busy on his phone. I was itching to talk to him about Pat and the case, but I was on the job myself.

"Take a quick break while you can, Turner." I smiled at my hardworking assistant.

"That would be good," he said with a look of relief. He tossed his apron in the box and strode to the men's room.

I quickly threw together another triple batch of biscuits, kneaded and rolled them out, and set up three pans full of the disks that would become tall, flaky puffs of heaven when baked. I unloaded the dishwasher, keeping the silverware in its caddy, and loaded it again. After Turner returned, I took my own quick break.

"How's the supply of pancake batter?" I asked him when I came back.

"Low. I was about to mix up some more."

"Perfect. Can you also please get the pot of chili out of the walk-in and start heating it on low? It's big and it's cold, so it'll take a while to heat up for lunch. I'm going to roll silverware and chat with Buck for a minute, okay?" As the boss, I didn't need to ask him for permission. But we were a team, and today a team of only two. Assuming something was okay—when it wasn't—could interfere with our relationship, and that was the last thing I wanted.

"Of course."

I took a minute to check my email, but still nothing had come in from Adele. I could only hope that not getting news was good news. I carried a stack of clean napkins in my store's royal blue and the caddy to Buck's table. "Join you?"

"Always, Robbie."

He observed my hands as I folded one of the cloth napkins in half diagonally. I set a knife, fork, and spoon near the long edge, folded the two corners over the silver ends, and rolled it tightly away from me.

"I'd offer to help," he began, "but that looks too complicated for a clumsy duffer like me."

"Thanks, but I'm fine." I'd done it enough to be fast at the job, too.

"No more from your mysterious texter?" he asked.

"Not since the last time I checked, which was five minutes ago." I glanced around. We were far enough from other diners not to be overheard, but I lowered my voice anyway. "The message said, '*We* know about you.' Do you think that means it was from Upton and Tina?"

"Can't say. It coulda been the old royal 'we,' right? That is, a single person trying to fake you out."

"I thought about that, too." I frowned, rolling. "How'd your conversation with Pat Blake go? She didn't look very happy to see you."

"She wadn't."

"What were you asking her?"

"If she was at the fireworks Friday night."

That is, at the scene of the crime.

"I didn't see her," he went on. "But Nanette maintains Pat attended. Not setting with the old folks, even though Pat is one, but acrost the park."

"And what did Pat say?" I asked.

"It was like pulling infected teeth out of a ornery, demented boar," he said, wagging his head. "She finally acknowledged as to how she was, in fact, there."

I thought back to that night. "It would have been quite a stretch for her to travel across the park in the dark with all that crowd. She would have to have stabbed Vi and moved far enough away again not to be noticed after the light show ended."

"Yes, it would. She pointed that out herself, as a matter of fact."

After the light show ended. "Buck, I think I told either you or Oscar that Upton and Tina were sitting a short distance from Abe and me that night. Afterward, he said to her, 'Don't you want to go say good-bye to Mom?' Why would he say that if he knew Vi was dead?" I drummed my fingers on the table. I hadn't realized their little exchange might be significant.

"Maybe he said it for public consumption. Already trying to cover his tracks, so to speak. What did his sister answer?"

"She told him no and said she needed to leave. 'To get out of there,' I think were her exact words."

"I'll file that in the database." Buck grinned and pointed at his head.

"And you'll tell Oscar?"

"I will inform our esteemed detective."

I thought of one more thing. "Also, Nanette was sitting on the other side of Grant, who was in the middle of the two women. Wouldn't she have seen the killer?"

"You'd think so. She claimed she was snoozing during the fireworks. I'm not so sure I believe her, but that's what she says."

CHAPTER 21

I was still sitting with Buck when the bell on the door jangled a few minutes later. Corrine strode in in all her statuesque, mayoral splendor: black dress, red blazer, red heels, red lipstick, flaming hair in Farrah Fawcett layers from another century. She beelined right for us and dragged over another chair.

"Golly, it's hot out there." She dragged the first word into about four syllables.

"Good morning, Corrine," I said.

"Madame Mayor," Buck said.

"Howdy, Robbie, Buck," Corrine drawled. Her phone vibrated. She glanced at it and blushed, exactly like she had the other day.

"Is that the new man?" I asked.

"What new man?" Buck followed up.

Corrine was busy answering her text, so I murmured, "She's dating someone. Met him online, apparently."

"Well, butter my butt and call it a biscuit." Buck wagged his head. "Never thought I'd see the day."

"Oh, hush up now, Buck Bird." Corrine set down the phone. "You and Thompson working that case? It needs solved, you know, and fast."

"I know." Buck's phone rang. He wrinkled his nose at it but jabbed the device on. "Bird." He listened, then swiped it off and stood, rummaging in his pocket for money. "Gotta run, ladies. Duty calls."

She narrowed her eyes. "Anything I should oughta know about?"

"Not at this time, ma'am. Catch you both later." Clapping his hat on his head, he hurried out at a pace way faster than his usual one.

A development in the case? I hoped so. "How's Danna doing?" I asked Corrine.

"The poor thing. She was suffering last night, but this morning it wasn't so bad. The miracles of modern medicine."

"I'm glad." I started another roll. By now, I had an impressive stack of finished ones, and the pile of clean napkins was down to about five.

"She said she's going to try to come in and work lunch."

"Really?" I asked. "I told her to take as long as she needs."

"Yes, but you know her. She hates to leave you and Rao in the lurch." Corrine peered at her phone. "No emergency, I guess." She held it away at arm's length. "Dang it, Robbie. There's no getting around it."

"Around what?"

"Getting me some of them reading glasses. I'm warning you. Don't get old."

I laughed. "Yeah, but think of the alternative. Anyway, you aren't old."

"Hon, I'm closer to fifty than forty."

"Think of it this way, Corrine. You can get red readers with rhinestones. It'll be a fashion accessory."

Her expression brightened. "My dear, you're brilliant, you know that?"

"To change the subject, do you know anything about Kristopher Gale? Danna said you had mentioned him in passing."

She tapped her cheekbone. "I've met the man at a bluegrass jam session. But that's about all."

"Thanks." On top of everything else she did, Corrine had her own bluegrass group.

"Now, can I get me a cup of coffee and a plate of blueberry pancakes as a midmorning snack?"

I finished the roll. "Of course. I'll be right back." Corrine and Danna were both so tall they could eat almost as much as Buck without gaining an ounce. I gave Turner her order and returned with a full, steaming mug of coffee. Everybody at the tables still looked content, so I sat again.

"I expect you're helping the boys with this homicide," Corrine said.

The boys. Oscar and Buck, of course.

She doused her coffee with cream and sugar. "Am I right?"

"I'm thinking a lot about it, for sure, and seeing what I can discover."

"Ask me anything. Ain't nobody I don't know in these parts, and all the history, too."

"Okay." I gave a nod. "What else do you know about Stitch and Bitch?"

"That's a good one to start with. 'Course, those ladies are a heap older than I am, and I never was much of a one for that kind of busywork. But there have been rumors over the years." She sipped her coffee.

"About what?"

"Shady practices. Something like that."

"Shady practices in a women's knitting group? That sounds, I don't know, far-fetched."

"It was more so like a cover-up for something shady."

I stared at her. I opened my mouth to ask for more details when the front door opened to a woman accompanying two younger people. Several more followed her, and I could see even more behind, with two additional older adults. I stood. "Tell me more later, please."

Corrine nodded, then pointed her chin toward the newcomers. "Those are the folks from that day program in the old theater building." She smiled. "They all have different kinds of mental delays, but most of them are as sweet as they come, especially Melissa."

I took another look. One girl had the typical look of a person with Down syndrome. A young man next to her was a big fellow with a huge grin on his face. Two other men held hands, the shorter one moving with a vacant look on his face and the other picking at a thread on his sleeve. A light-haired girl in a pink jacket walked with a stiff, flat-footed gait. I hurried toward them.

"Good morning, and welcome to Pans 'N Pancakes. I'm Robbie Jordan."

Many of the newcomers mumbled, "Hi, Robbie."

The woman in front started to speak when the young woman in pink said, "We chose here for today. We get to choose." Her big brown eyes focused intently on me.

The staffer smiled. "Hi, Robbie. I'm Leanne, and I hope this is okay. Our participants at Cornerstone Connections do get to select an outing each day. We like to give them agency over their decisions, and several were eager to visit here. I thought this might be a less crowded time for us to invade."

"It's fine, and I'm glad you came," I said. "As you can see, you picked exactly the right time of day."

"I brought my Disney comic books," the big, beaming dude said. "Do you want to see them, Robbie?"

"Not now, Nathan. Robbie's busy," the staff person said in a gentle tone. To me she added, "We have four staffers and twelve clients."

"Do four tables of four work for you?" I asked.

"Perfect."

I got them seated and took drink orders from those who could speak. "We're short one person today, but I'll do my best," I explained to Leanne, then took the orders to Turner and told him about the group.

"How cool is that?" he asked. "Letting them decide where they want to go."

"It is pretty cool."

"Corrine's flapjacks are ready. I'll start on the drinks."

I headed toward Corrine with her plate. When I passed the girl in pink, she pointed at me.

"I saw you at the fireworks, Robbie." She wore an intense look, almost a frown. "I went with my dad and my grandma."

I smiled. "Yes, I was there. What's your name?"

"Melissa." She proceeded to tell me the names of the others at her table.

"I'm pleased to meet you, Melissa, and all of you. Did you enjoy the fireworks?" I asked her.

She drew her mouth down as she covered her ears and shook her head. "Too loud. Too scary." She flapped her hands, muttering, "Bad things."

Bad things? A chill passed through me. Bad, like murder?

CHAPTER 22

Accompanied by Josie, Danna walked through the door at eleven thirty. Josie sat at a two-top while Danna made her way to the kitchen area.

"Danna, what are you doing here?" I asked.

"Yeah, dude," Turner said. "You should get better first."

"It's not catching, bro." Danna took a long drag from a water bottle labeled *Brown County Volleyers*, the name of the volleyball team she played on. She wore a store T-shirt and jean shorts, not her usual eclectic fashion ensemble.

"Well, you look terrible." He shrugged and ladled chili over two grilled hot dogs in toasted buns. They nestled into the paper boats we served them in, which were also handy for catching chili drips.

He was right. Danna's face was pale, and the beige bandanna she'd tied around her burnished-gold dreadlocks didn't help. The expression on her face was pinched, as if she was in pain.

"I didn't want to leave you guys shorthanded." She started scrubbing her hands. "But, Robbie, I might need to take lots of breaks."

"Of course." I bobbed my head. "Promise me you won't overdo it? And that you'll go home whenever you need to."

She smiled a wan version of her usual beam and held up the first three fingers of her right hand. "Girl Scout's honor." She tied on an apron.

"Who wants to cook, and who wants to bus?" I asked. "I'd like to take orders for a while. I want to chat with Josie for a minute while it's still pretty quiet." The Cornerstone Connections group had left a few minutes ago, and so far, we had only a smattering of early lunchers. I hadn't asked Melissa what she'd meant by "bad things." I hadn't wanted to further upset her, and I'd had too much to do to dwell on it.

"I can bus," Danna offered. "Might make it easier to hit the head when I need to, which is, like, often." She wrinkled her nose.

"You got it." I headed over to Josie, who was leafing through a newspaper. "Good morning, Josie."

She glanced up. "Hi, Robbie." She folded the paper. "Can you sit for a sec?"

"Sure."

"Sorry about our girl, there. She asked me for a ride and refused to stay home where she belongs."

"She's conscientious. I made her promise to leave when she needs to."

"And I'm sticking around so I can take her when that happens. I can assure you, it will happen."

"I'm glad you are." I took off my store ball cap and re-fastened my ponytail.

"Any progress in Vi's case?" She tilted her head, re-garding me.

"I don't think the police have made any, but they might not tell me. I've been trying to poke around a lit-tle—carefully—but I'm not sure I've learned anything useful." I threaded my hair back through the hat and fit-ted it onto my head. "I did visit Buck's grandmother yes-terday."

"Simone is still alive? She must be, what, a hundred by now?"

"Exactly a hundred. And all clear up here." I tapped my head. "She told me about her daughter's murder."

"Yolande." Josie shook her head with a sad move. "I didn't meet her until she moved up here, but we were friends. Vi, too."

"And Pat Blake and Nanette Russo?"

"Yes, although I didn't know them as well. Nanette's always been a bit odd. And you've heard about Pat and what happened to her husband?"

"I read about his homicide last night. Do you know how he died?" I asked.

"I'll have to think about that. It was a heck of a long time ago."

When the door jangled and five people walked through, I stood. "Can I get you coffee or tea? Lunch? Chili dogs are the special."

"I'd love me a chili dog. Sure, give me one, please, and coleslaw, plus a glass of skim milk."

"You got it. I'll be back."

I busied myself welcoming and seating the hungry

newcomers. I gave Josie's order to Turner, but Danna seemed to be missing.

"Danna?"

He pointed to the restroom, then turned two dogs. He flipped a patty and laid a slice of cheddar on it.

"Gotcha." We didn't have any tables to bus right now, anyway. I loaded a hamburger plate, a turkey burger, two bowls of chili, and two chili dogs onto a tray and delivered them, took money from a man who had eaten fast, and jotted down orders for more lunches. By the time I bussed the single guy's table and delivered the new orders, Josie's order was ready.

I wanted to ask her what she'd meant by Nanette being "odd." It was too bad Josie didn't remember how Pat's husband had been murdered. Buck would know. In fact, I could have asked him earlier this morning, but I didn't think of it. I glanced around, but Danna still hadn't emerged. I thought of knocking on the restroom door, but I didn't want to embarrass her or draw attention to one of my employees not feeling well. Both restroom doors were in full sight of the diners, an issue I hadn't thought of when I'd renovated the store. I resolved then and there to put up a shielding wall in front of that area to screen it from sight.

As I headed to Josie's table and set down her food and the glass of milk, Danna emerged, propping open the door with her hip while she tossed the paper towel in the restroom's trash receptacle. My assistants and I had developed strict hygienic practices, including not touching a door handle with clean hands. She slipped her apron back on.

"She was in there awhile." Josie frowned in Danna's direction.

"I know. You might want to eat fast. I don't think she's going to be able to keep going, and I don't want her stressing about being at work." More new diners set the bell jangling. "I don't have long, Josie, but can you explain what you meant by Nanette being 'odd'?"

"I don't know. She always seemed to be hiding something. And she would make bets on everything. If you ever objected, she'd laugh and say it was only a friendly bet." She took a big bite of chili dog. Unlike Buck, she leaned carefully over her plate, so drips and drabs of chili landed there, not running down her forearms.

"What kinds of bets?"

Josie swallowed. "They were both silly and serious. Who would win the governor's race. Which of the Stitch and Bitch girls would finish their project first. The year some random person was born."

"Were the bets for money? Did she usually win?" I asked. This was absolutely my last question. Newcomers were milling around looking hungry. I needed to greet, seat, and take orders.

"Yes, she usually won. The bet was either for money or lunch at our favorite Nashville diner." She shook her head as she sampled a bite of coleslaw. "I refused to play along after a while. I didn't have time for baloney like that."

The bell jangled again. "I have to get to work. Thanks for explaining. Enjoy your lunch."

She narrowed her eyes at the door. "There's another odd one. 'Unscrupulous' might be a better description."

I turned to see Kristopher hovering just inside. I looked back at Josie. "You know Kristopher Gale."

"You bet I do. I told you I was part of Vi's mystery

book club. That man is despicable." She drank down half her milk.

"I want to get back to you on that."

She nodded. Danna bent over the sink and let out a whimper I could hear from here. Josie grabbed her purse and rushed to her side. Kristopher folded his arms, glaring at Josie. *Why?* I didn't think she noticed. I plastered a smile on my face and headed to the entrance, even as Josie ushered Danna out through the service door.

"Welcome to Pans 'N Pancakes. I'll get you all seated right away. Welcome back, Kristopher."

He cleared his throat and greeted me in the most perfunctory of ways. That is, he gave a nod and muttered, "Robbie."

"A table for one?" I asked him.

He nodded again, this time without speaking. *All righty, then.* I got everybody settled. I jotted down orders and took them to Turner, even as I felt terrible for poor Danna. I wondered what kind of conflict Kristopher and Josie had had. He'd aimed quite the look at her.

CHAPTER 23

By one o'clock, the restaurant was full, with ten people waiting to eat. I'd had to supplement my from-scratch chili with two of the big cans when it ran low. Who knew chili would be so popular on another hot day? I hadn't had a minute to step outdoors, but all the customers wore summer clothes. More than one came in fanning themselves with a piece of paper or blotting sweaty necks and brows with a handkerchief. I was pretty warm, myself.

Kristopher had nearly finished his grilled cheese and tomato on sourdough when Buck moseyed in. It seemed like he'd just been here, but, of course, this morning was hours ago. My arms were full of the detritus from a recently vacated table, so I couldn't even wave. Buck didn't make eye contact with me, instead making a beeline for Kristopher. *Interesting.* I checked the people waiting.

None were solo diners, so Buck taking the extra seat at Kristopher's table didn't really constitute jumping the line.

It took me a while to get over there. I bussed, wiped down, and reset tables. I seated and took orders from the hungry hordes and delivered plates full of lunch. But I took a second to thank Turner.

"You're awesome," I told him as he ladled and flipped and did all the rest of it.

"Just doing my job, boss." He flashed me a quick grin.

"And then some. With any luck, Danna will be back tomorrow."

"Man, let's hope so."

We'd each grabbed a bite to eat earlier, thank goodness. Despite my aching feet, sitting would have to wait until closing time. Coffeepot in hand, I finally made it over to the two men, where Buck slouched back in his chair. Kristopher drummed his fingers on the table next to a plate now holding only a half-eaten dill spear.

"Howdy, Robbie," Buck drawled.

I nodded at him. "Coffee?"

"Please."

"How was your lunch, Kristopher?" I poured Buck's brew.

"Excellent." He looked up at me. "Could I have my check, please?"

"Of course." I laid it on the table. I don't know what I'd expected. Actually, I'd wondered if he would be upset by Buck helping himself to the other chair, but it didn't seem so.

"We was having ourselves a little chat about the bookstore business," Buck said.

"It can't be an easy one," I said.

"No, ma'am, it isn't," Kristopher said.

"What do you do now that Aunt Agatha's is closed?" I asked. He didn't know Oscar had told me he was a CPA.

He studied me through narrowed eyes for a moment. "I was never involved in the day-to-day operations, of course. I do this and that."

Buck stretched out his long legs. "Thought you was a tax guy, Gale."

"Yes, that's one of the things I do. I'm a certified public accountant." Kristopher stood and handed me a twenty. "Thank you. I don't need change. Good day, Lieutenant." He strode toward the door.

Buck gazed after him. "He got outta here faster than a one-legged man in a butt-kicking contest. I wonder why."

I cringed at the expression and hoped he never used it around someone who'd lost a leg. "It seemed like he didn't want to talk about whatever he does for work." The ready bell dinged. The diners at a six-top stood. A seated customer held a coffee mug aloft. No time to think about it now.

I pocketed the twenty and picked up Kristopher's dishes. "Chili dogs?" I asked Buck.

"Thanks. Can I get me a burger on the side?"

I jotted it down, marveling at his capacity. "How's your dad, by the way?"

He made a seesaw motion with his hand. "So-so. He sure liked you, though. Was asking me when you might be by again."

"I enjoyed visiting with him. I'll try to ride out there again this afternoon." I headed to the kitchen area. I had liked Grant, a lot.

What with the rush, it was ten minutes before I got back to Buck with his lunch. At least I'd gotten all the waiting diners seated, and a few cleared tables remained empty.

Oscar now sat opposite him. I hadn't seen him come in. "Hey, Oscar. Would you like to order lunch?"

"Yes, please. I would like a vegetable and Swiss omelet, with a glass of nonfat milk."

"What kind of toast?" I asked.

"No toast, no meat." He peered up at me from behind his thick glasses. "Can I substitute coleslaw?"

"Of course." He wasn't as skinny or tall as Buck, but the low-cal, low carb order surprised me. His robust-of-figure fiancée was the one on a pre-wedding diet. Maybe he was eating the same way out of solidarity. "Do either of you have any ideas about who might have sent me that text last night?"

"I'm afraid not," Oscar said. "I'd ask to see your phone, but I don't have the technical skills to learn anything from it."

"Buck, were you questioning Kristopher after you joined him?" I asked.

"Gale was in?" Oscar asked him.

"Yup," Buck drawled. "Was about to tell you, Thompson. I wadn't exactly grilling him, Robbie. Sounding him out, more so. You know, bein' friendly and all."

"Right." I drew the word way out. I gazed from one man to the other. "He certainly didn't seem to want to talk about his occupation, did he?"

"Nope. He did not."

"I'll go put in your order, Oscar."

"After you return, you'll share what new information you might have learned, if you please," Oscar said.

"Sure." I closed my astonished mouth and went about my job. This was a new side of Oscar, asking for my help.

But had I learned anything since yesterday? I wasn't sure. Kristopher hadn't looked like he liked Josie much. Corrine had hinted at shady practices with the craft group, whatever that meant. Josie had mentioned Nanette's habit of betting.

Oscar's lunch was ready a lot faster than Buck's had been. When I set it down, the detective thanked me.

"Set with us a spell, Robbie?" Buck asked.

"I can't, sorry. One thing I learned, Oscar, is that Upton Perkell is a junior, and he owns a leather-working business in Evansville, an artisan shop his father—by the same name—apparently started. I believe they use supersharp piercing tools in that trade."

"So noted. Thank you." Oscar took a bite of his omelet.

"I wasn't able to learn anything about his sister, Tina," I said. "Have either of you?"

"School librarian down to Boonville," Buck replied. "Not far from Evansville. She didn't seem none too happy about her job, neither." He popped in his last bite of chili dog, dripping chili onto his uniform shirt. Maybe he was the reason the SLPD wore navy blue, to keep their second-in-command from embarrassing himself more than he already did with his sloppy eating. Buck never seemed to care. He cheerfully swiped at the drips with his napkin. Too bad he didn't use his lean-over technique when he was eating.

"Did Buck tell you that Vi, Pat Blake, and Nanette Russo were in a needlework and knitting group called Stitch and Bitch?" I asked.

Buck chuckled at the name. Oscar blinked.

"You mentioned that a couple few days ago," Buck said.

"Corrine said she thought it was a cover-up for something shady," I continued. "She didn't know what."

Buck whistled. "Them ladies getting up to criminal activity? Stranger things have happened." He frowned, tapping the table with his long, bony index finger. "Seems to me I have a faint glimmer of a recollection about that. I'll check the records back at the station."

A customer caught my attention. "I have to get back to work, gentlemen. Take care."

"You too, hon," Buck said.

Oscar nodded, his mouth full—and closed.

CHAPTER 24

After Turner and I cleaned up, he offered to help with prep for the next day.

"Nah," I said. "Go home. I'll come back this evening and do it, or I'll show up early tomorrow." I locked the door after him, and the door to the upstairs, too. Edna would use the outdoor stairs to go in and out of the B&B area until I opened up in the morning.

I did a quick assessment of our supplies. We had plenty for breakfast. If I put in an order now for delivery tomorrow morning, for a lunch special we could offer an orzo salad like the one Abe had made. And we still had loads of blueberries, so a quick and easy blueberry muffin could be our special on the breakfast menu.

By four o'clock, I was cycling out to Jupiter Springs after changing clothes at home and spending some much-needed playtime with Birdy. I rode what I thought of as my around-town bike. This wasn't going to be a hard exercise ride, and the hybrid cycle had a big basket on the front. I would pick up a rotisserie chicken, salad greens, and a baguette for dinner on the ride back.

"How's my favorite chef?" Grant asked twenty minutes later. He sat in a big tan recliner in his apartment. The décor was in browns and greens, but it wasn't oppressively masculine. A framed cross-stitch, with the word *Home* surrounded by flowers, hung near Grant's chair, and a striking watercolor depicted a riot of phlox, irises, columbines, and peonies blooming near a pond.

I perched kitty-corner from him on a small couch with a wooden frame. A Shaker-style desk was against one wall. It and several end tables were similar to the furniture my mother had crafted.

"I'm fine, thank you," I said. "Your pieces here are lovely, and they remind me of some of my own furniture. Did you make them?"

"I made all the furniture in here. The school never minded me going in on the weekends to use the shop."

"You must have taught at the same time as Pat Blake."

"Mmm."

"I heard about the business with her husband's death. How was he killed, do you know?" *Oh*. Maybe I shouldn't have brought up another homicide. Too late now.

He folded his long-fingered hands in his lap. "Frank was shot in his sleep."

Shot. "Do you know why?" I asked. "Did he have enemies?"

"Enemies? How about the man never met someone he couldn't pick a fight with, including his wife, most of all. She was accused of the crime but acquitted."

"How did that go over at the school?"

"They didn't like it a bit," Grant said. "But after she was cleared, the administration was obliged to let her teach again. Some of my colleagues weren't too happy about her reinstatement, but I didn't care. She was a good teacher, and she really helped some of the girls excel at sports."

"Hearing about another homicide must have been hard for you, coming, what, five years after your wife's death?"

"Not really. Pat, she was friendly with Yolande, while she was alive. They were in that group together." His smile was a sad one, and he pointed in the direction of the cross-stitch. "My wife made that pretty thing. But her talent didn't end with needles. She painted the spring scene on the wall there, too. I can picture it in my mind, even though my eyes don't see it."

"It's very pretty. Is it of Pike's Pond?"

"You know your Brown County. That's exactly where she painted it. She would sit outdoors in all kinds of weather, painting. Took Buckham along with her until he became a teen and had his own activities. He would bring home frogs and all whatnot."

"I keep learning new things about Buck." I'd have to ask him about the art excursions.

"He's a good son, he is." Grant stroked the cushioned arm of the recliner and gave a little laugh. "I made all the furniture in here except this comfy boy, of course. Buckham convinced me to buy it. Do you know, Robbie, it came with a remote control? If I end up too poorly to stand up on my own, it even has an ejection setting to tip me out."

"You seem to get around fine so far. How are you doing? I mean, with your grief about Vi?"

His smile slid away. "It's not easy to find new love at this age. To lose it is even harder."

I reached out and touched his knee. "I can imagine. Would you like to tell me happy memories about her? I know that helped me when my mom died."

He patted my hand, then leaned back and interlaced his fingers in his lap. "You are a thoughtful person, Robbie. I would like to talk about my Vi. Why, there was one time when . . ."

I let him talk on, his face aglow with thoughts of happier days. I knew the feeling. A picture of the two of them sat in a frame on the desk. Grant and Vi stood beaming, arm in arm, in an area bedecked with summer flowers.

He stopped only when his phone, sitting on the low coffee table in front of him, gave two *dings*.

"That's my five-minute dinner warning." He boosted up to standing without the benefit of the remote. "I thank you for listening, dear. I'm sorry to cut short our visit, but they like us to be on time for these ridiculously early dinners. Will you walk an old man out? I have one of those canes, but it only gets in the way."

I stood, too, and took his proffered elbow. "Of course."

He switched his hand, tucking it through my elbow.

As we passed the open door of the room next to his, he paused. "This was Vi's room." He stepped inside and ran his hand across a floor-to-ceiling bookshelf adjacent to the door. "Look, Robbie. This holds only mysteries."

I followed him in and gazed at the titles. "What a treasure." I pulled out an Erle Stanley Gardner title and opened it. A signed first edition. Same for hardcovers by Rhys Bowen, John Grisham, Tana French, and Ann Cleeves, plus she had shelves full of historical and contemporary cozy mystery titles. "This is an amazing collection."

"It is. Anymore, I can only 'read' with audio books." He put finger quotes around the word *read*. "I tried to learn Braille after I lost my sight ten years ago, but I'm too old to pick up such a complex system, I think. All these smart devices like my phone read everything out to me, anyway." He lowered his voice. "The folks who run this place are all over Vi's children to clear out the room, and I've overheard those two arguing about what to do with the books."

"Isn't there a library here?"

"There certainly is, and it's well stocked. I think they would welcome the addition of Vi's collection. But Upton and Tina? They quarrel about everything, including which of them is responsible for their mother's debts."

"She had debts?"

"I didn't think so. According to them, she did. Or maybe they're anticipating funeral costs."

Funeral. "Do you know when Vi's service will be?"

He shook his head and led me back into the hallway. "My son says the state police have to release the body first." His voice caught on the last two words.

I squeezed his arm. Right before we reached the dining room, Grant pulled me to a halt.

"Robbie," he whispered. "I picked up on the oddest sound on Friday night."

I stared at him. "Like what?"

"It was during a pause between fireworks explosions. I do believe I heard my Vi being murdered."

CHAPTER 25

What? Time seemed to stand still. From the open dining room door came the perfectly normal sounds of
laughter, silver on porcelain, murmured conversations.
Two women passed us, one leaning on a walker, the other
walking with a gray cane.

I searched Grant's face, his sightless eyes the color of
faded cornflowers. A patch of thin white stubble on his
jaw where he must have missed it shaving. His salt-and-
pepper eyebrows, with a long, rogue silver hair curling
out of the left one.

I swallowed. "Grant, what did you hear?" I whispered.

He turned his face upward, as if thinking, conjuring up
that night. "It's like this, Robbie. It was noisy as all get-
out, naturally. Poor old Horace wanted to sing. Nanette
kept telling him to shut his fool trap, which didn't do a

lick of good. The man doesn't have a mind at all anymore. He just knows he loves the old songs. The more patriotic, the better."

Adele and my mom had talked about their father, the grandfather I'd never known. He'd died from Alzheimer's, but he'd hung on to his beloved choir pieces until nearly the end, remembering the tunes and all the words. It was a horrible disease, and Grandpa Fred's love of music had been the only thing that could comfort him.

Still, I needed to know more about what Grant had picked up on during the fireworks. "But you heard something."

"I did. I mean, I think I did." He also kept his voice low. "There was this moment when the noise paused. All sound went quiet, which never happens."

True. If I closed my eyes and listened to the world, something audible was always happening. Always.

"At the time, I didn't understand it," Grant continued. "It was the smallest of noises, but I swear I heard something. And later, Robbie, when I learned what had happened to Vi, I put it all together."

What would a needle going into a neck sound like? Would Vi have gasped? Struggled? It was awful even to contemplate.

A staff person approached to escort Grant to his dinner table.

"Have you told Buck?" I asked Grant, my words tumbling out.

He shook his head. "I couldn't. Not with what happened to his mother. Will you inform him for me?"

"Of course."

I watched Grant disappear into the dining room. Right

then and there, I sent off an urgent text to Buck telling him he had to talk to his dad again about Vi's murder. Even though Grant was vision impaired, there had to be more to the story. Had he smelled the person's scent? Picked up on a voice, a cough, a grunt, a whispered farewell message? What exactly had he heard?

CHAPTER 26

I texted Danna from the store at seven that night.
How are you feeling?

I'd sent her a message before I rode out to see Grant,
simply telling her to rest and be well. Still, I had a restaurant to run, and another day like today would be brutal for
Turner and me. I needed to know if I should rope in additional help.

Way good. Meds are working. See you in AM.
Awesome. Glad to hear it.

It really was good news. And I needed some after what
I'd learned from Grant. The two hours since then had
been occupied with riding home and a quick, grocery-
store take-out dinner with Abe before he left for banjo
practice. I'd then driven here to the store to do meal prep
for tomorrow.

Now flour was on my hands and opera was on the

speakers, which helped me to both work and think. I was yawning, too, so I needed to work quickly and get home to bed. Even if we did have all hands on deck tomorrow, any day in the restaurant tended to be hectic.

When my phone buzzed, I nearly ignored it. After I dusted off a hand and read the text, I smiled, hurrying to the door to unlock it.

"I bear gifts of sweetness," Phil proclaimed, arms full of brownie-laden trays.

"I return gratitude." I returned his smile, as well his flowery formality, and let him in.

"That flour on your nose tells me I interrupted something." He set down his trays. "Can I help?"

"Always. First things first." I opened the door to the walk-in. "Let's stash those and get ourselves a drink. Tea and Four Roses?"

Phil held forefingers to temples. "Mind meld."

Two minutes later, he perched on a stool opposite me, rolling silverware while I cut butter into the biscuit dry ingredients.

"Any word on how Samuel is?" I asked. "I didn't get an update from Adele."

"Doing better every day, thank the Lord."

"I'm so glad."

He finished a roll and lined up the silverware on another napkin. "Don't you think it's kind of nuts for old people to go wandering around in the tropical wilderness?"

"Dude, Mumbai might be tropical. But it's so not wilderness. You know it's a huge, modern city, right?"

"I guess." He took a sip of his bourbon-laced tea. "What's happening closer to home? I mean, with that lady's murder."

"Nothing, as far as I know." I drank from my own mug. "It seems to be a mess of past history, family resentments, maybe some financial wrongdoing. Hey, Phil?"

"Yes?"

"Will you look something up for me?" I gestured toward his phone with my chin.

"Sure. What?"

"Check out a place called Ginny's Gobblers. A turkey farm."

He laughed. "I don't have to do that. It's in Beanblossom. Your pal Martin owns it, the Mennonite dude. That is, his mother does. She's Ginny. Why did you want to know?"

"Nanette used to work there, a long time ago. Interesting. I'll have to give Martin a call."

"Is that guy involved in the murder? The one we were talking about the other day—somebody Gale?"

"Kristopher Gale. He might be, but I'm not sure how. Did you ever run into him in Bloomington? He says he's a CPA, but he seemed evasive about it."

"A CPA?" Phil blinked, frowning a little. "Now the name rings a bell. I think my parents might have used him for their taxes for a while. Then they switched to someone else. They had a reason, but I can't remember what it was. Lemme text Mom and ask her." He paused his rolling to pull out his phone.

I lightly kneaded the biscuit dough, formed it into several large disks to stash in the walk-in overnight, and wrapped them in plastic.

Phil looked up. "Mom says Gale charged them way too much and missed some important deductions they could have taken on their taxes. When they confronted him, he claimed it was due to a software glitch, and he refused to give them a refund. She suspects he cheated them."

"Whether he cheated them on purpose or not, to refuse them a refund is a bad business practice."

"Would it be more help right now for me to roll napkins or to dig further into this guy?" He cocked his head.

"Dig, please."

He dug, while I mixed dry ingredients for pancake batter. When that was done, I turned on the oven, then greased a half-dozen twenty-four-count tins. Even if I baked them tonight, the blueberry muffins would still be plenty fresh tomorrow. I'd filled two tins with batter when Phil glanced at me.

"This is crazy," he said. "It's a gossip column, from the looks of it, and it claims Gale has something to do with a gambling ring."

"He doesn't have a criminal record?"

"Not that I've found. But the craziest part is that the gambling is associated with a bunch of women knitting and stuff."

Whoa.

"Get this," he went on. "The name of the group is—"

I interrupted him. "Stitch and Bitch."

"How'd you know?" Phil asked.

"Danna's grandma told me, plus Corrine knows about it. It's a long-running craft group that Vi and a couple of other South Lick women founded. They probably have dues and everything." I scraped out the bowl of muffin batter, topping up the last tin, then slid the pans into the oven. "I'd heard there was something shady about the group. She also said Nanette made bets on all kinds of things."

"They might have needed a money guy like Gale."

"Maybe. Or maybe they'd wanted to keep it quiet." Kristopher had been enmeshed with the finances of Vi's store, and possibly with a gambling group. Had his involvement also stretched to murder?

"Anybody else you want me to check into?" Phil asked.

"Maybe in a few minutes. I have a car full of cookware I still need to unload and price. Can you help me with that first?"

"You bet."

I set the timer for the muffins, and we headed out. A few minutes later, a couple of tables were covered with my purchases. I set to dusting them off and adding price stickers.

"MacDonald's Research, at your service." Phil grinned, his thumbs ready on his phone.

"Can you look for Buck's mom, Yolande Bird? She was murdered, like, thirty years ago, and it's still unsolved."

"One of those 'cold' cases."

"Yes." I hurried to the oven when the timer *ding*ed. "She died in Floyds Knobs, down on the Ohio." Muffins out and Sharpie in hand, I headed back to my pricing.

"You got it." Phil thumbed and poked and read. "Here's a few stories with lurid headlines. 'Hen Party Homicide.' 'Fireworks Fiasco Ends In Fatality.' 'Area Mother Murdered.' And worse."

"Ugh." I stashed the whisks and flippers in a crock and labeled it, "One dollar each."

"Here's another. 'Police Stymied in Fatality.'"

"What papers carried the story?"

"The *Indianapolis Star* and the *Louisville Courier-Journal* seem to have covered the story for the first couple of days," he said. "It was the local papers—*Floyd County News and Tribune* and the *Brown County Democrat*—who kept reporting."

"No details on who or why, though?" I asked.

"Nope. And the story seems to just die after about a week."

"Weird, huh?"

"Not really. No news is no news. I bet that even back then, newspapers were short-staffed. And if the police didn't come up with anything else to report on, then there's nothing to report."

"I guess." I settled the set of nesting bowls on a shelf. But why hadn't the police ever solved the case? That was the more interesting question.

CHAPTER 27

"I'm so glad you're feeling better, Danna." And I was. She'd arrived promptly at six thirty the next morning while I was in full setup mode. Now, at a few minutes before seven, the restaurant smelled as good as it always did, with scents of bacon, biscuits, berries, and baking batter filling the air. Plus fresh coffee, of course.

"Me too, boss. I have my trusty cranberry juice in hand." She grinned, lifting a bottle of the red juice to her lips. Today she was styling magenta overall shorts over a fluorescent yellow biking shirt, with high-top tennies in turquoise. A turquoise scarf bundled her dreadlocks out of the way. The color in her cheeks and her energy were back to normal, too. "I still might have to take breaks more often than usual."

"Whatever you need to do."

"Thanks." Danna flipped three sausages. "So, no real progress on the murder case?"

"Not really." That was the question of the week for people to ask me. I only wished I had a better answer. I pulled out one sheet of puffy biscuits and slid another into the oven. "A few bits and pieces of info, but it's not really hanging together."

"You're staying safe, right, Robbie?" She gave me a concerned glance. "I mean, in the past you've been in, like, danger."

I wrinkled my nose. "I did receive a threatening text the other night. Phil came by last evening with brownies and to help. He followed me home in his car, to be sure I got there safely."

"Good." She pushed around a pile of mushrooms sautéing in advance of omelet orders. She pointed her chin at the big school clock on the wall. "Yo. It's seven."

"Oh! So it is."

"I'm ready if you are."

I gave her a thumbs-up and headed for the door, unlocking and opening it to see Buck and Oscar first in the line of a dozen hungry diners. "Good morning, gentlemen."

Oscar nodded and headed to Buck's table. Buck held back, letting those behind him stream in.

"Sit wherever you'd like," I greeted the others. "I'll be around to take your orders right away."

When we were alone, Buck pointed at me. "You're staying safe? No new texts?" He gazed down his nose at me, his brow knit in worry.

"Safe, yes. And no new threatening messages. I'll try

to carve out some time to talk with you and Oscar, but it might be tight until Turner comes in at eight." I'd gotten home last night at the same time as Abe. Texting a homicide investigator about Kristopher Gale had been the last thing on my mind.

"I hear you."

"No developments on your end?" I shifted from one foot to another. Diners gazed at me in search of coffee, if not also breakfast.

"We'll talk." He stuck his hands in his pockets and ambled toward Oscar.

I blew out a breath. I pointed myself toward the coffee carafes and my livelihood.

When Buck and Oscar's orders were ready, I carried them over, amused to see the two ignoring each other. Instead they were both focused on their phones, like teenagers and half the other diners in here. Didn't people talk to each other over a meal anymore? I set down a Kitchen Sink Omelet—which included ham, cheese, and all the veggies—for Oscar. He must have been hungry today, because he'd included bacon and toast with his order. Buck got his usual onslaught of food, plus three blueberry muffins.

"I don't have long," I began in a low voice. "Have you checked out Kristopher Gale's connection with the Stitch and Bitch group?"

Oscar nodded. Buck, his closed mouth full of pancakes but leaking maple syrup at one corner, appeared bewildered.

"Also, Phil MacDonald's parents had a bad experience with Gale as their accountant," I said. "You might want to talk with them."

"You can connect us with these people?" Oscar asked.

"Of course." I nodded. "Buck, did you talk with your dad last night?"

"I tried," Buck mumbled around a bite of muffin, having the grace to hold his hand in front of his mouth. "He'd already gone to bed."

I leaned closer to the table. "He told me he thinks he heard Vi being murdered. You have to go out there and find out why he thinks that."

Oscar blinked behind his glasses. Buck looked stunned. I glanced at the grill to see a panicked-looking Danna signaling me.

"Enjoy your meals." I hurried to Danna.

She tore off her apron. "Sorry."

"I'll take over." I checked the orders, flipped three pancakes, and poured out beaten eggs for two omelets. When I glanced at the clock, I swore under my breath. It was only seven thirty. Every table was full, and a party of six had come in a couple of minutes ago. Edna had trotted downstairs shortly after seven and had ordered a simple breakfast of oatmeal and fruit, plus a muffin. Now she stood from her two-top and picked up her dishes, silverware, paper menu, and napkin, and carried her detritus to the sink.

"Edna, you didn't have to do that," I protested.

"It's not a problem, and I can see how busy you are. Is your assistant all right?"

"Yes." I kept it to that. The last news I wanted to get around was that Danna wasn't feeling well.

"I'd love to help, and I know my way around a kitchen." She set her hands on her round hips. "Can I go around and pour coffee? Clear tables?"

I tilted my head and gazed at her. "You really don't have to."

"But I'd like to."

I didn't have time to politely protest. "That would be awesome, and thank you. Grab yourself an apron. My second person comes in at eight, so the pressure will be off soon."

Her laugh was a cascade of bells as she tied the store apron behind her back. "I admire you for running this place so well, Robbie." She washed her hands, then grabbed the carafe and headed out among the tables.

This lady was getting a free night's stay, on me. Sure enough, having a third hand on deck made all the difference. When Danna emerged, she said she would take orders and deliver food. I took a second to introduce her to Edna when she returned an empty coffee carafe.

Danna set a new one to brew. "Thanks for helping out."

"It's my pleasure." Edna sidled closer to me at the grill. "Robbie," she murmured. "That fellow, Grant, whom you were talking with the other day. He told my sister to be careful around Nanette Russo. Do you know why?"

"Mmm." I laid three rashers of bacon on the grill and gently turned two fried eggs. How should I answer her without getting into a lot of speculation? "Grant has known Nanette for a long time. She and his late wife were friends, and Nanette was in a craft group with Vi Perkell."

"The lady who was murdered."

"Yes."

"Joan has heard a bit about Stitch and Bitch," Edna said. "Quite the name, isn't it?"

I smiled. "Yes. Anyway, Grant is our local police lieutenant's father. If he thinks Joan should tread lightly around Nanette, he's probably right."

Edna frowned. "Do you think it's safe for my sister to live there?"

"Of course. It's a well-run place. I'm sure she'll be fine."

"It had better be. I have to drive home tomorrow. I'd hate to leave her in a residence where homicide is a possibility."

"You're right that Vi was a resident, but she wasn't killed there at Jupiter Springs. It's a safe facility."

She bobbed her head. "I expect it is, but I'm glad to hear you say so, too."

I plated four orders and dinged the ready bell. Danna hurried over, sticking three new orders on the carousel. The door admitted five more hungry customers. Buck waved at me.

"Edna, could you please get those?" Danna gestured at two vacant tables needing bussing.

"I'm on it." My B&B guest shot me a concerned look before bustling off, rag in hand.

"Danna, we're running low on biscuits already. I think there's one more disk in the walk-in, but as soon as Turner comes in, we'll need to mix up and bake more, stat." Personally? I was running low on reassurances. Was it safe for Joan to live at Jupiter Springs? Was it even safe for Grant, if he'd heard the murder take place?

CHAPTER 28

We hit a true lull around ten thirty. "Hey, gang," I said to Turner and Danna. "I forgot to go to the bank on Monday. I'm heading over there now. You guys okay with assembling the orzo salad? The olives and orzo came in with this morning's order. We should have everything else."

Turner picked up the recipe from the counter where I'd left it. "Sounds awesome. We can handle it."

"Thanks." I tossed my apron into the dirty-linen box.

Danna nodded her agreement. "Did you create the dish?"

"Not I." I laughed. "Abe made it for dinner the other night. It's easy and tasty and can be served at room temp. A triple win." I washed my hands and grabbed the bulging bank envelope I'd extracted from the safe in my apartment. "I won't be long."

I pondered as I walked the few blocks to the bank. Unease walked with me. I hadn't had a chance to talk with Buck and Oscar again. Our lifesaver, Edna, had left looking a little worried. I finally had the mental space to think about what Phil had uncovered.

Kristopher Gale was a couple of decades younger than the senior citizens in Stitch and Bitch, but maybe they'd only started the illegal stuff more recently. How had they roped him in? And what exactly did they gamble about? Did they rig bets? On what, how many stitches someone would drop? A giggle slipped out of me, making a passing couple shoot me an odd look. Josie had mentioned Nanette liked to make bets.

But this had to be more serious than gambling on knitting. Didn't it? It occurred to me that maybe Kristopher was behind the gambling. Maybe he'd roped the ladies in rather than the reverse. But what were they betting about?

Clouds overhead glowered. The red-white-and-blue bunting the town had hung from the lampposts for Independence Day whipped in the wind. If my thick hair hadn't been threaded through my store cap, the wind would have taken the hat. We were in for a rainstorm pretty soon.

I pulled open the heavy, etched-glass door to the restored Art Deco building that housed South Lick First Savings Bank. It was one of several around town built in the historical style, with its rounded geometrical lines, and I loved that the buildings had been preserved rather than torn down.

I accomplished my banking at a teller's window. Making a big deposit always gave me a rosy feeling. A lot of it would go right back out, to my employees' salaries, to pay the food supplier's invoice, to zero out the utility and insurance bills. But not all. Pans 'N Pancakes had been operating in the black for nearly the whole time since the day I'd first opened and welcomed in the public. My country store would be four years old in a couple of months. I smiled to myself, pocketing my deposit slip. I should throw a birthday party in October.

As I turned to go, I heard a voice I thought I recognized. I slowed my step, listening.

"It's not right," the voice protested from within one of the walled-off offices.

Was that Vi's son, Upton?

"Mr. Perkell." The speaker bit off her words.

Bingo.

"We can't possibly release it to you at this time." A woman in the bank's signature green blazer ushered Upton from the office. "We'll be in touch after matters are finalized."

"But—" he began.

The banker turned and went back into her office. The door clicked shut behind her. Upton glared at it with clenched fists. He muttered under his breath and gave his shiny head a shake before turning away.

He caught sight of me and curled his lip. "What are you looking at?"

"Hello, Upton." I smiled in a perfunctory, polite kind of way. "I'm not looking at anything. I finished my banking and saw you, so I thought I'd say hi."

"Sorry." He peered at me. "What was your name again?"

"Robbie. Robbie Jordan."

"Right. From the country store." He glanced back at the closed office door, then strode toward the exit. He wore a crisp blue Oxford shirt tucked into fashionable jeans—with a pressed crease—secured by a belt in a tooled dark maroon leather.

I followed close on his heels until we stood on the sidewalk. "I couldn't help but overhear a little of your conversation in there. Did they give you trouble with your banking?"

"With my mom's banking, more so. I'm not sure this is best institution to trust with your money, Robbie."

"Oh? I've always had excellent service with First Savings. What seems to be the problem?"

He finally looked me in the face. "I can't go into it." He let out a sigh and began to turn away.

"Do you and your sister have a funeral planned yet? I would like to pay my respects."

"Not yet. But thank you. I'm sure you'll hear about it." He stopped and stared at me. "You seem to hear about everything, Robbie Jordan." His tone was suspicious, challenging.

I lifted a shoulder and dropped it. "I run a restaurant where everyone in town comes to eat. I do hear a lot." I swallowed. Time to change the subject, in case he was my threatening texter. "That's a striking belt you're wearing, by the way. Where did you buy it? My husband's birthday is coming up, and he would love something like that."

"Thank you." The aggressive look slipped off his face, replaced by one of pride. "I made it of Moroccan leather. My company produces fine leather products." He extracted a card from his shirt pocket. "We can custom-craft a belt for your husband, made right here in the U-S-of-A."

"I like to support Hoosier businesses." I glanced at the card for Perkell's Fine Leather before pocketing it. From the change in the business name, I guessed Upton must not have a son to pass the business to. "Evansville. Do you ship?"

"Of course. Anywhere in the world, in fact."

"Awesome. I'll be in touch. For now, I'd better be getting back to work. I hope you and your sister will come in for a meal while you're in town."

He only nodded before striding away in the opposite direction. Had I diverted his suspicions? I sure hoped so.

CHAPTER 29

Things were picking up in the restaurant by eleven thirty, although a few empty tables still awaited lunch diners. My crew had worked their magic on the orzo salad, and I'd treated my stomach to a small bowl of it when I returned.

"It's perfect," I told Danna at the grill.

"It was easy peasy," she said.

"Lemon squeezy," Turner chimed in.

"Piece of cake." Danna grinned at him.

"No sweat," he returned.

I laughed. "Is this what you two do when I go out? Compete for the best cliché?"

"Like water rolling off a baby's back." Turner scrunched his nose.

"Or the worst mixed metaphor." Danna pointed the spatula at Turner. "That one was bad, bro."

He shook his head but smiled as he headed off to bus a table.

I washed my hands and aproned up, still thinking about Upton and his displeasure with the bank. It had sounded very much as if he wanted to withdraw from Vi's accounts before her estate was settled. He was probably in for a long wait. My mom's finances weren't fully finalized until at least a year after she died.

My senses stood at alert when Tina Perkell stepped into the restaurant with a tentative air. I was on greeting-and-order-taking duty, so I bustled over to her.

"Good morning, Tina." I smiled. "Are you here for lunch?"

"Um, I think so." Dressed for the weather in navy Capris and a white sleeveless top, she glanced around. "Did my brother come in?" She clutched the handle of a soft, cream-colored leather purse slung on her shoulder, made by Upton, no doubt.

"No, but I saw him at the bank downtown about half an hour ago," I said. "He seemed unhappy about what they told him."

"Are you freaking kidding me?" She gave me an incredulous look as she folded her arms, which made the bag slide down to the crook of her elbow.

"I'm not."

"I told him not to even ask. It's pointless for us to try . . ." She gave a little start, as if realizing whom she was speaking to, and let her voice trail off. "Well, never mind. Sure. I'd like to eat, while I'm here."

"Please follow me." I led her to an open two-top. "I'll be back in a minute to take your order. Coffee?"

"No, thanks." She sank onto the chair. "Is it too late— or early—for a Bloody Mary?"

Here was a woman after my own heart, except I had to disappoint her. "Sorry. We don't serve alcohol unless you bring your own."

She twisted her mouth at that. Her phone buzzed, and she held up a finger as she read it. She tapped back a quick reply, then looked up. "Do you have tomato or V8 juice?"

"Of course."

"Please bring two big glasses of it, then, but not all the way full. And someone will be joining me."

Bringing vodka, I assumed. I'd have to wait to see whether Upton would show up or someone else.

"You got it," I said.

"Plus hot sauce, if you have some."

I gave her a nod. I took three orders at the next table, poured coffee at a four-top, and seated a party of six hikers with flushed cheeks and sweaty hair.

I was on my way back to Tina with her V8s when the Cornerstone Connections staffer hurried in. She caught my eye and gestured for me to head in her direction, which I did after I set down the glasses in front of a phone-absorbed Tina.

"Robbie, I only have a second." The staffer's brow was knit, and she rubbed her thumb and fingers together.

"Not a problem. I'm sorry, I can't remember your name from the other day."

"I'm Leanne. Leanne Ilsley." She glanced around and leaned toward me. "Remember Melissa, the girl who said she saw you at the fireworks?"

"Of course. What's up?"

"Melissa told me she saw a skinny person do a bad thing that night."

I froze. And peered at her, blinking. "She didn't say whether it was a man or a woman?"

"She didn't. But I've heard you're kind of a detective, and I thought I should let you know."

I ignored the detective bit. "What do you think Melissa meant? What kind of 'bad thing'?" *Murder?* Melissa had also said "bad things" when I'd asked her about the fireworks. This mention of one person doing a bad thing provided more detail. Kind of.

"She won't say." Leanne shook her head once. "Or maybe she can't. After she told me, she became agitated. I don't dare ask her again for details."

"You need to let the police know."

"Because of the murder." She sucked in a breath. "That could get very complicated. She doesn't do well with men in authority."

"Her parents should help her through that."

"Melissa doesn't see her mom. She lives with her father, Quinton Blake."

Quinton Blake. Related to Pat?

"So you haven't told him?" I asked.

"No."

The cowbell on the door jangled. Kristopher walked in, holding a paper bag. Leanne glanced at the clock and muttered a mild swear word under her breath.

"I have to get back." She reached for the door handle.

"You need to tell the police." I grabbed one of the store business cards from the holder by the door. "But if you can't, please call or text if she says anything else."

She nodded. "Even if she doesn't, I'll text you from my cell so you have my number."

"Thank you." I stepped onto the porch and watched her drive away. *A skinny person did a bad thing.* I pictured my drawing of circled suspects and lines. While perhaps not skinny, none of them was overweight. And for a young person like Melissa, whose cognitive functions hadn't kept up with her age, "skinny" could be a default description. A real detective needed to know he had a witness, albeit one who would need to be treated gently and by professionals.

"Robbie?"

I turned to see Turner inside the screen door.

"We need you," he said.

"Coming." Back inside, I surveyed the tables to see where Kristopher had ended up. *Huh*. Two of my circled names now sat together with an unopened bottle of clear alcohol on the table between them. I had figured Tina and Kristopher would know each other peripherally, but well enough to eat lunch together over drinks? That surprised me and made me want to know more. A lot more.

CHAPTER 30

"**Y**ou can double that." Tina looked at me and pointed at her glass.

I poured a second shot of vodka into her glass on top of the first one.

"Hit me with the same, please." Kristopher pointed to his glass.

"Certainly. Please remember you aren't allowed to serve yourselves." I filled the shot glass again and added it to his V8. With any luck, they wouldn't want another round of alcohol. "What can I get you to eat? The special is a Mediterranean orzo salad."

"I'd like a turkey burger with no bun, but extra lettuce and tomato, please," Tina said in her high voice.

I wondered if she'd been plagued by the nickname Tiny Tina in her past. As I gazed at her, Melissa's description echoed in my head. Tina was definitely skinny. I suppressed the shudder running through me at the thought of her killing her own mother.

Tina shook a few drops of hot sauce into her drink. Her lunch order was certainly guaranteed to keep her tiny. And maybe she figured the V8 canceled out the vodka's calories.

"I'll have the orzo special with grilled Swiss and ham on rye." Kristopher looked thirstily at his glass instead of at me as he spoke.

"Coming right up." I jotted down their orders. "Tina, you're from out of town. How do you and Kristopher know each other?" I kept my tone light so it didn't echo the intense curiosity behind my question.

Now Kristopher looked at me. "We've known each other for a long time." His gaze defied me from delving deeper.

All righty, then. "Cool. Enjoy your drinks."

The two didn't wait for me to leave before clinking their glasses.

"Are they having Bloody Marys over there?" Turner asked when I brought their lunch orders to the kitchen area.

"They are. It's legal, but for the most part, customers want to enjoy wine or beer. This is the first time someone has brought in their own hard liquor." I kind of hoped it was the last. I never minded when one of my regular customers brought in a bottle of celebratory bubbly or a special wine. And I had hosted Beer and Bible Friday night gatherings last winter, at Samuel's request. Non-regulars usually didn't even ask about alcohol with breakfast or lunch. I preferred it that way.

Danna, who had been ringing up a retail purchase at our register near the door, hurried over. "Get ready, kids. Tour bus time."

I sucked in a breath. "How big of a bus?"

"Forty, maybe." She glanced toward the door. "It just pulled up. Kentucky plates."

I surveyed the space. "I hope they're here to shop, too. They're going to have a bit of a wait." The only empties were one six-top, two four-tops, and Buck's usual table in the back. I sure was glad I'd gotten the new cookware priced and onto the shelves last night.

Speaking of Buck, he pushed through the door—ahead of the forty tourists—at the same time that a text buzzed in on my phone. I gave a little whistle. It was a text from Buck's grandmother, Simone.

I had another thought about past and present. Can you visit again?

I liked the sound of that. I texted back.

I'll try. Super-busy at store right now, will call later.

Buck used a fast version of his amble to reach his two-top. Smart man.

"We've done this before, guys," I said to my team. "I'm going to grab a quick word with Buck before that door opens again."

"We're on it, boss." Turner exchanged a fist bump with Danna as I bustled away.

"Hungry again?" I smiled at Buck.

"How long have you known me?"

"Almost four years. Listen, I don't have long. There's a girl who attends Cornerstone Connections. Well, a young adult. Her last name is Blake. I don't know if she's related to Pat, but she was at the fireworks with her dad and grandmother. She and a group from that organization came in yesterday, and Melissa—the girl—told me she saw me at the park."

"That's nice. Why are you telling me about her?" He squinted at me.

I filled him on what Melissa had said to me when I'd met her. "Because she later reported to the staffer that she saw a skinny person do a bad thing. Buck, she might be a witness to the murder. And she must have a good memory for faces if she recognized me."

He stopped squinting and took on an alert expression. "That Cornerstone outfit does good work. We think of their clients as kids, because of their mental age, but they're not. Name of the staffer?"

"Leanne Ilsley."

"I'll talk to her."

"You'll have to be really careful if you want to interview Melissa. Leanne said she got agitated even remembering Friday night."

"I hear you. My nephew goes there. Big teddy bear of a guy called Nathan. He's thirty, but you'd think he was six by the way he acts."

I smiled. "A cheerful guy into comic books and Disney?"

"Around the clock."

Our forty customers from the Bluegrass State began filing in.

"Oh, boy," I murmured.

"You go on now, Robbie. Bring me a mess of food when you get the chance. And don't worry none. We'll be gentle with Miss Melissa. I might could talk with her and Nathan together. That boy can calm anybody with his

Buddha smile." He stretched out his legs, gazing around the restaurant. He put the brakes on when he spied Kristopher and Tina. "Them two been here long?"

"About half an hour. Just so you know, they're drinking vodka in their V8. Alcohol they brought in themselves, of course. I poured it." I knew Buck wouldn't suspect me of going behind the law's back, but it never hurt to be clear.

"I'll keep me an eye on them." He nodded, as if to himself. "Oh, yes, I will."

I headed toward the busload. The visitors, a mix of couples and singles, all seemed to be over sixty, with plenty having the wrinkles and postures of those well over seventy.

I introduced myself and greeted the group, now milling around near the door. A half-dozen women had already made a beeline for the antique cookware, what was left of it after the last tour bus.

"It's going to be a bit of a wait for most of you, but we'll get you seated and fed as soon as we can," I said. "We have a few tables available now. Do any in the group need to sit and eat right away?"

A tall, silver-haired woman stepped forward. "Hi, Robbie. I'm Susan, and kind of the wrangler for our group, at least for today. We're from Whitesville Senior Living. It isn't far from Owensboro, right across the river from y'all here in Indiana. We have thirty-eight in total." She pointed to a few in the group and lowered her voice. "Gil needs to eat for his blood sugar, and his wife will want to sit with him. I'm sure Dottie and Dolly there would like to sit soon. And Queenie should, although she'll never admit it. Do you have tables for them?"

"Sure. I can put them all at the six-top over near the wall. Can you add one more to fill the seats?"

"Of course." She turned to the group and summoned the ones she'd mentioned. "Red, why don't you join these folks?" She whispered to me, "He'll make sure Queenie comes along. She's crazy in love with him."

The wizened Dottie and Dolly, leaning on matching blue walkers as they made their way toward me, looked like identical twins. A ruddy-faced man with thin reddish-white hair extended his arm to a woman in pearls who wore a brooch on her blouse and a brimmed hat reminiscent of those favored by Queen Elizabeth. She even carried a handbag slung royal-style over her crooked elbow. The only things missing were gloves.

"Come with me, ladies and gentlemen." I smiled and led the way along the least-obstructed path I could find toward their table. I seated the twins and the couple, but Red and Queenie had stopped at the table next to the six-top, where Tina and Kristopher talked in low tones as they drank.

"If it isn't my favorite Boonville librarian," Red's voice boomed as he beamed at Tina.

Buck had said Tina was a school librarian in Boonville. Maybe Red had grandkids in the town and visited often.

Tina looked up with a sharp move of her head. Her eyes narrowed for a moment, then she smiled, but faintly. "Hello, Red. What are you doing up here?"

"Having an outing with my best girl and the other kids at the old folks' home."

Queenie blushed and clutched his arm even tighter.

"Is this your boyfriend, then?" Red asked, gesturing toward Kristopher. "Your partner in crime, so to speak?"

Tina looked panicked. Kristopher gave Red a cold stare. Neither spoke.

"Or maybe not." Red gave an unperturbed shrug. "You'd mentioned some gent you were in business with. Y'all have a good lunch, now." He led Queenie to the last two spots at the six-top.

Tina was in business with someone? Why had Red asked if Kristopher was her boyfriend? This was getting interesting.

I inquired at the six-top about coffee and said I'd be back to take their orders. As I headed off to grab the carafe, I glanced at Buck. The whole restaurant had to have heard what Red had said to Tina. I expected Buck was going to be looking into the relationship between Tina and Kristopher in some detail. I might, too.

CHAPTER 31

I'd never been more thankful for a great team. By one o'clock, the last of the Whitesville residents were finishing their meals. We were once again pretty much sold out of cookware, which was fine, although I'd have to hit the next antique fair or revisit the barn and pick up more. We hadn't had a big rush of locals for lunch, so we'd managed, although by now only a few grains of orzo remained. Buck had kept a close watch on Tina and Kristopher. After they'd eaten and paid, he slapped some bills on his table and followed them through the door.

Things seemed under control in here. I stepped out onto the porch for a breath of air. To my right, the twins sat next to each other in rockers, hands in their laps, sound asleep. The rain I'd expected this morning hadn't materialized yet, but the air was even heavier, and the clouds were about to explode. I sniffed smoke and peered at the far end of the porch to my left. Red sat in one of the rocking chairs holding a lit cigarette between his fingers. Queenie was nowhere to be seen as he raised his hand in greeting.

I moseyed toward him and leaned on the railing. "Did you enjoy your meal?"

"Very much, thank you." He held up the smoke. "You don't mind?"

"Not out here, which is why I have ashtrays around." Vintage ashtrays on stands, of course. "I don't mind the smell of smoke in fresh air, as long as I don't have to inhale it or sweep up butts off the ground." People who were going to smoke were going to smoke. As long as they didn't bring it indoors—which was against the law, for restaurants, anyway—I'd decided to make it easy for them to be tidy about their habit.

"I appreciate that. You get to be my age, it's hard to change. I try to keep the numbers down, but one good smoke after a good meal means a lot to me." He inhaled the last puff. He exhaled away from me before stubbing out the cigarette. "And that was a darn good lunch y'all served up."

"Thank you. I'm glad you enjoyed it." I kept my voice casual. "So, you know Tina Upton?"

"Yes." He frowned. "I have family in Boonville, you see. I live on the other side of the mighty Ohio, but I visit scenic Boonville a lot."

"Is it scenic? I've never been there."

"Why, yes. They preserved and renovated many of the antique buildings downtown, including the Warrick County Courthouse and the old jail, one of the fanciest set of cells I ever set eyes on. The storefronts are looking good, too, and they recently redid the square. Fancied it up to make it welcoming."

"Sounds like the residents appreciate history."

"They surely do. You should pay the town a visit when you can. At any rate, I'm a voracious reader, so I took out a library card there using my daughter's address." He patted the hardcover book in his lap.

"What do you like to read?"

"I like historical biographies, but mostly I read crime fiction. Give me an exciting international espionage story or a legal thriller any day. Le Carré, may his soul rest in peace, is always a good read. But so is anything by Grisham or Patterson, and a lady named Hank Phillippi Ryan has had a couple of good ones lately." He held up the book. "I'm especially liking the ones Patterson writes with a fellow named Brendan DuBois. Top-notch stuff."

I needed to steer this chat back to Tina before I got steered back to work inside. "Somehow I thought Tina was a school librarian. But you know her from the public library?"

"Yes." His nod was a somber one. "I'm not sure what the trouble at the school was, but I think it had to do with that man she was here eating with."

"Kristopher Gale."

"That's the gent's name?"

I nodded.

"Well, she was persuaded to leave the school to take a reference job at the public library."

I blinked. *Trouble*. With children? That sounded bad.

"My grandgirls are in college now. But I remember hearing something from them, and then reading a few vaguely worded articles in the local online news site."

"There were no criminal charges?"

He shook his head. "Why are you so interested in Tina?"

I leaned closer and lowered my voice, even though there was nobody else nearby, at least not anyone awake. "Her mother was murdered last Friday."

His eyebrows, the same formerly red color as his hair, rose nearly to his hairline. The bus started up. The silver-haired wrangler ushered the rest of the group out. Queenie spied us and rushed toward Red.

"I didn't know where you'd gone, darling Red."

Red stood, surreptitiously rolling his eyes at me. He held out his hand. "Good talking with you, Robbie."

"Likewise." I shook his hand, then found a store business card in my apron pocket and handed it to him. "Please contact me if you think of any other details."

"I do believe I will." He again held out his arm for his lady friend.

I followed them down the steps and waited until all but the tall woman had boarded. "I hope you'll come back," I said. "Just so you know, you'll get faster service if you—"

"If we come an hour earlier?" She laughed. "I know. We'd planned an eleven o'clock arrival, but sometimes sh—I mean, stuff happens." She smiled and climbed aboard.

Stuff sure did happen, and too often. I took a moment to text Oscar and Buck about doing a deep dive into Tina's past as a Boonville school librarian. I hit *Send* as loud thunder rolled. I scurried up the steps and under the overhang. Almost immediately lightning cracked. The clouds finally let loose. Those seniors got out of here just in time. I hadn't even gotten Red's last name. But I knew where to find him.

CHAPTER 32

All the locals apparently decided to seek shelter from the storm, too. As soon as I got back inside, the cowbell on the door didn't stop jangling for a full half hour. One of the prospective diners was Josie, someone I'd been wanting to talk with. I was also dying for a few quiet minutes alone to think about what Red had said. That wasn't in the cards until later today, though.

"Go figure." Danna shook her head after I stuck six orders on the carousel. "After we already fed all those Kentuckians."

"Good thing I erased the special from the board before this crew started demanding orzo salad." Turner pointed at the now-blank blackboard.

"Is there anything I should run to the market for?" I glanced around the restaurant, which had every table filled and four people waiting. Josie sat alone at a two-top reading what looked like a professional magazine. It definitely wasn't the kind of publication you'd find in the grocery store checkout lane.

"I think we're good. Right, Dann?" Turner asked.

"For an hour?" She flipped two beef patties and laid slices of cheese on them. "Yeah. But, Robbie, you probably should order now for, like, everything. We'll legit run out of all kinds of things tomorrow if you don't."

"Will do."

"Turner, those three plates are ready for the four-top in the corner," Danna told him.

I headed for my desk to grab the iPad I used to submit orders. I might as well order enough to last us through Sunday. I took a second to peek out through the glass in the door. The din of the rain beating on the metal porch roof only added to the clatter in here of conversation, silverware clinking on plates, and various bits of lunch sizzling and popping on the grill. The storm showed no sign of letting up.

After I fired up the tablet and clicked open the ordering software, I let the door to the walk-in clunk shut behind me. Both the silence and the chill were a welcome respite. But I knew I couldn't indulge myself with musing about a case having nothing to do with my livelihood. Instead I ordered buns for burgers and hot dogs. Tomatoes, lettuce, and onions. Red and green peppers. Cheese, milk, eggs. Ketchup, mustard, relish. Beef, turkey, and veggie patties. Sausages, hot dogs, and bacon. Plus white, wheat, and rye bread. I would add another order after my guys and I put our heads together about specials for the next four days.

My finger hovered over the *Submit* button. What had I forgotten? We had lots of oatmeal and grits. Neither were as popular during the warmer months as they were when the temperatures dropped. And I had plenty of white and whole wheat flour, which made me think of banana-walnut pancakes. I snapped my fingers. Fruit, that was what I was missing. I ordered bananas, strawberries, and melons. I hoped I could get to the farmers' market early Saturday morning to pick up some local produce. I'd learned that having a backup was a wise practice, in case events conspired to prevent purchasing from area farmers.

I pressed the button. A loud *crack* resounded that I heard even in here. The overhead light flashed off, leaving only the low-wattage emergency light above the door. *Wonderful*. There went the power. With a full restaurant. I let myself out in a hurry, making sure the door shut tightly behind me. The generator outside kicked on. It wasn't strong enough to power the whole place, unfortunately. I'd gotten one only sufficiently big to keep electricity running to the walk-in, so it would prevent the food from spoiling. The gas to the grill would work until it was turned off. It was only two o'clock. Despite the storm clouds, there was enough light in here from the windows for diners to see their food. Fresh coffee would be a no-go, but otherwise? I didn't see why we couldn't feed this crowd.

"Yo!" I waved my hands in the air. "Can I have your attention, please?" When the place quieted and most faces were focused on mine, I said, "Obviously the power is out. We won't be able to make more coffee. But you'll still get your meal. Pans 'N Pancakes is here for you. Right, team?"

Danna and Turner each raised both thumbs.

"Please bear with us if we're a little slower than usual." I headed for the kitchen.

A man yelled, "We love ya, Robbie."

The woman next to him chimed in. "We love all three of you!" She started clapping.

A second later, the whole place was applauding. I made it to the kitchen area, but my throat was thick, and my eyes threatened to overflow. I sniffed back the emotion. Grabbing Turner's hand on one side and Danna's on the other, I raised my arms and murmured, "Take a bow, guys." We bowed like the pros we were, except the kitchen was our stage instead of the theater.

Turner shot a look at the grill. "Flip those babies, girlfriend, and quick."

"Oopsies." Danna turned two turkey and two veggie patties.

He headed out to bus tables, and I followed him to take orders.

"What can we get you, Josie?" I asked when I reached her.

She glanced up. "Hi, Robbie. I'd love a grilled cheddar and tomato on wheat, with a brownie, and a good old-fashioned Coke. In fact, can you bring the brownie first?"

I smiled. "Of course. Dessert before the meal?"

"Hon, I come by my silver hair honestly. At this stage of life, I figure I can do pretty much what I want, as long as it's legal." She winked. "And sometimes when it isn't."

I smiled. I wasn't touching that one. "Adele says the same thing. I'll go get your brownie." Josie actually didn't have that many white hairs in her short dark do. But now that I was looking, she had sprouted a lot more in the almost two years since I'd met her.

She touched my arm, no longer smiling. "I'd like to talk with you for a minute when you come back."

"Sure."

It took me a while to get back to her table. By the time I did, Oscar had joined her. I didn't realize they knew each other. Would she still want to tell me whatever it was? I set down her drink and dessert. "Hey, Oscar."

"Robbie," he said.

"I invited Oscar to join me," Josie said. "He should hear what I have to say."

"Okay." I stuck my hands in the pockets of my knee-length denim skirt. I didn't have time to sit, and there wasn't a free chair in the place, anyway.

Josie cleared her throat. "You remember I told you about Stitch and Bitch?"

"Yes."

"I was exchanging emails with an old friend last night, and we were chatting about times gone by. When she asked me if the poker games were still going on, it sparked a memory."

"Poker games, Ms. Dunn?" Oscar leaned toward her.

"Oh, for corn sake, Oscar. Would you call me Josie, already?"

"Very well." He let out an aggrieved breath. "As you were saying?"

"What I remembered, with the help of my friend, was that Nanette Russo and Yolande Bird were running a gambling scam. Under cover of meeting to knit and do needlework and such, they ran poker games. With betting."

"That's illegal." Oscar sat back, looking incensed.

Was he upset because it was against the law, or because it violated his sense of cultural propriety that crafting moms would be crafty enough to run a gambling ring? I couldn't tell. Maybe both.

"Obviously," Josie said. "What's worse, they rigged the results."

"How?" I asked.

"I don't know," she said. "My friend thought they skimmed the bets, too. She said Nanette and Yolande were vying for who would lead the organization."

"So, it's been going on for a long time, if Yolande was involved," I mused. Kristopher couldn't have been involved at the start.

"Yes," Josie said.

"Do you think Buck knows any of this about his mother?" I asked. And had Yolande threatened to expose Nanette and been murdered for her efforts?

"I wouldn't know," Josie said. "As you can imagine, I didn't want to tell him directly."

"You did the right thing by telling me," Oscar said. "Bird will want to know, I expect. Or need to, anyway."

Danna arrived carrying her grandmother's sandwich plate. She and Turner must have switched jobs.

"Thank you, sweetie," Josie told her. "How are you feeling?"

"I'm all right. Detective, would you like to order?" Danna asked.

"Might as well. Been a while since breakfast. Hamburger and coleslaw, please, and a ginger ale."

"Coming right up," Danna replied to him, but the look she gave me included a frown and a glance at the restroom.

Right. She was still recovering. "Thanks for sharing that, Josie. I'll talk to you both later." As Danna and I walked back toward the grill, I held out my hand for Oscar's order slip. "Give me your apron and take a break."

She complied and hurried across the store to the loo. I added Oscar's order to the carousel and Danna's apron to the soiled linens bin. But even as I bustled about the business of running a restaurant, I wondered if Nanette had killed Yolande all those years ago. So many questions remained. Why hadn't that murder been solved? Was the gambling enterprise still operating? Could the earlier murder be tied to Vi's? Was Tina's crime related to these, and how was Kristopher involved? And, perhaps most urgently—although not homicide-related—when would we get power back?

CHAPTER 33

After Josie left, Oscar lingered on at the two-top. He kept glancing up as if he expected someone to join him. I headed to the door at two thirty to turn the sign to *Closed*. I had to snatch my hand back when a drenched Buck appeared in the entrance.

"I was about to lock the door, Buck."

His face took on a sorrowful look. "So, I can't get me a pile of lunch? My stomach's got a hole in it bigger than the Grand Canyon with no tourists, and it needs filled."

I laughed. "Yes, you can eat. And I think Oscar might have been waiting for you." I let him in and then finished my closing tasks, turning the sign and locking the door for exit only. I needed this workday to end as much as my team did, but I couldn't refuse Buck his lunch. Plus, once the rest of the diners cleared out, I might be able to grab a quick powwow with the two officers. "I'm sorry there's no coffee, though. As you can see, the electricity is out, but the grill is still working."

"Food's all I need, hon."

I smiled. I knew some women would be upset at a random man using an endearment like that. I actually loved it, at least from Buck. He certainly wasn't a random male, although I didn't mind any of my customers calling me that, male or female. It made me feel as if I belonged here.

Ten minutes later, I arrived at Oscar's table carrying two double cheeseburgers for Buck, as well as the last two biscuits, smothered in sausage gravy. The last customers—present company excluded—had paid and left. I set down the extra plate I'd brought, holding my own single cheeseburger and dish of coleslaw, and sat. I'd cleared this break with Turner and Danna, promising them they could leave promptly at three and I would finish whatever cleanup remained.

"Looks like it's still raining out there, Buck," I said.

"Shooey, is it ever. It's a regular frog strangler." Buck laid his phone on the table and bit into his first cheeseburger.

I fixed my gaze firmly on Oscar, in case Buck was getting messy with his food. "Oscar, did you tell Buck what Josie said?"

"Yes."

Buck, mouth full, nodded and pointed to his phone.

"Part of it." Oscar shot me an intent signaling look.

I assumed it meant he'd omitted the part about Buck's mom. Telling a fellow officer that his murdered mother might have been involved in illegal activities before her death—when he was in his teens—wasn't news-appropriate for a text message. And maybe we didn't need to get into it now, either.

Buck swallowed and swiped his mouth with his napkin. "Disturbing, wadn't it? Them little ladies running a fixed gambling ring. Who'da thunk it?"

"I guess anybody's capable of wanting more than they have and risking arrest to get it." I took a bite of my burger.

Oscar flipped open his palms but kept his mouth shut.

I swallowed. "Have you found the murder weapon yet?" I asked.

"We have not." Oscar pressed his lips together.

"Buck, your grandmother told me about Nanette working at a turkey farm in those early years, at Ginny's Gobblers. I dug in a little and found out it's in Beanblossom. My Mennonite friend Martin Dettweiler and his wife own it." I sold Martin's jars of delicious honey in the store, a popular item.

"So who the heck is Ginny, and why should we care?" Buck asked.

"She was Martin's mother, but his wife runs it these days. Simone said Nanette worked for them cooking turkey dinners." I nibbled on my pickle. "Have either of you ever roasted a turkey?"

"Can't say I have," Oscar said.

Buck, having just taken a huge bite of gravy-laden biscuit, shook his head instead of speaking.

Grateful for small blessings, I went on. "Cooks often stuff the cavity, but you need to close it so the stuffing doesn't fall out. You can sew it shut, but you can also use small lacers to weave the skin closed."

"Lacers?" Buck asked.

"They're skinny little skewers about five inches long and either bent at one end or with a loop." I held my index fingers that far apart. "But they're super-sharp at the other end, to pierce the skin."

Oscar and Buck exchanged a look.

"Sounds like it would do the job in a little lady's neck," Oscar said. "Ginny's Gobblers?"

"Yes."

The detective poked a note into his phone.

"Did either of you get a chance to look into Tina Perkell's past?" I asked. "That guy I talked with, Red, seemed to think she'd been banned from being the school librarian."

"We haven't yet, but thanks for the tip," Buck said.

"He also thought Kristopher Gale was her business partner. What have you learned about him?" I nibbled a bite of coleslaw.

"Not enough," Oscar said.

The overhead lights flickered on. The drinks cooler and under-counter refrigerator hummed back into life. At the sink, Danna shot a fist into the air.

"Power to the people!" she announced.

I smiled. "What a relief."

"I'll bet," Buck said.

As my shoulders dropped, I was a little surprised at the tension ebbing out of me, a strain I hadn't realized I'd been holding. Maybe I should put a larger generator on my wish list.

Buck cleared his throat. "Gale popped in to see me at the station a little bit of a while ago."

My ears perked up. "You followed him and Tina out of here after they left earlier."

"Yup. Wanted to be sure them two didn't just hop in a

car and drive while intoxicated. Instead, they walked to the park, so I let 'em alone. Anyhoo, he claims he saw Nanette Russo stab poor old Vi."

Whoa.

Oscar nodded as if he already knew.

"What are you going to do?" I asked Buck.

"Nothing yet." He stretched out his legs. "I can't say I'm a hundred percent confident he's telling the truth."

Oscar frowned. "I would have to agree."

"Why do you say that?" I asked. "Do you think it's a kind of smoke screen?"

"Might could be." Buck bobbed his head.

"And why didn't he report it until now?" I tapped the table as I thought. "Why not find you, Buck, or another officer, and let you know? Or call it in? Sitting on what he witnessed doesn't make any sense."

"I asked him exactly that," Buck said. "He nattered on about how he didn't realize what he'd seen until later."

"He's trying to distract us," Oscar added. "No doubt about it."

CHAPTER 34

At three thirty, as I loaded and started the dishwasher, the discoveries of the day overtook my brain and roiled it, especially Buck's last piece of news.

Kristopher claimed to be an eyewitness. Seriously, why had he come forward only now? His former business partner had been murdered five days ago. Like Buck and Oscar, I wasn't sure I trusted his account of witnessing the killing. Had he and Tina concocted the story after their lunch drinks to cover up their own wrongdoing?

And what about Tina? Red's allusions to her misdeeds made me want to shirk my responsibilities and Google the heck out of her. Or call him. Or both. Except I couldn't, not right then. I wiped down the counter, wishing I'd asked Buck and Oscar if they'd learned anything about Upton or about Pat Blake. Was Melissa Pat's granddaughter? Who had the girl seen, and what had the "bad thing" been? Was someone with developmental delays a reliable witness? I had no answers to even a single one of these questions.

I blew out a breath and stuffed the dishrag into the bag of dirty store linens. I wasn't going to resolve any of this right now, and I needed to drop the bag outside by four for the laundry truck.

I paused on my way to the service door. I loved being alone in my store. The place still smelled, in the best of ways, of bacon and baking and burgers. Precipitation continued to hammer onto the porch roof. Danna and Turner had cleared out at three o'clock, with Buck and Oscar leaving not long after. I loved my livelihood, my coworkers, my customers. I also loved it when they were all gone—but only because I knew I'd see them again tomorrow.

I smiled to myself. Once, when I was about ten, my mom arranged for the first time to put me alone on a nonstop flight to spend a week with Aunt Adele here in South Lick. Mom's friend had asked her, in my presence, if she wouldn't miss me terribly, then added that she'd never spent a night apart from her then-teenaged children. My mother replied, "Of course I'll miss my girl. But she'll be back. And it's good for both of us to mix it up a little." I'd adored my aunt and knew her well. I had looked forward to the trip and the excitement of traveling solo.

As an adult, I came to realize my mom had needed time by herself. Who didn't, as long as it wasn't permanent? Mommy had no way of knowing she'd be leaving me forever—involuntarily and irrevocably—a decade and a half later. I shook off, for the moment, my grief. It had lessened but never truly left.

I also wanted to call Simone but finishing up my work

had to come first. I unlocked the service door—after having been attacked by a malicious person who came in through this very door, I no longer left it accessible to the outside—and dragged the bag out, leaving it under the overhang.

It was definitely still raining. The air bore that fresh scent of wet pavement, saturated dirt, and something else. My Mennonite farmer friend had told me once of the beneficial effect lightning had on the soil, that it fixed nitrogen, whatever that meant. Maybe that was what I was smelling. Whatever it was, I loved the scent. Rain had been so rare where I grew up, I still delighted in it here. Power outages, not so much.

By the look of the clouds, the storm wouldn't let up soon. Rain was good for area farmers, as long as it wasn't a weeklong deluge. Drops splashed off the hinged top covering the enclosure where I kept the trash cans. A memory splashed unbidden into my mind of the time Danna and I had tried to hide the rat droppings someone had planted in my restaurant to discredit me. I'd been able to prove the whole thing had been faked.

I waved at the driver when the food supplier truck pulled up. Perfect timing, except it brought another memory from only a few months ago, when poisonous mushrooms had been included in my order—on purpose. I'd changed suppliers immediately. Feeding toxins to my customers was not part of my business plan. This supplier hired hip young drivers, who trundled in my boxes and bags on a handcart and always had a smile for me.

It was four o'clock by the time I had the order put away and the floor swept. Exhausted, I sank into my cushioned swivel chair at the desk. I still needed to do breakfast prep. What I wanted was a long chat about anything but murder with Abe. He was my respite, my comfort, and my excitement all in one handsome package. We'd planned to go out to our favorite Japanese noodle restaurant in Bloomington tonight for dinner. He'd served as a medic in the military in Japan, and he loved the cuisine as much as I did. Right now, though, the forty-minute drive west into the university town didn't seem that appealing.

Speaking of Abe, a text buzzed in from him.

Sorry, sugar. With the lightning strikes, we're all on overtime tonight. Rain check for dinner? I'll be home when I'm home. XXXOOO

A rain check, indeed. I blew out a breath. Such was the life of an electrical lineman. I, as the wife of same, was on my own for supper. I texted back.

Stay safe. Love you, R.

For a breakfast special in the morning, Turner was going to reprise his popular Indian-spiced roasted potatoes, and we were going to do up a Cajun shrimp and grits for a lunch special. I had until whenever to do prep for our usual breakfast offerings. I retrieved a local IPA from my apartment fridge and settled back into the desk chair to finally call Simone Walsh, eager to know what she'd wanted to tell me.

"I'm sorry I can't get down there this afternoon to visit in person," I said after we exchanged greetings.

"Of course you can't, hon. You shouldn't be driving in this storm."

"That's kind of what I thought, too. I would like to see you again soon, though."

"This old lady appreciates that."

The clink of ice on glass came over the line. Was centenarian Simone indulging in a four o'clock cocktail?

More power to her if she was. Or maybe it was only a soft drink.

"You said you had thought of something you wanted to tell me." I sipped my own four o'clock drink. "About past and present. Are you willing to talk about it over the phone?"

"Why not?" She gave a low chuckle. "When you're as old as I am, Robbie, there's no time like the present. I might not be alive tomorrow."

"I certainly hope you are." And I did.

"It's just, I got to musing, you know." Her ice clinked again. "About that Stitch and Bitch group, and what happened to my girl all those years ago."

"I'm all ears."

"Well, now. It was thinking about my dearly departed husband that brought up a memory. I recalled Mr. Walsh always maintaining it had to be Pat Blake who did in our Yolande."

Wow. "Really?"

"Indeed. Leastwise, that's what he said after she murdered her own husband. Did you know about that?"

"Yes. She wasn't convicted, though."

"We always thought she got off on some kind of technicality. Nobody knew why she married Blake in the first place. He was a mean-spirited fellow, no two ways about it." She chuckled. "It's not Christian of me to say so, but his death was a case of good riddance, after a fashion. If she'd divorced him, he would have gone on to abuse another family."

"Do you mean he was mean to his child, too?"

"That poor boy. I'm surprised Quinton has done as well as he has as an adult, what with his past and all."

Melissa's father. "How old was he when his father was killed?"

"Six or seven, I do believe. He's a good ten years younger than Buckham."

"Did something else happen in his past after he lost his father?

"You'd best believe it. First he got picked up for stealing. Then he turned to drugs. Why, he—" Simone broke off and spoke away from the phone as if she were talking to someone in her room. "Robbie, the aide is here to take me down to our weekly bridge game. It keeps the mind lively, don't you know?"

"I understand. Take care, Simone."

She disconnected. I sat staring at nothing. Would Pat have murdered again? But why would she kill Vi? And what else had Quinton done?

CHAPTER 35

I was itchy to learn more about this case, to unwrap some of the secrets. It felt like every time I got close, something intervened. Simone's card game starting. Red having to leave on the bus. Josie not knowing how the group had rigged the bets. And then there were the hints. Upton's dissatisfaction with the bank. Grant's warning to Joan about Nanette. Buck following Tina and Kristopher out, ostensibly to make sure they didn't drink and drive. I wasn't so sure that had been the real reason.

If I could get to Jupiter Springs at around five, I might be able to eat dinner with Grant. Places like that usually welcomed guests at meals. I could have a chat with him and perhaps keep an eye on Nanette, too. Yes. That was a good plan. I freshened up in my old apartment, where I also kept a few clean pieces of clothing for situations like this one. I didn't have time to go home and change.

The rain had eased to a gentle patter by the time I locked the store behind me. Clad in a summery top and swingy skirt under my rain jacket, with my hair brushed out and wearing a touch of lip gloss, I hopped in my car. I'd swapped out tennies for sandals, too. The quickest way to Jupiter Springs was straight through town. I slowed when I caught sight of the old Strand Theater, which had been renovated last year to house the Cornerstone Connections organization. I pulled into a diagonal parking space in front of it. Would they let me have a friendly, casual visit with Melissa? Would she be willing? I had only one way to find out. The clock on the bank next door read four thirty. If I was late for the senior dinner hour, so be it.

Leanne opened the door. "Robbie, what can I do for you?" Behind her stretched a big open room with tall windows. In one corner were several clients in wheelchairs. At a long table several others were cutting pictures out of magazines and pasting them into blank books. I spied Nathan on a sofa laughing at one of his comic books. He pointed to something in it, showing a young man with Down syndrome sitting next to him. The friend smiled. Melissa sat on an exercise ball, rocking back and forth as she stared through a window at the rain outside.

I greeted Leanna. "I was passing by and wondered if I could say hi to Melissa."

She narrowed her eyes. "You can't question her about the fireworks."

"I promise I won't." Of course I hoped the young woman would volunteer some bit of information that could unlock a piece of this frustrating puzzle. I knew my chances were slim.

"All right. But I should warn you, everybody's tired. They go home at five."

"Got it. I won't stay long." I made my way toward Melissa. When I passed Nathan, he glanced up and gave me a big grin and held up his palm.

"High five, Robbie."

I slapped his big, soft hand with mine. "How are you, Nathan?"

"I'm great! Do you want to see what Mulan did?" He started to hold up the page he'd been looking at.

"I can't right now. Maybe another time."

"Okay." He smiled.

I wondered if this joyful fellow ever had dark times. I hoped not. Melissa stared at me as I approached. I pulled up another exercise ball and sat facing her.

"Hi, Robbie." Her gaze was as serious and intense as it had been the first time we'd spoken. "You like to sit on a ball, too."

"I actually never have before, but it's comfortable, isn't it?"

She nodded. "I like swinging, too. When I get home, I'll swing until dinner."

"That sounds fun. Do you swing in the rain, too?"

"If Dad lets me, I do. But not if it's too cold." Her gaze never left my face. She kept up her rocking. "I saw you at the fireworks."

"I remember you said that. They have them every Friday night. I really like the colors in the dark sky."

Her eyes widened. "I'm never going again." She lowered her voice to a whisper. "Bad things happen, Robbie. You should stay home, too."

"Okay. But I didn't see anything bad last week."

Which was true. I only saw the aftermath. I wanted her to keep talking, and I couldn't ask her directly.

"I did." Her hands fluttered at her sides, and she stopped her back-and-forth movement. "It was when I went to the bathroom."

"Did you go by yourself?"

"Yes. I know the way." She resumed rocking, at a faster rate than before. "Somebody hurt a lady."

"That's too bad." I clasped my hands together so I would look calmer than I felt.

"Somebody skinny."

Skinny. The same as what Leanne had reported to me. Tina, Upton, and Kristopher all qualified. Even Nanette. Especially her.

"Not like Nathan," Melissa went on. "It was dark. I had to get back to my gran."

"Your grandmother Pat?" Slender, trim Pat qualified as having a "skinny" profile, too.

She nodded again, her focus returning to the window.

It seemed she'd said all she was going to. Thinking about the fireworks had agitated her, but at least her hands had stopped fluttering.

"It was nice seeing you, Melissa." I stood. "Take care."

She didn't answer. When the outer door opened, she turned her face toward it. A slow smile spread across her face, transforming it into a ray of happy. I glanced at the entrance. A tall, burly man stood just inside, scanning the young people for someone. Judging from the girl's reaction, this might be Melissa's father.

It was time for me to leave. Leanne was busy with a client, so I headed for the exit. I nodded at the man, who gave me a quick, dimpled smile. I blinked. This was the guy who'd spoken about the poker games at the antiques place in New Pekin.

"Are you one of the new volunteers?" he asked in the same low, kindly voice I remembered from the barn.

"Not exactly." I thought fast. If this was Pat's son, I would love nothing more than to pick his brain about what Melissa had seen. But not here. Not now. "We spoke down at the antiques barn a couple of days ago. I'm Robbie Jordan." I extended my hand.

He took a second look. "So we did. Quinton Blake." His big hand was warm and callused, as if he used his hands for his livelihood. "I've heard of you. You own the country store."

"I do."

"And you're a kind of PI. What were you talking to my girl about?" He gestured with his chin toward Melissa, but his tone was curious rather than suspicious.

"I'm not a detective, not at all."

He tilted his head as if he didn't believe me, but he didn't speak.

"The Cornerstone group came into my restaurant this week," I went on. "I just stopped by today to see where they hang out, say hello. I'm considering signing up to volunteer." Suddenly I wanted to make that a true statement.

He peered down at me. "Good. The clients enjoy new faces." He focused on his daughter again. His face lit up as he took a step in her direction.

"It was nice to meet you, Quinton." I slid out, happy I hadn't gotten a cold reception from him.

I wasn't really any the wiser about what Melissa had

experienced the night of the fireworks. It might be significant that she had mentioned how the person she'd seen wasn't like Nathan. Or it might not be.

I froze in place on the sidewalk, ignoring the drops pelting the hood of my raincoat. If the killer had been Pat, Melissa would have recognized her. Wouldn't she? Pat was her own grandmother. Or had Pat snatched the opportunity of her granddaughter's taking a walk to the restroom and killed her longtime friend?

+

CHAPTER 36

My Jupiter Springs dinner plan worked. Sort of. Grant was happy to see me and welcomed me to eat with him. Unfortunately, the only free table already had Joan seated at it.

"I've been inviting her to sit with me," he explained as a high-school waiter in black pants and white shirt ushered us there. "As a friendly gesture."

"That's sweet of you."

And it was, except I wouldn't be able to dig into the murder and what led up to it with her listening. I'd have to stick around until I could speak with Grant alone. I was glad I'd cleaned up. Grant wore a sports coat. He also carried a cloth bag. Had he brought his knitting to dinner? All the other residents were nicely dressed, too. White tablecloths covered the tables, and each was decorated with a small vase of fresh daisies in the middle. A paper menu sat at each place next to heavy silverware and yellow cloth napkins.

We passed Nanette sitting alone at a table. Her chin rested in one hand, and she drummed the fingers of her other hand on the table. If Pat had killed Vi, Nanette must have seen her do it.

"Nanette, would you like to join us?" Grant asked.

"No, thanks. Someone is coming to eat with me." She did a little double take when she saw me. "Slumming with the old folks, Robbie?"

That was one way to put it. I smiled. "Enjoy your dinner." At our table, I greeted Joan.

"Nice to see you, Robbie," she said.

Grant pulled a bottle of pinot noir out of his bag and handed it to the boy.

Ah. Wine, not knitting.

"Three glasses, please," Grant said. "Right, ladies?"

Joan nodded.

"Yes, please," I said. "This is very elegant, Grant."

"They told me they want us to feel like we're dining in a restaurant," Joan said. "It's nice, isn't it?"

"The food actually isn't bad, either." Grant tapped the menu. "Robbie, read me the specials, will you, please?"

I read off the menu items: a grilled salmon with baby roasted potatoes and asparagus, a beef tenderloin with polenta and mushroom sauce, and chicken Florentine with pesto-tossed pasta. "Those all sound delicious." The menu also listed a burger, a grilled cheese sandwich, clam chowder, and a few other offerings under a heading of *Every Day.*

"I've only been here a few days," Joan said. "I'm impressed with the dinners."

"On the other hand," Grant began, "the hot breakfasts are nothing to write home about. They're never very hot, for one thing. And who wants to eat cold scrambled eggs?"

"That's too bad," I said.

"I'll probably stick with cold cereal and fruit," Joan said.

"Speaking of home, Joan, your sister said she's returning to Connecticut tomorrow," I said to her. "I thought she might be here tonight."

"Edna's having dinner with my son and his family. She'll come by in the morning before she hits the road."

A staff person clearly over twenty-one arrived with the open bottle of wine. As she poured for us, Pat Blake walked in and made a beeline for Nanette's table.

Interesting. "Grant," I murmured after the staff person had left. "Pat Blake has joined Nanette at her table."

"Yes, they eat together at least once a week."

I didn't ask how he knew, not being able to see them. I'd had a blind friend in high school, and she'd surprised me all the time with pieces of information she picked up. She tutored elementary-age blind kids and saved her money to buy a tandem bicycle. We'd had a great time cycling around the area together, me steering on the front, her in the back pedaling away and enjoying the wind on her face. I remembered I'd thought of checking into someone to tandem-ride with Grant but had forgotten all about it.

Grant smiled sadly. "My Vi used to dine with them. They called it Girls' Dinner."

"Here's to Vi." Joan lifted her glass. "I wish I had known her, Grant."

"To all those who have gone before, including my Yolande, as well as your mother, Robbie." Grant lifted his.

"And my late husband, too," Joan added.

I clinked my glass with theirs. The teenage boy brought three salads and took our dinner orders. We chatted about this and that. I stole an occasional glance at Pat and Nanette. They were not drinking wine, and their conversation looked like a serious one. At one point Pat sneezed three times in a row into a handkerchief.

"Grant, have Upton and Tina finished with Vi's room?" I asked. "They're Vi's children," I explained to Joan.

"I do believe they have. Vi had done the needlepoint on a small pillow I was fond of. I can feel the pattern, you see, and I wanted a keepsake from her, one her hands had created. When he was in the room, I asked Upton if I could have the pillow." He shook his head.

"And?" I asked.

"The man nearly threw it at me, or that was what it felt like."

Joan made a *tsk*ing sound.

"I ran into Upton at the bank this morning," I said. "He was trying to clear out Vi's accounts, which, of course, is way too soon. He wasn't happy with their refusal."

"Is the man hard up for money?" Joan asked. "That can make anyone irritable. I certainly went through a time of barely making it, when I was younger."

"Vi might have mentioned something of the sort," Grant said.

"He owns a fine leather company in Evansville." I took a sip of wine.

"I'm not sure the market is strong for fine leather goods right now." Grant sipped, as well. "People willing—or able—to pay for American-made products are becoming ever more scarce."

Our entrées arrived, salmon for Grant and chicken for Joan. I'd ordered the beef, partly because I adore polenta anywhere, any time, in any form. We three dug in. The next time I peeked at Nanette, her plate held only a triangular half of a grilled cheese sandwich, while she nibbled on the other half. I wondered again if she was ill. She was quite thin, and she didn't appear to have much of an appetite, plus earlier I'd noticed the sallow tinge to her skin. Pat was making her way through a salad topped with grilled shrimp.

I narrowed my eyes as I gazed at Pat. Had she also been part of the gambling operation? What if she and Nanette had conspired to kill Vi, because Vi was going to shut them down? Or turn them in?

Pat must have felt my mental focus on her. She turned her head and stared at me. I smiled and gave a little wave, then aimed my attention squarely on my food and my dining companions, as it should be.

Fifteen minutes later, my plate was nearly empty. Nanette and Pat stood. We were sitting next to the main aisle. I opened my mouth to greet the two as they passed, but Nanette walked straight by.

I spoke more quickly to Pat. "Pat, I don't think I told you I met your granddaughter, Melissa."

She stopped short, her eyebrows raised. "Where? Why?"

"Her group decided to come to my restaurant for a meal a couple of days ago. She told me they got to choose their own outings."

Pat's face relaxed. "They do. Cornerstone is a great organization."

"Melissa said she saw me at the fireworks," I continued.

"Yes. I took her, but I'm afraid she didn't have a very good time."

Because of the fireworks, or because the girl had witnessed a murder?

"Oh?" I kept my tone casual, concerned. "Why not?"

"Never mind. Good night."

CHAPTER 37

I hadn't dared to press Pat in the public milieu of the dining room on what Melissa had said after the fireworks. About why she hadn't had a good time. Maybe the girl hadn't spoken to her grandmother at all about what she'd seen.

After dessert—sugar-free vanilla ice cream for Grant, dark chocolate for me, and a brownie for Joan—and decaf, I walked Grant back to his room. He tugged on my arm when we reached Vi's room. The door again stood ajar.

"Hang on a little minute, Robbie." He stepped into the room. "The place is empty, isn't it?" He wore a sad, resigned look.

"Nearly. There's still a bed, plus a bookshelf here next to the door."

He reached for my arm, facing me. "Robbie, do you see a folder around anywhere? A file, like?"

"A paper folder?"

"I think so. I never saw it, of course, but my Vi said she, uh . . ." He cleared his throat. "She purloined it from Nanette's room." The last words came out in a wobbling whisper.

A folder. Stolen from Nanette. A file. Files normally contained information people wanted to keep. This could be important.

"I wonder if her children found it." Grant kept his voice low. "I hope they didn't."

"Let me look." I scanned the large room, which was designed like a studio apartment. At the other end was a nook serving as a bedroom. A kitchenette faced the bathroom door, and the sitting area was in front of us. It smelled faintly floral, perhaps from a perfume Vi used. What I didn't tell him about was the detritus. Bits of paper, a cheap hairbrush, and an open jar of facial cream littered the room. A tattered paperback by Mary Higgins Clark lay on the floor. Maybe Tina and Upton knew they would get hit with a cleaning bill, anyway, and decided not to pick up after themselves.

My gaze froze. A foot away, the corner of a green folder stuck out from behind the bookcase.

"There's something stuck behind this piece of furniture." I wiggled out the folder. My eyes widened when I saw the label, *Stitch and Bitch*.

"What did you find?" Grant asked.

"An old folder that was jammed behind the bookcase." I took a quick glance at the first page, which looked like nothing more than a knitting pattern.

"Does it have a title? A label?"

"Yes. Stitch and Bitch."

"Will you take it?" he asked. "I'd like you to keep it safe. Read through it if you'd like, but let Buckham have it tomorrow."

"I promise."

"And, Robbie?"

I waited. He seemed to struggle to find the words. While I waited, I stuffed the folder into my bag to study later.

"Don't tell my son I know about the file."

I scrunched up one eye as I thought about this request.

"He's apt to chide me for not informing him myself. I'm his father, but our roles in life are more and more reversed. I can't abide being chastised by the son I raised."

"That's got to be hard." I touched his arm. "Don't worry. I'll figure out something to tell him."

"I appreciate that, hon. Now, this old man is tired." He hooked his hand through my arm, and we made our way to the door of his own room.

"I need to be getting back to my store to prepare for to-morrow's breakfast. But can I ask you a question first?"

"Please."

I kept my voice low. "Joan's sister mentioned you had cautioned Joan about Nanette. Why was that?"

"I've known Nanette for a long time. I can't put my finger on any one thing in particular, but there's an aspect to her I don't trust. It's what you might call a gut feeling."

"All right." *Too bad.*

"But you might learn something from the folder that will shed light on what she was up to."

I ventured another question. "At dinner we were talk-ing about Upton's finances. You don't know any specifics about his money problems?"

"No. But I recall Vi saying she was worried about him."

"Did she ever talk about Tina having issues at work?" From what Red had said, Tina had problems of her own.

"No." Grant cocked his head. "Why do you ask about that?"

"It was something a visitor to my restaurant said today. I'm sure it's nothing."

"Very well."

"I'd better let you go." I touched his arm. "It was good to see you again."

"Likewise. You're always welcome, you know."

"Thank you for trusting me," I murmured, but he didn't seem to hear. I watched him feel his way to his recliner and fumble for the television remote on a side table. "Good night, Grant."

CHAPTER 38

I made my way to the exit. Outside the rain had stopped, but heavy clouds still darkened the summer evening sky. A car door slammed as I took a step toward the parking lot. I stopped when I saw Buck amble toward me, hands in pockets. *Uh-oh.*

"Evenin', Robbie. Was you visiting with Pop?"

"I was. I ate dinner with him."

"The food here ain't bad, is it?"

"It was delicious." Except . . . who had told me it wasn't worth eating? Nanette? No, it had been Tina. Maybe she'd simply gotten the chef on a bad day. Or maybe she'd sampled one of the less-than-stellar breakfasts.

"And lemme guess, you was snooping around a bit, too." He gave me the side-eye.

"I wasn't snooping." Although the folder was burning a hole in my bag. Still, I wanted to take a look at it. Grant had asked me to. I didn't need to turn it over right now. Did I? For all I knew, the whole thing was a file of knitting patterns having nothing to do with the case. "But aren't you and Oscar frustrated with this case?"

"You could say that."

"Did you check out Tina's work situation?" I asked.

"Seems somebody made a couple few accusations about her at the school, which she claimed were false. They came to a mutual agreement for her to move over to the public library."

Accusations. "What kinds of accusations?" I asked.

"Some inappropriate behavior."

I felt like I was grilling him, maybe because I was. But he didn't show any signs of continuing inside, so I pushed on. "Have they found the murder weapon? It seems like that would be the most important part."

"I don't believe so, no."

"And you don't know what it was."

He cast his eyes up in a give-me-a-break look. "It was a thin, sharp object, Robbie. That's all we know."

"Have they searched Nanette's room? Her needlework bag? The trash cans at the park?"

"You can't up and search somebody's personal possessions without a reason, Robbie. A judge won't sign a warrant without cause."

"Doesn't Kristopher's accusation provide a reason? 'Cause,' as you put it?"

"His word ain't enough."

I blew out a breath. "What about the trash? Here and at the park." If I had killed someone, I'd want to ditch the weapon as soon as I could.

"A public park's one thing. I do believe Oscar's people went through the barrels there, to no avail. This here is private property. Again, we'd need cause, and Oscar don't got it yet."

"Too bad." I shook my head. "Buck, I talked with Simone this afternoon. She was starting to tell me something about Quinton Blake, but she got called away. I haven't had a free minute to research him. Has he been in trouble or something?"

"Why are you asking about him now?"

"Just in case he helped Pat or . . . I don't know. I guess I want to leave no stone unturned."

"I do not believe he is involved in this case. He had a rough childhood, no question. But he's on the straight and narrow now, and from all reports, he's a responsible father to that girl of his."

"Good." That was one question answered. Quinton might have had a troubled youth, but he certainly seemed like a responsible person to me. He'd been nothing but polite and congenial to me, in a modest kind of way. He clearly had a job, and he was a caring father, to boot. Some people found their way to getting clear of their past. That was a good thing. "Did you talk to Melissa?"

"Not yet." He peered at me. "You didn't get no more threatening texts, now, did you?"

"No, thank goodness. Are you headed in to see your dad?"

"That I am. And possibly do a bit of my own snooping, unofficially." He smiled.

"Good luck. I'm heading back to the store to do prep for tomorrow."

His smile vanished. "You take care, Robbie. I mean it. Lock your doors and such."

"No worries, Buck. I'm being very careful."

He headed in, and I made my way to my car. Even

though the sun wouldn't officially set for another two hours, it was creepy out here with the cloud cover and the darkening woods surrounding the parking lot. Why had I parked at the far perimeter? I shivered as I hurried. Whoever sent the threatening text could be watching me right now. They could be lurking on the far side of my car, crouching, waiting. My scalp crawled. I hovered my thumb over the *Unlock* button on the key fob, waiting to push it until the very last minute.

I slid into the driver's seat as fast as I could. The *click* of the doors locking me safely inside my car had never sounded so good.

CHAPTER 39

In Pans 'N Pancakes twenty minutes later—with the doors firmly locked and all the outside lights on—I sang along with the aria I'd cranked up. I didn't speak Italian, or not much, and I could barely carry a tune, especially one from *Tosca*. But, hey, with audience-free solo singing, I figured I could do whatever I wanted. And I wanted to belt out arias, even ones sung by men.

I hadn't forgotten about the folder in my bag. The Stitch and Bitch file Grant had asked me to take from Vi's room, which Upton and Tina had clearly not noticed hiding behind the bookcase. The papers I should have promptly turned over to Buck without poring over them, despite Grant's request. The information I was itchy to read. But my work came first. Of course I would turn it all over to Buck and Oscar after I'd learned what I could. Tomorrow would be soon enough. Wouldn't it?

I didn't have to do prep for the roasted potatoes. Turner had promised to come in early and take care of them. I pondered whether to defrost and shell the massive bag full of shrimp tonight for tomorrow's lunch special. I should, in case we didn't get a lull during the late morning. I dumped them into the biggest colander I had and ran cool water over them to start the defrosting. At least grits cooked fast and didn't need any prior preparation.

Meanwhile, I had the usual biscuit dough and pancake mix to prepare, and the perennial silverware rolls to get underway. Edna's car hadn't been parked outside when I'd arrived, so I knew I was alone in the building. Before I covered my hands with flour, I texted Abe that I was in the store and should be home by eight. Eight thirty at the latest. When the last thing a police officer says to you is, "Be careful," it was prudent to let at least one other person know of your whereabouts and plans. Abe being my adored and adoring husband, I would have let him know even if there wasn't a murderer on the loose.

By seven thirty I'd finished all the flour-based prep. I separated the thawing shrimp from each other and did another rinse, this time with warmer water. Hot would start them cooking, but I did want to get the shelling done before I headed home. The job was nearly impossible while the tasty crustaceans were still frozen, not to mention that I would be guaranteed to come down with a painful case of icy fingers.

I settled in at a table with a tall stack of napkins, a full silverware caddy, and a brain full of thoughts. Fold the napkin. Place a fork, knife, and spoon in the middle. Fold in the ends. Roll. Snug the roll into the end of the high-sided tray. Fold, place, fold, roll, snug. As usual, the repetitive motions made thinking easy.

Why hadn't I asked Buck what *would* be cause to search Nanette's room for a weapon? Or, for that matter, to search Kristopher's residence, or those of Tina, Upton, or Pat? I frowned at the current napkin. Where in South Lick did Kristopher live, anyway? Abe had been going to find out for me via his music circles.

I felt like I'd barely seen him lately, and I missed my guy. I decided then and there to carve out a week in August when we could get away somewhere, with or without Sean. With Len's help, my capable Pans 'N Pancakes team could get along without me. Abe and I had gone away for a long weekend after our wedding, but it hadn't been a full-fledged honeymoon. We were saving that for a trip to Italy next year. Still, we needed a vacation.

When an email dinged on my phone, I had flash of premonition. I took a glance after sending up an intention to the universe that this not be bad news from Adele or my father or anyone else. I sucked in a breath when I saw it was from Adele.

"Samuel's better, but we're coming home early out of an abundance of caution. Phil picks us up in Indy Friday 7 pm. Love, Adele."

Whew. I tapped out a quick reply. "Safe travels. Love you both."

I would touch base with Phil, and I would also plan to be at Adele's at eight Friday night. I could pick up groceries to restock her fridge and bring a ready-made meal the travelers could eat on the spot or later.

I focused on the rolling again. When I didn't have help, this task was becoming more onerous every time I did it. It sure sped up our process of re-setting tables during our busy times. But maybe we needed to resort to simply having a supply of pre-folded napkins and making sure we separated the three main categories of flatware. I would brainstorm with my team tomorrow. Paying the laundry service to deliver folded napkins, if they offered such a service, might be worth the expense.

I had only a few more napkins to go when my cell played its incoming-call tune. I froze. Another threat? This time while I was alone in a store with big front windows and all the lights on. The call could be from whomever had texted me. I shot a glance to the phone on the table. I didn't know the number. Should I answer? It could be perfectly innocent store business from someone who had no idea I was here by myself. Or it could be Leanne or Red, both of whom I'd given my store card to. I knew I was feeling vulnerable, but I swallowed hard and connected the call. "Hello?"

"Robbie, it's Pat Blake."

"Hi, Pat." I relaxed. A little. I didn't know why she was calling me, but at least she was a known quantity. I put the call on speaker so I could keep working. "How can I help you?"

"Listen, Buck Bird was poking around Nanette tonight. Do you know why?"

No beating around the bush for her. "I don't. Are you still at Jupiter Springs?"

"No, but Nanette called me. I know you're buddy-buddy with Buck." Her tone was terse as she bit off her words. "If you two are thinking Nanette killed Vi, you're dead wrong."

So to speak. "Pat, you are aware I'm a chef, not a detective or a police officer, right?"

"I know that's what you say, but..." She let her voice trail off.

"I say it because it's true."

"I'm serious. You tell your police pals that Nanette Russo isn't well, and they should effing lay off. She never would have hurt Vi. Ever."

"I'm so sorry Nanette is ill. I didn't know." Nanette was sick, as I'd thought. Was she on hospice and Pat was providing her with wellness services, whatever those were? "But you really should call the police yourself."

"They won't listen to me." Pat sounded bitter.

"I can try to pass along your message."

"And one more thing." Pat cleared her throat. "You've upset my grandgirl, and I want you to stay away from her." She disconnected.

Whoa. I heard her "or else" loud and clear.

CHAPTER 40

It wasn't until I arrived home at a quarter past eight and dropped my bag on the kitchen counter that I let myself sit down with the purloined folder. Abe still wasn't home. Before I opened the folder, I texted him where I was. I got up again to feed Birdy and pour myself a glass of cold whole milk. Okay, milk laced with Kahlúa. Now that the storm had passed, I wanted to sit outside on the patio and watch dark fall in the coming hour. Let my mind wander where it would. Gaze at the fireflies coming to life, signaling each other with their little lights. Were they courting, talking about predators, or sharing information about dinner? I had no idea.

Instead I stayed indoors with the sliders locked and the drapes again drawn over them. It was going to be me, the couch, the cat, and the craft group until Abe arrived. I sipped and stroked. Birdy purred at maximum volume, happy to have a human home after a long day alone in the house and yard.

Staring at the folder, I wrinkled my nose at my own deception by omission. Was I really going to—tomorrow—tell Buck I had accidentally found it? Lying didn't sit well with me. I could always claim I'd thought it only held knitting patterns. I knew I didn't want to betray Grant's trust. Adele had said getting old wasn't for wusses. I'd never considered how hard it could be to be dependent on one's children and have them scold you. I was Adele's niece, not her daughter, but I'd found myself chiding her a couple of times in recent years, a situation that bore further musing. But not now.

I thought about Vi shoving the folder behind the bookcase. Had she done it on purpose? She could have been trying to keep it hidden from someone. Specifically Nanette, since Vi had stolen it from her room. If the file detailed illegal activities, Vi wouldn't have wanted the staff to see it. Or maybe she'd dug up dirt on Nanette or Pat and didn't want them to know. It occurred to me that my fingerprints were now on the card stock that formed the folder. I could go don gloves, but it was a bit late for that. I doubted one could wipe prints from paper, anyway. I would fess up. Tomorrow.

I opened the cover and flipped past the knitting pattern. The second page, the paper yellowed from age and now crinkled with my mistreatment, was titled *Stitch and Bitch, South Lick Chapter. Chapter?* This was official. Maybe there was a national organization by the same name.

The second page was a list of founding members. It included the four I knew of—Yolande Bird, Pat Blake, Vi Perkell, and Nanette Russo—plus another half dozen I'd never heard of. Next to each name was listed that person's preferred needle craft, including knitting, embroidery, cross-stitch, crewel, and quilting. A short section was titled *Minutes*, with a date from nearly forty years ago. The group had elected officers, collected dues, and set meeting places and dates for the year to come. They'd selected Nanette to be the treasurer, and next to her name was a note about First Savings Bank. So the group had an account.

I flipped slowly through the pages. After the first year, they'd stopped taking minutes. Instead, every year had a single sheet listing the meeting date and location for each month. After the page for the third year, a program for Yolande's funeral was tucked in. I turned it over. The picture of her was fuzzy, but I could see similarities with both Simone and Buck. I could have dwelt again on how hard it must have been for Buck to lose his mom in his teen years—to murder, no less—and for Grant to lose his wife and the mother of his son, his only child. But my goal tonight was to learn all I could from this folder.

I cruised past notices for Brown County Quilt Guild meetings and a needlework exhibit in Indianapolis. Signups to carpool to the Indiana State Fair in Indy the following month. An invitation to a cross-stitch club in Bloomington. New members joined, original members dropped out, with Nanette, Pat, and Vi remaining the constants. The first page had listed what kind of crafting Pat did, but I hadn't taken notice. I also hadn't come across a funeral program for her husband, but that wasn't odd. She was the member, not him.

As yet, nothing looked fishy. This record of a decades-old group seemed reasonable and aboveboard. I certainly hadn't come across any suspicious coded messages about gambling or skimmed funds.

I frowned at the sheet for the current year, the last one in the folder. At the top was written, *Dates TBA*. Maybe they weren't meeting regularly anymore. Running my hand down the page to smooth it, I readied to close the folder and accept that I hadn't learned one useful thing. Except . . . my fingers encountered a flat bump under the page. I flipped it over and stared.

A slender booklet stuck out of an envelope taped inside the folder's back cover. I carefully extracted the booklet. Someone had neatly printed *S&B Accounts* on the front cover. But it wasn't a bankbook from First Savings. This was a homemade ledger. And it was full of those coded messages I'd been looking for.

Columns of handwritten numbers and initials filled the otherwise-blank lined pages. None of the columns included a heading. I peered at them, trying to decipher the meanings. The first column could be dates. The number 514 could be May fourteenth, 1002 October second, and so on. The numbers never began with anything larger than twelve. If they were dates, they didn't include the year. The digits in the second column, while not preceded by dollar signs, might be amounts of money. I didn't see any sum that ran to four digits, and many were under a hundred. The third column was possibly the most interesting.

NR

PB

VP

NR

NR

PB

VP

Didn't these have to be Nanette's, Pat's, and Vi's initials? I sat back, thinking. Yolande's initials weren't included. The others might have started their gambling ring after she died, or maybe Grant's wife was never part of it. Simone had said how much her daughter loved crafting and being home with Buck.

I flipped through the pages. *VP* didn't occur after the first few, so maybe Vi had wanted out. How had she gotten the folder? She'd stayed in the craft group, though. Could she have known about the scam and let it go on? Maybe Pat and Nanette had assured her they would stop—but didn't. Never having played poker, I didn't know the first thing about how to cheat at it or any other card game.

I thought back to when Nanette claimed Vi was a liar. Maybe Vi had lied to her about having the folder. She must have known it contained incriminating information. My thoughts flashed onto Quinton. He'd have still been at home in the earlier days of the group. They'd met in members' homes. Quinton had been in trouble when he was younger. After learning how to cheat at gambling from his mother? Or had he been stealing to pay debts from losing? He was apparently an upstanding citizen now and certainly seemed to be a caring father for his differently abled daughter. But maybe I was wrong about him.

When a noise sounded outside the side door, I started, then swore under my breath. I was home alone pondering a murderer's identity. I had no weapon. Sweet Birdy was hardly a guard cat. My heart pounded. I grabbed my phone, hovering my finger over the *Emergency* button, the one that would summon 911. The papers in my lap slid to the floor. I tried to swallow, but my throat was too thick with fear. My clammy hand nearly dropped the phone.

The lock clicked. The door swung open to reveal a tired-looking but smiling Abe.

"Honey, I'm home."

CHAPTER 41

" **A**m I ever glad to see you." I hurried toward Abe, arms extended.

"Likewise, sugar." After a welcoming kiss, he said, "I really need to shower off the day before I can relax."

"Of course." My heart rate returned to normal. I blew out a shaky breath. "Are you hungry?"

"Boy, am I. I barely had time to eat."

"Me chef." I pointed at my sternum, then turned my index finger toward him. "Make food for husband."

"I love you, dear wife. An easy sandwich would be fine."

I was so relieved both that he was home and that I hadn't been attacked by an at-large murderer, I would have made him a four-course dinner.

Now, at nine fifteen, Abe wandered barefoot into the kitchen with damp hair. He sported soft cutoff jeans worn to a pale blue and a green T-shirt reading *Pluckers Unite*. The shirt was illustrated with stick-figure drawings of a banjo player between a farmer in overalls plucking a chicken and a cosmetologist extracting eyebrow hairs from a reclining customer. He sank onto a stool on the other side of the counter.

I slid his grilled Gouda, ham, and Dijon on sourdough out of the skillet and onto a plate. Setting it down in front of him, I added a full pint glass of his favorite beer.

"You're the best." He squeezed my hand.

"Everything's all repaired?" I poured myself a little bourbon and cut myself a piece of cheese. Dinner with Grant seemed like a long time ago. I came around to keep Abe company. I perched on the next stool and swiveled to face him, letting my knees nudge his thigh. "The county has power?"

"Mostly. A transformer blew over the county line to the west, but it affects some Brown County folks. Hoosier Energy is working on it. They should have it fixed soon." He lifted his glass. "Cheers, sweetheart."

I clinked my glass with his. "I'm glad you're home safe."

He took a bite of his sandwich. "Mmm."

Abe ate. I sipped. He sipped. The adrenaline from my fear had ebbed as I cooked, and now I stifled a yawn.

He took a deep breath and let it out. "Boy, this hits the spot. The sandwich and the beer, both."

"Good. Any more word from the boy?"

"No, but I don't expect to hear anything. He's always spent a lot of time with my folks, and they enjoy each other's company." Abe tilted his head. "Robbie, hon, you looked a little shaky when I came in. Is everything all right? Tell me about your day."

I gazed fondly at him as I pondered which parts of my very long day to share. "Now that I think back, quite a lot happened, and I'm still in the dark about Vi's murder." I held up my palm. "Just so you know, I'm fine. I was never in danger." *Maybe*. "What do you know about cheating at cards?"

He had just taken a big bite of sandwich and covered his laugh with his hand. "Maybe I shouldn't ask why you need that kind of information."

"Maybe not quite yet. I'm serious, though. I've never played poker and haven't the slightest idea about how to rig a game."

"Well," he began, taking me at my word. "Sometimes they mark the cards on the back. That wouldn't fly in Las Vegas or with anyone who plays for high stakes. But this is southern Indiana. Are we talking amateurs?"

"I would say so."

"So, if whoever is running the scam knows which are the high value cards, they can also see what the other players are holding."

"How do they mark them?"

"There are lots of ways. One is to ding the card itself on both ends."

"No matter which end is up, the cheater will know it's a high card," I guessed.

"Yes, or they add a small colored dot to a particular place on the back. With the pros, of course, the dealer has to use a new sealed pack. For small-potato players, I'm sure they can mark cards and then reseal the pack so it looks new." He popped in the last bite of sandwich.

"I've heard of counting cards. Is that a thing?"

"It certainly can be, for someone with an excellent visual memory and a grip on the numbers."

Nanette would have a grip on the numbers. Wasn't that what actuaries dealt in?

Abe continued. "They have to remember every card that was played and by whom. They have to know the card's value relative to their own hand as well as their own prospects for winning. It's a pretty specialized skill, and it's actually more useful in other games than in poker."

"What about palming a card? You know, the kind of thing magicians do."

"If you're good—and wearing long sleeves—you can slip a card out of a hand and hide it in your sleeve or under your leg until you need it. You have to be good, though. False dealing is another method, where the dealer might pre-stack the deck and deal the second card instead of the top one, keeping it for himself."

"Or herself."

"Of course. And if two cheaters work together, they can really make out. But you have to have a trustworthy cheater as a partner."

"'Trustworthy cheater' sounds like an oxymoron, doesn't it?" I took a taste of my whiskey. Two of the Stitch and Bitch members could have been helping each other cheat the others. "Should I even ask how you know all this?"

He threw back his head in a classic Abe move and laughed. "No, I don't have a sordid history of being a brilliant beater of the odds, Robbie. I watched a documentary on that kind of gambler. That's all."

"I never suspected you for a minute."

"I didn't think you had." He leaned over to give me a light kiss. He drained his beer glass and stood. "Thank you for the super supper, darlin'. It's time for this puppy to . . . oh, wait. I need to tell you about a thing tomorrow."

"A 'thing'?" I also emptied the last of my bourbon and held my hand over my mouth opening on another yawn. Sleep and I were so overdue for a good, long visit.

"A musician social thing. It's kind of last-minute, but the South Lick bluegrass players are having a cookout and jam session tomorrow at five. Significant others and families are invited." He touched my cheek. "You'll come, won't you?"

I wouldn't know anyone there, and I would have been working all day. Still, I looked at his smile, his eagerness. "If you want me to go, I will. Do we need to bring food?"

"I'll check. Probably a side or dessert." He took my arm. "You'll have been cooking all day. How about I make another orzo salad as our contribution?"

"Sounds good to me. Where's the party?"

"You might be interested in this. Kristopher Gale is hosting it as a kind of housewarming, even though he moved in last year."

My antennae went on full alert. "I am interested. Where does he live?"

"Over near Corrine. He said he hasn't had guests since he moved in. His girlfriend—Tina—will be there, too."

His *girlfriend* Tina? If I'd been at all reluctant before, I wasn't now. Seeing where Kristopher lived, watching him interact with others? No-brainer. Plus, this Tina had to be Vi's Tina, didn't she? It wasn't a super-common name. Now I knew why the two had been at my restaurant together drinking vodka over lunch. Finding out how she and Kristopher became an item would just be the frosting on the proverbial cake.

CHAPTER 42

To my surprise, Josie was one of the first customers waiting outside when I unlocked the door to Pans 'N Pancakes at seven the next morning. I didn't think I'd ever seen her in to eat so early.

"Robbie." She grabbed my hand after the dozen other early birds had entered. "I need to talk with you."

I'd also never seen her not wearing lipstick. I gazed at her mussed hair.

"Sure. Are you . . . ?" I gestured toward the restaurant.

"Um." She looked startled. "What?"

"Are you here for breakfast? Because I'm sorry, but I can't linger and talk right this minute."

She stared at me, then nodded. "I so need some coffee. Of course. Breakfast."

"Josie, are you okay?"

"Yes." She hurried inside.

What was up with her? I shook my head. As I'd told her, I seriously didn't have the leisure time right now to stop on the front porch and chat, not even with both Danna and Turner on shift. After coffee was poured and everybody's orders taken, maybe.

Before I could follow her in, Oscar and Buck climbed out of Buck's cruiser. The first thing that popped into my head when I saw them was "Mutt and Jeff," instead of their real names. Which really wasn't a bit fair, because Oscar wasn't short and round, but I had to stifle a giggle. Two more cars pulled up. It was shaping up to be a busy morning. I waved at the officers, pointed inside, and hurried through the door.

To my own credit—sort of—I'd texted both Oscar and Buck about the folder last night before I'd gone to bed. I'd said I would bring it to work with me, and I had. The folder now awaited them in my desk drawer. Did I also need to tell them I had used my phone to photograph all the ledger pages? Maybe, but they would obviously do their own scanning of the information. I hoped they had better luck figuring it out than I had.

I headed for the grill to grab the coffee carafes. Turner was already taking orders. Danna looked worried.

"What's up with my grandmother?" Danna pointed across the room with her chin as she flipped one pancake after another.

"I don't know. She said she needed to talk with me."

"She does not look like herself today. I can tell even from here something's the matter."

"I can cook if you want," I said. "So you can ask her what's wrong."

Danna narrowed her eyes for a moment, thinking.

"No, she said she wants to talk to you. It's gotta be about the murder, don't you think?"

"I don't know. Maybe." I held up the caf and decaf carafes. "Off I go."

Buck and Oscar had taken Buck's usual table.

"Good morning, gentlemen." I poured for both of them. "The folder is in my desk. I'll get it as soon as I can."

"'Morning, Robbie. We'd appreciate that."

"Turner is taking orders," I said.

"Good," Buck said. "'Cause my stomach's about to growl louder than yesterday's thunder."

I left Josie for last so I could grab a quick word with her. "What's wrong?" I asked in a murmur.

"Robbie, we don't know each other well. I can tell you I'm not easily shaken."

"I can't imagine you are."

"After we spoke yesterday, I got to thinking. Last night I was going through some old papers, trying to whittle down my possessions so my Corrie won't have to when I kick off."

"You're not ill, are you?" I asked.

"No, nothing like that. But I need to keep at it while I can. Anyway, I ran across a newspaper clipping about Frank Blake's death. His murder."

I nodded slowly. The bell on the door jangled. Seated customers were starting to look hungry. Turner was moving as fast as he could. I seriously needed to get to work.

"And?" I asked.

"He was a mean son of a b—Well, you know. And we all thought Pat was justified in killing him."

"Except she wasn't convicted."

"That was a technicality." She batted away the thought.

"She claimed she wasn't home, and an intruder did it. Too, lots of people wondered why she'd married him the first place. Not because he was such a jerk, but because we thought she might have preferred women."

"Pat's gay?" I asked.

"I don't know. Maybe not. And it's a tired old cliché, of course, the lesbian gym teacher. I'm just telling you it was whispered about."

"She never remarried?"

Josie shook her head. "But what I'd forgotten was that Frank was shot to death. While he slept, Robbie."

As Grant had mentioned.

Josie leaned toward me. "What if she . . ." Her whisper trailed off.

I cleared my throat. "Do you have the clipping with you?"

"Yes. I wanted to give it to you." She started to reach for her bag.

"No." I gestured with my thumb toward Oscar and Buck, even though I was sure this wouldn't be news to them. "It's those two who need it, not me. All right?"

Her hand froze. "I don't want to spoil their breakfast."

"Josie, listen to me. They probably already know, but you should give it to them."

"Could you?"

"Huh-uh." I gave my head a sharp shake. "I need to get to work. Promise me you will?"

"All right."

I hurried away, pouring coffee into mugs as I went. I had no idea why she didn't want to pass along a newspaper clipping from decades ago. It was part of the public record. I imagined one of the two officers already knew how Pat's husband died, if not both. I shook my head. As

Josie had said, she and I didn't know each other well. She'd always seemed like a together, competent woman. She was successful in her consulting company. She was fit, attractive, and congenial, the whole package. It couldn't be that she didn't like police. She'd invited Oscar to eat with her yesterday, hadn't she?

I didn't have time to worry about it. I had a restaurant full of people to feed and make happy. And a folder to convey to Buck and Oscar.

CHAPTER 43

Turner's Indian roasted potatoes were a popular order, and he'd made loads of them. Forty-five minutes later, we were in no danger of running low. Josie, having downed a quick scrambled egg with toast, got up to leave. Before she headed toward the door, I was glad to see her hand Oscar an envelope I assumed held the clipping.

Danna watched her go. "What was up with my grandma? She didn't even say hi to me."

"She found an old newspaper clipping and seemed kind of shaken by it. It might have to do with Vi's murder, and I told her she had to give it to Oscar. You'll have to ask her. Her reaction seemed kind of out of character to me."

"Thanks. I will ask her, or maybe sic my mom on her." She frowned. "Josie's been acting a little bit funny lately. I hope she's not getting Alzheimer's or anything."

"I hope she isn't, either." Dementia? That would be awful.

Edna trotted down the interior stairs, giving me a little wave. She pointed at an empty two-top with a questioning look. I gave her a thumbs-up and grabbed the coffeepot.

"Good morning, Edna." I filled her mug. "Are you heading out?"

"Hi, Robbie. Yes. My car's all packed, and I left the key card in the room, as you said to do. Before I go, I'd like a quick bite, if I may."

"Of course. And remember, your room receipt will be in your email."

"That's fine. I think I'd better have the Hoosier biscuits and gravy. They don't really offer that at diners in Connecticut." She smiled. "Plus one scrambled egg and a dish of fruit to offset the gravy."

"You got it. Let me go put your order in." After I did, I surveyed the place. Everybody was fed and nobody was waiting to be seated. I finally had time to grab the folder. After I slid it onto Oscar and Buck's table next to the envelope, the detective glanced up.

"What'd you think of that reporting?" he asked me.

"I didn't even see the clipping. Josie wanted to give it to me. I told her you were the two who needed to see it."

"Thanks, Robbie." Buck wiped his mouth with his napkin. He peered at the article, which lay on the table next to one of his empty plates.

"Did you guys already know that information, about how Pat's husband was mur—I mean, how he died?" I stood with my back to the rest of the tables and tried to keep my voice low enough so other diners didn't hear. "I mean, you must have been looking into her, right?"

"I'm not at liberty to say." Oscar lifted his chin.

Gah. That sounded like a "no" to me. Hadn't he said a few days ago that he was keeping his eye on Pat?

"Well, anyway, you'll want to check out the little notebook in the back of the folder," I said. "Please let me know if you figure out the code."

Buck looked up from the article. "What code?"

"It's what the letters and numbers seemed like."

"You say you found this in Vi Perkell's room?" Oscar tapped a finger on the still-closed folder.

"Grant and I popped our heads in after dinner yesterday." I had omitted the timing of my find from my text last night and had also not included Grant asking me to look for the folder. I winced a little, but forged on, crossing my fingers behind my back. "Upton and Tina left a mess in there when they cleared out her things. I happened to see the folder stuffed behind a bookcase. When I noticed the label read *Stitch and Bitch*, I thought it might be useful."

"Wait a chicken-pickin' minute there, Robbie." Buck gave me as close to a glare as he ever got. "I met you in the parking lot after that. You didn't think to mention it? Hand over the goods, so to speak?"

"It plum slipped my mind, Buck." I smiled brightly as I threw in one of his favorite adverbs on purpose. "And now you have it. If you'll excuse me?" I hurried off to the kitchen area, where Danna was pouring and flipping away. "Switch with me, would you?"

She gave me a suspicious frown. "Sure." She glanced at where I'd been and back at me. "Something up with Buck? He's shooting you a dirty look."

"I'm in a teensy bit of hot water." I did not let my gaze wander in Buck's direction. "It'll be fine."

She snorted and slid off her dirty apron. "Have at it."

Turner arrived with a load of empty plates and used silverware.

"I'll bus, bro," Danna told him.

"You got it," he said. "Robbie, do you have a lunch special planned?"

"Yep. Cajun shrimp and grits. The shrimp are all shelled and marinating in their Cajun-ness."

"*Laissez les bon temps rouler?*" Danna asked.

Turner looked surprised. "You have a good accent, Dan."

Danna lowered her voice to a growly nasal and twirled the tip of a pretend mustache. "*Ho-ho, merci, mon ami.*"

I laughed. "Get out of here, you two." I read an order and added a half-dozen sausages to the griddle.

When I finally dared to check what Buck and Oscar were up to, they had their heads down together over the little ledger. Good. I hoped it would bring some kind of progress in the case, even a resolution. An arrest. I wasn't sure how, but one could dream.

CHAPTER 44

By ten thirty we had a good lull, and both my helpers had already taken breaks. I carried a small plate of spiced potatoes with a fried egg on top into my old apartment at the back and sat at the small round table.

What I wanted to do was drive to the turkey farm and ask about Nanette's time with them. But jaunting off to Beanblossom midmorning was not the move of a responsible restaurateur. I'd have to save that particular field trip for this afternoon, maybe combined with a bike ride. Still, there was nothing wrong with a little quiet alone time. I couldn't linger back here long, but sitting and being still felt good.

Breaking the yolk into the potatoes, I took a bite and savored the flavors. *Mmm*. This was a great combination. Maybe we could come up with a baked dish dotted with

the equivalent of fried eggs. No, the yolks would probably overcook in the baking.

So many questions about Vi's murder—and Yolande's—were tapping at my brain. My fork slowed
halfway to my mouth. Nanette had casually mentioned
early on that she'd gotten rid of her husband. Surely via
divorce and not murder. I hoped. Nanette and Pat were
definitely close. Were they in a long-term relationship, as
Josie had implied? I shrugged. Their personal lives were
none of my concern—unless it had to do with homicide.

While I was here, I might as well take a couple of minutes to do a bit of research. One person I wanted to learn
more about was Upton Perkell. Pulling out my phone, I
tapped in his name. I still didn't know why or even if he
was having financial problems. And if he was, would
they lead him to do the unthinkable—kill his own
mother?

I tapped and ate and read. By the time my plate was
empty, I knew Upton's father had filed for bankruptcy.
And I'd learned a leather supplier had sued the current
Upton for failure to pay an invoice for goods. I couldn't
seem to get any further than that. So, yeah, he had money
woes. Except lots of people did, and they didn't knock off
their moms to pay their debts. I couldn't remember who,
but somebody had said Vi herself had debts. If she did,
Upton killing her wasn't going to solve his problems.

The questions about Yolande's death still bugged me. I
didn't think there was any way someone could stab her in
the neck without her friends seeing. Truly, the same ap-
plied to Vi's murder. Grant couldn't see, but if anyone
other than Nanette had killed Vi, Nanette would have noticed. Wouldn't she? She was sitting in the next chair.

I gazed at the smears of spice-flecked yolk on my plate. I was tempted to lick them off, but I restrained myself. Instead, I pushed away the plate and started a deeper dive into news coverage of Yolande's murder. I'd talked with Simone about her daughter's death, and Phil had found those few articles. There had to be more.

And then . . . *bingo.* I happened across an article by a journalist who had interviewed Pat and Nanette after Yolande's funeral. They each stated they'd seen nothing. Nanette had no idea why someone would murder her friend. Pat said Vi had gone off to the restroom. She and Nanette had stepped away to chat with two friendly young gentlemen, leaving Yolande alone in her chair. They both insisted neither had seen a thing. Who were these young men?

The reporter's writing conveyed a sense of breathless, bewildered innocence from the women. Sure, they'd been a lot younger. But I couldn't imagine Pat or Nannette as breathless or bewildered. Innocent? Maybe, maybe not.

The story ended by saying that both Vi Perkell and the widower, Grant Bird, had declined requests for an interview, and that the authorities continued to search for the person responsible. I reread the passage and wrinkled my nose. The wording held the slightest suggestion that there was something wrong with Vi refusing an interview. Was he implying it was because she was guilty? Because maybe she hadn't been in the restroom during the killing, after all. Somehow I was more willing to believe Vi than Nanette and Pat, but I wasn't sure why.

Darn. I wished I could read the police reports. Nobody could refuse an interview with the authorities. I wouldn't want to bug Buck about the investigation into his mother's murder, but maybe Oscar could dig up the reports.

My phone buzzed with a two-word text from Danna. One with an unmistakable message.

Tour bus.

I grabbed my plate and stashed my phone. Musings on murder were over. It was all-hands-on-deck time.

CHAPTER 45

The tour bus hadn't been one of the huge ones. We'd had no trouble accommodating the twenty Japanese visitors. We'd started our lunch service a little early when two of them noticed Danna adding Cajun shrimp and grits to the Specials board and wanted to order it. Luckily, Danna had started the grits while I'd been dawdling in my apartment.

I'd delivered the shrimp and grits to the two gentlemen and went back to see how they were doing a few minutes later.

One sucked in air through his teeth. "Hot." He fanned his mouth with his hand.

"They are a little spicy," I agreed. "Would you like something else?"

"No, sank you." He took another bite.

"It's like kimchee," his companion said. "We like hot."

He patted his forehead with a handkerchief and also dug in for more Cajun yumminess.

I liked the spicy Korean fermented cabbage, too, a condiment Abe had introduced me to. It was apparently popular in Japan as a bar snack. I had to admit, kimchee paired well with a cold beer.

Now, at noon, the tourists were shopping in the retail area, and I was gladly taking their money. One woman brought a butter dish to the counter. It was painted black and white to look like a Holstein cow, with the top featuring the cow's head at one end.

"*Kawaii soo*," she exclaimed to her friend.

"That's means 'cute'," the friend explained to me.

I wrapped the dish and the lid separately in tissue paper and passed it to the purchaser in a paper store bag with a handle. I hoped it would get back to Japan intact, but that was up to them. I didn't stock cushiony packing materials.

The bus left just in time. We were shortly thereafter hit with the mother of all lunch rushes. The three of us became a whirlwind of order-taking, cooking, delivering, bussing, and starting the cycle over again. Turner was on the grill. Danna had her arms full of dishes. I had pen to paper at twelve thirty waiting for a solo diner to make up his mind about what he wanted for lunch when Corrine strode in. The dude finally decided on a cheeseburger and a ginger ale.

I waved at Corrine as I hurried the order over to Turner. "This guy took five minutes to decide on a cheeseburger, bless his heart."

Turner laughed. "All it did was put him five minutes behind everyone else."

The mayor signaled she'd seen me, then leaned against

the wall near the door and bent over her phone. Eight people were ahead of her for a table. Danna exchanged some kind of wordless communication with her mom and kept on working. Corrine appeared to be here to see me. It took me ten minutes of pouring coffee—and making more—along with delivering food before I had a minute to approach her.

"Sorry we're so busy," I began.

"No worries, hon. I do have me a hunger, but I can wait my turn. Buck might could show up in a little minute, too."

"Sure."

She pointed to her phone. "Something I heared you was interested in."

"What is it?"

Corrine turned her back to the door and held the phone in her palm. "This business of Frank Blake?"

I turned my back too, even as the door opened to let in new hungry customers. "Yes?" This was not my usual storekeeper mode, but I was too curious to ignore Corrine.

"Read this," she whispered. "It's about the investigation into Pat getting rid of her husband once and for all."

"Does it have to do with the article Josie found?" I whispered, too.

"Yes." Corrine pointed at the phone again. "You're going to want to see this." She passed me the device.

I took it carefully, so I didn't remove whatever it was from the screen. My eyes went wide when I saw mention of an Indiana State Police Homicide Investigation. I glanced up at her. "The police report?"

She nodded once. "Imma go say hi to my girl. Take your time." She clicked off on her high heels.

As if I had time to take right now. Still, I couldn't help myself. I read a little and was swiping to read the next screen when a low-register voice spoke nearly in my ear.

"What's so interesting?"

I jumped, whirling. Pat Blake stood behind me. Like, close behind me. *Yikes*.

"Hello, Pat." Where had she come from? And how much had she heard? I quickly stuck the phone in my apron pocket.

"I heard you talking about a police report to Corrine." Her words were knife-edged. She set her fists on her blue polo shirt–clad hips. "Are you helping the homicide detective, Robbie?"

"Not at all." I glanced behind her at the new half-dozen diners, glad for their close proximity. I took a step back from Pat's threatening demeanor. "Are you here for lunch?"

"Why not?"

I returned a perfunctory smile to her and raised my voice, also addressing the other newcomers. "I'll get all of you a table as soon as I can." Turning away, I returned to my job, at least my official one. I took orders, delivered checks, accepted money, and answered questions. When I got back to the kitchen, Corrine had removed her blazer and was loading the dishwasher.

"Madam Mayor, you really don't have to do that," I said.

"Oh, it's only for a second." She straightened and dried her hands. "What'd you think of the report?"

"I didn't have a chance to get into it." I shook my head. "And I don't have time right now. Send me the link, all right?" I handed her the phone.

"You bet."

"Plus, I think Pat overheard us."

"Don't you be worrying your head none about her," Corrine said. "We didn't say nothing."

"What if she heard you talking about her getting rid of her husband?" I glanced at the group of folks waiting to be seated. Then peered. I didn't see Pat anywhere. "Hmm. It seems she decided not to wait."

"Not a problem. Anyhoo, all's I mentioned was the investigation into Frank's death. The court decided Pat didn't do the deed. What's she got to worry about?"

What, indeed? "But they never figured out who murdered him."

"They did not."

CHAPTER 46

Buck strode into the store at about a quarter to one. I'd seated Corrine at a two-top only minutes before, and she waved at him. Buck gave me a nod and headed over to join her. He held himself with a tense air that was completely uncharacteristic for the relaxed lieutenant. Something was up.

No other new customers had come in for twenty minutes, and Pat had slipped out before I'd had a chance to seat her. Her departure seemed odd—why come in to eat and then leave? *Whatever*. It made for one less thing I had to think about, especially considering her tone when she'd spoken to me. At least things were starting to get under control. I grabbed a full coffee carafe and poured my way to Corrine and Buck, making sure I saved two cups' worth for them.

Buck's face was tight as he drummed his fingers on the table.

"What's up, Buck?" I asked.

"Pretty much everything, Robbie."

I lowered my voice. "Do you mean about the case?"

"Yup. And my pop, well, he told me something that's got me to thinking."

"Listen, do you both want to order?" I asked. "By the time your food is ready, I should be able to sit down and listen for a minute."

"Sure, if I don't take and get called away," Buck said. "I'll have a cheeseburger with everything, and can you throw some bacon on it, too? Plus a side of grits without none of them Cajun shrimps."

"Will do. Corrine?"

"Give me a cheeseburger, too, if you will please, hon. No bacon for me. And a chocolate milk?"

"That sounds good," Buck said. "I'll have me a chocolate milk, too."

I scribbled the orders. "I'll get these up as soon as I can." As I headed to the grill with the slip of paper, I thought about how Buck was rarely upset or in any kind of dark mood. I'd seen him businesslike, of course, but he was nearly always congenial and relaxed about life. Whatever Grant told him must have really worried him. Plus, the case had been going on unsolved for a week—or it would be tomorrow. That couldn't be good for Buck, and especially not for Oscar.

I was waylaid by diners right and left. One wanted coffee, to which I had to respond that the next pot was on its way. Another asked for hot sauce for her shrimp and grits. A couple requested their check. It was nearly fifteen minutes before I carried Buck and Corrine's orders to them.

It was too bad now was when I finally had time to talk. I hoped I wasn't going to have to hear Buck's news through a mouthful of food. I set down the plates, then put my hand on the back of the empty chair. Danna caught my eye, signaling she was taking a restroom break. I nodded.

The cowbell jangled, admitting Kristopher Gale. Two women and six little kids followed him in, plus a screaming baby in the arms of one of the women. Turner cried out and jumped back from the grill, holding his hand to his cheek. The spatula he'd held clattered to the floor.

"Shoot," I said to Buck and Corrine. "I can't sit down, after all." I hurried to Turner. "Are you all right?"

"I was working so fast I forgot to prick the sausages and one exploded at me. I must have gotten a grease burn." He pulled his hand away. A red spot glared on his cheekbone.

"That looks like it hurts, but I'm glad it missed your eye. I'll take over here. Do you want to go to the ER?"

"I don't think so."

"Okay. Go grab the first aid kit and try to hold that spot under running cold water for a bit. Then pat it dry, and squeeze some antibiotic ointment on a Band-Aid, okay?"

"I'm sorry, Robbie."

"Hey, it happens to all of us." I turned on the water to scrub my hands. "Don't worry about it. Danna burned her hand the same way during our first year. When you're fixed up, please see if you can seat those newcomers. The sooner we feed the kids, the calmer they'll be, and make sure you bring them each crayons." I'd learned from experience to have little four-crayon boxes on hand for children to color their paper place mats. We always tried to get their food orders delivered promptly, too. One day

Abe and I would be trying to entertain our own little ones at restaurants. I was just paying it forward.

I gave Kristopher a glance but didn't have even a minute to talk with him. I wished I did. I still didn't know what his malfeasance had been. If he'd mistreated Vi financially or otherwise. Or what his connection was to the gambling craft group, if any. Not that I could plop down across from him and ask. I remembered the party at his house later today. Would I have a chance to talk to him then? Unlikely, but stranger things had happened.

I flipped two turkey burgers and threw a handful of Cajun-marinated shrimp on the grill. It didn't take more than a minute for them to be ready to top a plate of grits along with a drizzle of olive oil and a sprinkle of parsley. I slid the patties onto buns and loaded up those plates.

My hand hovered over the ready bell, except Danna wasn't back and Turner had also retreated to a restroom to take care of his burn. I couldn't leave the grill because food was cooking. My team and I had a strict rule about that, having learned a different lesson from experience. Setting off the fire alarms from burning pancakes had not been fun, especially not with a restaurant full of hungry morning diners.

The warming light would have to do for these plates for now. I groaned when the cowbell jangled again. I couldn't even look in that direction as I poured out beaten eggs for an omelet, threw on another handful of shrimp, and turned four rashers of bacon.

"Robbie, are you here by yourself?"

I whipped my head to the side to see Len, looking worried. "Hi, Len. No, but it's complicated."

He'd already grabbed an apron and was tying it behind his back.

"You don't have to do that," I protested.

"Come on, Robbie. I insist." He quickly washed his hands.

"All right. You're the best."

"Who gets the plates in the warmer?"

"That four-top." I pointed. "And can you start a pot of coffee, too, please?"

"I'm on it."

How many times over the years had angels like him swooped in to save the day? I couldn't even count. Corrine, Phil, Adele. Len's sister, Lou. B&B guests. Even Buck. I was one lucky cookie to have landed in a community like this one. Murders notwithstanding.

Danna hurried back to work a minute later. I filled her in on Turner, and on Len aproning up on the spot.

"Ouch, and awesome of Len." She shifted from one foot to the other and looked pained.

"Are you okay?"

She sucked in a breath. "I think I'm having a little relapse. I hate to ask, but could I go home early?"

"Of course. Go now. Do you have your car?"

"I do." When she stayed overnight at her boyfriend's, she drove to work, but otherwise it wasn't a far walk from Corrine's place.

"We'll be fine," I told her. "Turner said he didn't need to go to the ER. And I'll close early if I need to."

Len returned after Danna left. "What's up with her?"

"She's been a little sick. She'll be fine."

"Do you want me to stay until closing?" Len asked.

Turner, with a bandaged cheek, came back to the grill and repeated Len's first question about Danna. I repeated my answer.

"Len, if you can stay for maybe an hour, that would totally rock," I added.

"No sweat. I came in with a few buds to get a late lunch after class." He gestured toward three tall college boys, possibly basketball friends. Len elbowed Turner. "Bro here can give me a lift home later, right?"

"You bet," Turner said. "Right now I'm going to seat the families, and that Gale dude."

I'd forgotten about Kristopher. "Len, want to take the grill?" I glanced at Kristopher, who was bent over his phone.

Ten minutes later, I finally had time to sink into a chair with Buck and Corrine, who both had empty plates in front of them. My feet thanked me.

"Did you send me that link, Corrine?" I pulled out my phone.

"I did." She glanced at Buck and explained, "The homicide report on Frank Blake."

I swiped it open even as Buck started to explain.

"They never locked their doors, them Blakes." He wagged his head. "What it looked like was some stranger come in and killed old Frank."

"Nobody locks their doors in South Lick," I said. Except me, in the last year or three.

"Leastwise that's what the report says." He drained his chocolate milk.

"But there were rumors that Pat shot him." I gazed from him to Corrine and back.

"There surely were," Corrine affirmed. "The lady is a marksman. You know I do me a bit of hunting when I can. But Pat's more like a target shooter. Like it's a competitive sport or something."

"She must own guns, then," I said.

"She does, several of 'em. Or did back then. I don't know if she does now. Do you, Buck?" Corrine asked.

"No." He sat frowning.

"So what's going on with Grant, Buck?" I asked.

Buck leaned toward me. "Pop smelled a particular scent that night, when he says he heard Vi being killed. He thinks it was Nanette."

Whoa. Grant hadn't told me that. Maybe he'd only just remembered. Still, it was big news. I stared at Buck.

"What was the scent?" I whispered. I couldn't remember picking up on a scent when I'd been around Nanette, but I'd barely been near her.

"He wasn't able to describe it too well, unfortunately. We're working on it, Robbie."

CHAPTER 47

By one thirty things in the restaurant had calmed down considerably. Buck left, still looking worried. I didn't blame him. It was hard to describe a scent unless you had a specific item to anchor it to. A freshly cut orange. A waxy gardenia. Car exhaust on a foggy morning. The cologne your mother wore when you were a child. Mouthwash. Coffee roasting. Even spoiled milk. All unmistakable. So, what had Grant smelled?

Corrine lingered on at her table. She kept glancing between her phone and the door as if expecting someone to join her. The man she'd met online, maybe? I'd love to know who had captured this kick-ass woman's affections.

Kristopher left cash on his table and stood, settling a straw hat on his head. I had just rung up the sale of all three Knott's pie pans to a gentleman, so I already stood near the door.

"I hope you enjoyed your lunch," I said as Kristopher neared me.

"I did, thank you." He cleared his throat and shoved his hands in the pockets of his khakis. "Did Abe, uh, tell you about our gathering this afternoon?"

Why did he seem nervous? "Yes. Thank you for the invitation. We'll see you there."

His eyebrows rose. "Oh! Well, good, then." He hurried out.

Had he expected me to make an excuse about why I couldn't make it? I shook my head as the cowbell jangled with someone new pushing through the door. I smiled.

"Welcome, Quinton." I'd been about to address him as "Mr. Blake" but changed course at the last minute.

"Hello, Robbie." He removed a Cardinals ball cap and smoothed thick brown hair back into place. Today he wore a plaid button-down shirt tucked into much newer jeans than he'd worn previously.

"Are you here for lunch?" I asked.

"Yes, please."

"You can sit wherever a table is empty and set." I gestured.

"Thank you. I'm actually meeting someone." His gaze roved over the restaurant until his expression lit up brighter than a Roman candle.

I turned to see the source of the joy. A beaming Corrine was half out of her chair, waving at Quinton, who now hurried toward her. *Seriously?* If that wasn't an interesting matchup, I didn't know what was. But it made me smile. Last Christmas Danna had discovered her half-brother, Corrine's son, whom she'd given up for adoption soon after his birth. If Corrine and Quinton became a

long-lasting thing, Danna would gain a stepsister, too. I
knew she would love that.

Corrine had already eaten. I gave Quinton and her a
few minutes to catch up before I wandered over there.
The two held hands atop the table and murmured quietly.

"Would you like to order, Quinton?" I asked.

"Yes, thank you. The Cajun shrimp sound good."

"You got it. Coffee?"

"No, thank you. Just water."

I handed his order to Turner, but my brain was in over-
drive all of a sudden. Hearing his low, resonant voice had
shot me back to the antiques barn. He'd spoken about
poker and had condemned gambling. I reached for a glass
and filled it with ice water. Pat was his mother. Was his
negative take on poker because of the poker scheme? He
had to know something of it. Maybe not the cheating part.
Certainly the betting aspect.

After I set down water at their table, I cleared my
throat. "I'm sorry to disturb you, Quinton, but I have
something important I need to ask you."

He gazed somberly at me, his brown eyes as intent as
his daughter's had been when I'd first met her. "Go
ahead."

"No worries, hon." Corrine looked up with her thousand-
watt smile. "Pull up a seat."

"Thank you." I sank onto the edge of the chair across
from her, but I focused on him. "When we spoke in the
antiques barn, you seemed very down on poker and gambling."

"I am."

"Is that because you saw firsthand the effect of the
gambling operation the local women were running?" I

asked in a soft voice, even though no other diners sat near us. "Your mom and others?"

He stared at the table for a moment, then straightened his spine. "Yes. Exactly. Here's how it is."

Corrine squeezed his hand but stayed quiet. I glanced around. Turner and Len had the restaurant under control. I waited, the muted sounds of my livelihood all around. Diners conversed, dishes clinked, burgers sizzled—a lovely chorus. Quinton took a deep breath and let it out.

"This beautiful lady knows the whole story." He tilted his head toward Corrine. "I didn't have an easy childhood. My father was murdered. My mother was . . . well, anyway, I got into trouble as a young man. I own responsibility for what I did. I got myself straightened out while I was still living at home, before I moved out and got married. When I was younger, I knew Mom and the ladies had their Stitch and Bitch group. It wasn't until I was an adult that I realized what was really going on." He drained half his glass of water.

Again I waited. After what seemed like a long period of silence but might have been only half a minute, I asked, "And what was going on?"

"They were ripping people off. They all would stitch— and bitch—for the first hour, then they'd pull out the cards and poker chips. Mom and Ms. Russo—Nanette—rigged the card games."

"Did they always meet at one person's home?" I asked.

"The three ringleaders rotated."

I had my mouth open to ask another question when Corrine nudged him.

"Mom, Nanette, and Vi Perkell," Quinton said. "And, no, I didn't go to the police."

He was a mind reader, too. I gave him what I hoped was an understanding look. "Pat was your mom. You couldn't turn her in."

"Right." He looked relieved I hadn't accused him of anything. He went on. "Plus, I'd already been in trouble with the cops. At the time I figured they'd assume I was part of the ring. Instead I moved out. I got married, we had a high-needs daughter, my wife left, and here we are."

Here we were, indeed. I stood. "Thank you for being honest with me. I appreciate that more than you can know."

"I've been honest about everything for twenty years. It's the only way to live." He peered up into my face. "Let me say one more thing. Despite her flaws, my mother is a devoted grandmother. She spends time with Melissa, and frankly, I need Mom's help. Corrie here knows how hard single parenting is."

Corrine nodded. My mom had known, too. The *Ready* bell dinged. The cowbell jangled. My world came back into focus.

"Let me get your lunch, Quinton." And then I had a detective to call.

CHAPTER 48

By three the restaurant door was locked, and my team had gone home. I hit Oscar's number. He didn't pick up, so I left a message.

"Quinton Blake knows details of the gambling scheme. He told me his mom and Nanette cheated the players. Talk to him."

I couldn't do more than that. I'd fixed a grilled cheese sandwich before we cleaned the grill. After I locked the day's till in the safe in my old apartment, I carried the sandwich out to the little patio behind the building, along with a cold Pilsner. I sank into a lawn chair.

It was hard to enjoy this beautiful weather, though, with a homicide hanging unsolved in the air. I itched to make progress. Buck's news from Grant had been shocking. He hadn't had much else to say about it. Grant thinking he'd smelled something was hardly grounds for arrest.

I'd hoped to learn more from Kristopher, but all he'd done was eat and leave—not that I'd expected anything else. I hadn't had a minute to talk with him, but Abe and I would be at his place in a couple of hours. If I needed to slide in a few questions, I could do it then.

I popped in the last bite of sandwich. I did have a couple of things I could do on the case. I looked up Red's senior community in Owensboro and tapped the number. Two minutes later I was reminding him who I was.

He laughed. "I surely recall you, hon. What can I do for you?"

"I wondered if you'd remembered any more details about what happened with Tina Perkell at the school where she was working."

"I didn't remember so much as ask around town. It turns out she was caught necking with that Gale gent on school property."

"'Necking'?" I asked. "Making out?"

"Yes. In the stacks of the library, in full daylight, after school was out for the day. They were possibly in a state of undress."

"Oh, dear. I hope it wasn't a student who saw them."

He laughed. "Thank goodness, no. It was the janitor. But still."

"But it could have been a child, and of course it's inappropriate under any circumstance. Now I understand why they transferred her."

"As do I. Say, I need to be getting off. It's time for my daily swim."

I thanked him and rang off. As I sipped my beer, I

thought. For everyone's sake, I was glad Tina hadn't done anything wrong with or to a child. I had no idea why she and Kristopher were getting intimate in a school library, but a hot romance wasn't a crime, per se. And one small mystery was solved, although why anybody thought a public library was a better situation for her, I couldn't guess.

I gazed at the antique lilac bush next to the door. This was where Birdy had shown up and adopted me right around the time when I'd first opened the store. When he wouldn't go away and acted hungry, I began feeding him. He followed me inside, and that was that. I took him to the vet for a checkup and immunizations. The vet said Birdy hadn't been chipped, so I figured our relationship was meant to be. He definitely had a microchip now.

I found Martin Dettweiler's number and called it. We exchanged greetings for a moment.

"Martin, I'm curious about someone who used to work for your mother at the turkey farm some years ago. I know your wife runs the business now, but would it be possible for me to pay your mother a visit, maybe in a little while?" I would love to work a bike ride into my afternoon before the cookout Abe wanted me to go to.

He was silent for a moment. "Robbie, you could visit her where she rests, but she will be silent. She passed into God's arms these three months ago now."

Oh, no. "I am so very sorry to hear that, Martin. I hadn't heard."

"Mother had not been well. Please don't be distraught. It is a comfort to imagine her smiling down from heaven. And we accompanied her in her last hours on her final earthly journey."

"Well, please accept my condolences."

"I thank you. Now, which employee did you want to ask about?" he asked.

"I don't need to bother you with that."

"It's all right, Robbie, truly."

I cleared my throat. "I heard that Nanette Russo worked in the kitchens."

"Are you on another case?" Martin sounded delighted.

"Sort of, yes."

"I'll have to check the farm's personnel records. Can I get back to you?"

"Sure."

"Is there something in particular you seek to know?"

"I guess any mention of trouble with her. What kind of worker she was. Nothing specific." This was kind of a fool's errand, anyway. What, would he have a record of Nanette stealing turkey lacers years ago? And what did it matter? She could always buy some at the store.

"I shall investigate forthwith."

"I appreciate it, Martin. And thank you."

"Are you in need of any more honey?"

"I think we're good for now." The jars, from small to large, were a popular purchase from my retail area. I didn't stock a lot of items besides the cookware, but I liked to support the small-scale farmers and artisans of the area. I also sold maple syrup from Turner's parents' tree farm, the wool from Aunt Adele's sheep, greeting cards illustrated by Brown County artists, and a few other locally made products.

We said our good-byes and disconnected. That field trip was off, but I could still drive home and get out for a ride. A crow flapped onto a low branch of the redbud tree in the yard. It scratched out a series of caws as it trained its eerily yellow eye on me, making me shudder.

I glanced at the big barn at the end of the drive as I sipped my beer. I'd used it as a garage and all-purpose storage when I'd lived here, and as a workshop while I was renovating the run-down store into the gem it was today. With a cabinetmaker mom, I'd grown up knowing how to use carpentry tools. I knew the only way I could afford to fix up the store after I bought it was to do the work myself, so I had. I'd done the majority of the work upstairs on the B&B rooms, too.

I remembered I'd left an end table in the barn. The table, about twenty-four inches tall, was a garage-sale find that needed refinishing. It wasn't one of my mom's, but I really liked the Art Deco lines of the piece and the blue glass that formed the top. Summer was the best time to use furniture strippers. You could work outdoors and let the chemical odors float away. And maybe the rote motions of removing the old varnish would let ideas about a solution to Vi's homicide rise up in my brain.

Phone stashed in my pocket, I fished my keys out of my bag and headed to the barn, unlocking and sliding open the large door. I'd never kept it locked until a very bad person had used a tunnel that ran underground between here and one of my B&B rooms, a tunnel constructed in a previous century. I hadn't known about it when I bought the property. If the selling agent had been aware of it, she hadn't told me. The passageway was now closed off on both ends, but I kept the barn door locked for good measure.

Inside, I stepped out of the sunshine to the right and let my eyes adjust to the dimness. A few slivers of light slid in between the ill-fitting vertical sheathing boards that formed the walls, illuminating specks of dust floating like tiny fairies. The only window was high on the back wall, its light shaded by the tall old trees behind the barn.

The table was in here somewhere. I skirted a pile of old boards I'd ripped out during the remodel and never gotten around to disposing of. I moved carefully, since nails stuck up out of some.

At a noise from behind me, I whipped my head around. *What?* Was someone there? Then I laughed. It was only the crow who had followed me. It waddled a few steps into the doorway and cocked its head, keeping watch. I resumed my search.

Ah, there was the table. I bent over and swiped at the dust that coated the glass. At another noise, I stilled my hand. That sound had not been made by a crow. Unless crows stifled sneezes.

I picked up the table by the ends and whirled in one move, holding it across me as a shield.

From a yard away, Pat Blake stretched her hands toward my neck. "I told you to butt out, Robbie."

CHAPTER 49

"What do you mean?" My breath came almost as fast as my heart thudded. I took a step back. "Butt out of what?"

She matched my step. Her big, meaty hands reached for my throat. Her face was a dark mask of anger.

"Stop this, Pat." I swallowed. "I don't know what you're doing, but it's wrong. You're wrong." I had my phone, but I couldn't call for help while I held the table. And it was my only protection right now. "I don't know anything."

"As if."

I leaned back and extended the table away from me with sweaty palms, gripping my shield as tightly as I could. At least she wasn't gripping a gun, although she wore a long-strapped bag across her chest, and it looked heavy—like maybe it held a weapon.

"You're trying to put a sick old lady behind bars." She bit off her words. "I won't have it."

"What are you talking about? I can't put anyone in jail." Even if Buck and Oscar might be on that very path.

"I heard you going on with the mayor about Frank," Pat snarled. "I didn't kill him, you know. I was cleared."

"Of course." I took another step, but nearly fell over backward. Something half my height blocked my way. A desk? I tried to remember what else I'd stashed in this part of the barn. Maybe it was the antique blanket chest that sat atop the tunnel's trapdoor.

"I will not let Nanette be accused of murder." Pat's voice wobbled, a crack in her bravado. "My sister is the only person I've ever really loved."

I almost let go of the table. "She's your sister?"

"Half-sister. She's sick, and she's addicted. And you're trying to destroy her."

"I'm not, truly." The addiction had to be to gambling. "She can get help for her addiction."

"You shut up, Robbie Jordan," she growled. "You don't know the first thing about her private business or mine."

"Of course not." I mustered a faint smile. "And I don't want to. If you turn around and leave, I'll forget this ever happened. I promise."

"Sure, you will. As if." She stared daggers at me. "No, you'll call it in and have me busted for assault. Or much worse. Drop the table, Robbie."

That was so not happening. It was my protection, my only weapon. I had a life to get back to. A husband and a family. A business. With any luck, a baby or two. "Did you kill Vi?"

Her nostrils flared. "I said, drop it."

The table or the subject? Both, I guessed. "Sorry. Can't do that."

Pat was tall. She had extra-long arms. She made a quick move to grab me. She reached my throat and squeezed. A lifelong athlete, she had a grip to match, despite being over seventy. I tried to twist away. She kept her hold on my throat, even though she was forced to lean forward a little. Two of the short table legs pointed at her torso.

"Let go." My voice rasped.

She only squeezed harder.

I couldn't swallow. My vision started to blur. I had to do something, fast. I took in the deepest breath I could and tightened my abs. I summoned all my strength, pushing back against the chest behind me and forcing the table at her. The legs hit her in the solar plexus and below her waist. I pulled back and jabbed again. I put all my weight into it.

She cried out. Her hands dropped. She clutched her midsection.

I flipped the legs down and pushed her back with the top edge.

"Stop," she cried. For the first time, she sounded her age. She twisted sideways, her eyes on the door.

I didn't stop. I pushed her once more. She lost her balance and fell on her side atop the pile of boards. On the nails, rusty but still sharp. She screamed. A sharp report sounded, with a *thud* and an explosion of splinters in the old wood of the barn floor.

I dropped the table and raced toward the doorway, where afternoon sunlight had never looked so good. A puncture wound from a couple of old nails was unlikely to kill her. Let the authorities rescue her. Give her a tetanus shot along with a pair of handcuffs. I slid the door shut and locked it, shaky fingers fumbling with the key. My legs suddenly wobblier than a gel pillow, I slid to the ground, my back against the door. I leaned my head on my knees for a moment.

My avian observer, the crow, now sat on a fallen branch a few yards away. It stared at me. I waited until I had strength and breath enough to pull out my phone. The bird took two steps, then flapped away.

"I'd like to report an assault and attempted murder," my voice rasped. "Please let Lieutenant Bird know, ASAP."

CHAPTER 50

First came the sirens, with a lights-blazing cruiser roaring down the drive. Oscar jogged toward the barn after it. An ambulance pulled up behind the panda car. I'd told the dispatcher Pat would need one.

"Robbie Jordan?" the first officer asked, her serious-looking firearm at her side.

"That's me." I didn't budge from my seat on the ground. "The woman who attacked me is inside."

"Pat Blake attacked you," Oscar said.

"Yes. She surprised me in there, tried to choke me. But I got away."

The officer attempted to slide open the door.

"Wait. It's locked." My shakes were gone, but my legs were still weak. "Give me a hand up, and I'll open the door for you."

Germophobe Oscar kept his hand at his side, but the

officer extended hers. I stood. An EMT hurried to my side.

"I'm fine." I pulled out the key and turned it in the lock. "But I pushed Pat onto a pile of lumber with rusty nails sticking out of it. After she tried to choke me."

The first officer lifted her weapon toward the door. "Is she armed, Ms. Jordan?"

"I think she has a gun in her bag. It went off after she fell, but she didn't threaten me with any weapon except her hands." I sank down to sit again, my legs all jelly at the thought sinking in, finally. *A gun.* If Pat had aimed it on me instead of trying to choke me, I could be dead right now.

The EMT squatted next to me.

I waved him away. "I just need a minute." To the officer, I said, "Pat is over seventy, but she's in good physical shape." I had no idea if that was the kind of thing Oscar would have briefed them on—or even would have noticed.

"Thank you," she said.

"She's off to the right," I said in a rush. "Or she was when I left. It's dim in there, so you might want a light or time to let your eyes adjust."

"Miss, I'd like to make sure you are well," the EMT said.

"All right, but I'm going to go sit down." I let him help me up.

"Can I give you a hand walking?"

I headed on wobbly legs toward my patio. "Thanks, but I think I'll be all right." I sank onto the chair I'd vacated what seemed like both minutes and hours ago.

The EMT followed me, red bag in hand.

The second officer slid open the barn door and lifted

his gun in both hands. Both officers rushed in. I heard a shout of, "Police! Freeze." Oscar drew a weapon out of a side holster under his jacket and followed them. The second EMT hovered near the door but didn't enter.

My EMT buddy shined a little light in my eyes and took my pulse. "Does it hurt to swallow?"

I tried. "A tiny bit."

He ran a fancy thermometer across my forehead to check my temperature.

"Really, I'm fine," I said. "My throat's a little sore, but I didn't hit my head or anything."

"Glad to hear it. You're good to go. Please don't hesitate to call your primary care physician or the emergency department if you experience adverse symptoms."

"I promise."

He took his bag and joined his colleague outside the barn. I waited. Buck hadn't appeared. With any luck, he had Nanette in custody. I still didn't know which of the pair had killed Vi, but both were clearly implicated.

My phone buzzed with a text from Abe.

Are you coming home? The gathering is in an hour. And I miss you.

Gah. The bluegrass party. I tapped out a reply but chose my words with care. I didn't want to alarm him.

I might be late. I'm fine, but something came up here. I heard sirens. What's going on?

I was still reading his message when my phone rang.

"Robbie, darling," Abe said. "What happened? Are you sure you're okay?"

"I'm okay. Just a little shaken. I was getting an end table out of the barn, that one I want to refinish. Pat Blake came in and tried to choke me."

His gasp was audible. Oscar emerged from the barn

and spoke to the EMTs, who hurried in. The detective spied me and started toward where I sat.

"I pushed her away and locked her in the barn," I said. "I'm fine, sweetheart, honestly."

"I've never been happier to hear those words. Do you want me to come and get you?"

"Thank you, but no. Oscar needs to talk with me, and I'll lock up and drive home as soon as he's done. Okay? Go ahead to the cookout without me if you want."

"Are you kidding? I'll wait, wife of mine, and if you're not up for it, we won't go."

"You're the best." I held up a finger to the detective. "I have to go. Oscar's here."

"I love you."

"I love you, too." I disconnected. "How is Pat, Oscar?"

"In custody." He perched on the edge of the chair. "I'm sure you know the drill by now. Give me a thumbnail at this time of what happened, what she said. Tomorrow please visit the SLPD and make a formal statement."

I opened my mouth to respond, but he held up his hand.

"Also, I'm sorry you had to endure an attack. We were very close to detaining Ms. Blake. She, ah, evaded the officer assigned to track her movements."

"Do you think she killed Vi? I asked her, but of course she didn't admit to it."

"All in due time. So . . . ?"

"Okay." I kind of thought I deserved an answer after what I'd been through, but whatever. "I went into the barn. I left the door wide open. I had my back to it, looking for a small table I wanted to take home. I heard a stifled sneeze. Pat has bad allergies, in case you didn't know. She was right behind me." I shuddered, remembering. "I turned, keeping the table between us."

"What did she say?" He clasped his hands on his knees, rocking a little, as was his habit.

"She said I had been butting into her business." The words poured out. I so wanted to get this over with. "She told me Nanette is ill and addicted. I assume she meant to gambling. Did you know they are half-sisters?"

"I certainly did not."

"Me neither. Pat said Nanette is her half-sister, and she would not see her behind bars. She seemed to think I could make that happen. I assured her I couldn't." I filled him in on her attacking me in the barn. "After I pushed her away and she fell, a gun fired from her bag. The shot hit the floor, not me or her. That's all." I got shaky all over again thinking about my close call. My throat thickened, and my hands grew clammy.

Oscar peered at me. "Hey now, you take a few nice, deep breaths, okay, Robbie? We don't want you passing out. Maybe hang your head between your knees."

I made myself relax my shoulders. I reminded myself I was safe. A couple of deep breaths in through my nose and out through my mouth did the trick.

The officers walked Pat out, her hands cuffed behind her back. Her shirt was rolled halfway up on her right side, revealing a bulky bandage. The crossbag was nowhere in sight. The EMTs and their bags followed as the officers escorted her to the ambulance. She caught sight of me and glared, then lifted her chin and looked away.

"Thank you, Robbie. You take care now." Oscar rose. "I'll be in touch." He hurried toward his colleagues.

Abe rushed around the edge of the building. I stood, letting him fold his arms around me.

"I had to come," he whispered.

"I'm so glad you did," I murmured into his shoulder. "Let's get out of here."

I let the back door slam behind us. I didn't need to watch them all drive away. I didn't need to lock my barn, which was now a crime scene. I didn't need to talk with a detective. All I needed to do was get us both to the safety and comfort of home.

CHAPTER 51

At home I showered after being the beneficiary of lots of affection, both human and feline.

"Forget the party," Abe insisted as I towel-dried my hair. "We don't need to go. I don't need to be there."

"Abe, honey, I'm fine to go out." Admittedly, I was still a bit shaky. The visual of being attacked kept rerunning in my head. The thought of almost dying by gunshot, of losing my happy future, slammed me over and over. But it was all the more reason to be distracted by food and music. If we stayed home, I would keep rerunning the scene in my head, which was the last thing I wanted to do. Pat was in custody. Nanette probably was, as well. Their sad story was over. It was time for me to move on.

"We have to eat, anyway." I knew how much he loved music jam sessions. "And it's still such a nice day."

"Are you sure?" He cupped my chin in his hand and examined my face.

"Yes." At least, I thought I was. I found a turquoise silk scarf that felt like air to wrap around my neck. Bruises were already surfacing.

I sat at the edge of Kristopher's yard two hours later. With a belly full of grilled kielbasa and several salads, I held a red plastic cup of IPA and tapped my toe to the jam session. Abe picked his banjo, and Kristopher pulled and squeezed his accordion, with a fiddler, a guitar player, another banjo plucker, and an upright bassist playing along. Various spouses and significant others sat around. On the periphery of the yard, two dads played badminton with the half-dozen children who had come with their parents. It was a perfect summer's evening. I was glad I'd come.

Tina, wearing a flowered knit sundress that looked like it could have come out of the children's department, approached me with a hesitant air. "Can I join you, Robbie?" she asked in her tiny, high voice.

I gestured to the empty chair next to me.

"I got a call from the police," she began. "They said they believe they have my mother's murderer in custody."

"That's great news." I certainly hadn't gotten any call. "Who is it?"

"They didn't say. You haven't heard?"

"Why would I?" I took a sip of beer.

"I know you're kind of a private detective." She kneaded her hands, not looking at me. "And I know you've been asking questions about my brother and me."

What she didn't seem to know was that Pat had attacked me. I waited.

"We have our problems, Upton and me. But I want you to know that we loved our mother. We never would have hurt her."

"I'm glad to hear that." I watched Kristopher's fingers fly over the little white buttons on the left side of his red instrument as his other hand pressed the piano-like keys on the right side, pulling and squeezing all the while. Accordion players needed amazing motor dexterity.

She saw where I was looking. "And Kris wouldn't have hurt her, either."

I gazed at her face. "How do you know?"

"He told me!"

Yeah, that's always a reliable measure of the truth. It was time to change the subject.

"I'm glad to hear that," I said. "Do you live here, too? Or is Kristopher on his own?"

She smiled to herself. "He's invited me to move in. But I work in Boonville. It's over an hour's drive away."

"I heard you're a librarian. I'm a big reader. What kinds of books do you like?"

She launched into a list of recent women's fiction and historical novels.

Whew. The subject stayed changed until she excused herself to bring dessert out from the house. I didn't offer to help. I'd had my quota of helping for the day, locking Pat in the barn. And more.

I smiled as I watched the children running around. Yes, I would like more than one child with Abe, sooner or later. We could raise a whole passel of them. Start our own bluegrass group, not that I played an instrument. They would learn to cook from both of us. I could add a baby bike seat to my cycle and take him or her for windy rides. Abe could teach our little ones how to track in the woods and, after a while, shoot with a bow and arrow. Maybe Sean would even do some babysitting if he was willing.

The bassist crooned about losing his darling. Abe sang harmony in his rich baritone. I sipped and tapped my hand on my skirt and did not think about murder.

CHAPTER 52

In my store at eight o'clock, Abe handed me a mug with a healthy helping of Four Roses. After the cookout, he'd offered to help do prep for tomorrow so both of us could get home sooner.

"Here you are, my love," he said. "You earned it."

"You're not having any?" I asked.

He shook his head. "Designated driver. But I am good at mixing pancake ingredients."

"Or doing napkin rolls?"

"That, too." He grabbed the silverware caddy and took it to the nearest table. A knock at the door came before he sat. "I'll get it."

"That should be Buck. He said he'd drop by and fill us in."

But it wasn't my favorite police lieutenant. Instead, Phil handed Abe his armful of desserts.

"I'll get the rest." In a minute he was back.

"Thanks, my friend," I said. "Grab a drink if you want." To Abe, I added, "We can leave the door unlocked. In fact, only the screen door is fine. The air feels so nice." With the current and present danger in custody, I felt safe once again.

After the sweets were safely in the walk-in, Phil pulled up a chair and poured a little bourbon for himself.

"I thought you were going to be Buck," I said.

"Robbie, I will never be tall enough to be Buck."

I giggled. "No, I guess not."

"Or white enough." He grabbed a napkin and rolled with Abe. "So, why is Buck coming by?"

I sobered as I cut butter into the biscuit mix. "It appears they solved the case."

"That's good," Phil said. "Isn't it?"

"Of course," I said. "But nobody's told me any details of what's going on."

"And Robbie was assaulted out back today," Abe added.

"No!" Phil exclaimed with a worried look. "Are you okay?"

"I'm fine."

"My amazing wife locked her attacker in the barn," Abe said. "They should tell her if Pat Blake was also a murderer. Robbie deserves to know."

I nodded. Didn't I? All week, I'd passed along everything I'd learned. Oscar had actually asked for my help, or as good as. Maybe I'd finally overstepped my bounds as a private citizen, though. This morning, the last time I had seen Buck, he'd been upset with me for withholding the folder overnight. I'd thought we were friends. I hoped I hadn't damaged that.

As I worked, I thought about what a long, sad story Nanette and Pat had. One woman with an addiction to gambling. The other, deeply caring, who enabled her sister rather than getting help for her. Nanette ill, possibly terminally. And now both of them in deep trouble with the authorities for what they had done.

I'd finished the biscuit dough and was starting on dry ingredients for pancake mix when a uniformed Buck finally appeared. Hat in hand, he moseyed over to me. Was that a sheepish look he wore? Maybe I wasn't in the doghouse, after all.

"Evenin', Robbie. Howdy there, fellas."

"Have a seat, Buck." I gestured with my chin toward the table. "The bourbon's open if you're off-duty."

"As a matter of fact, I am, despite my getup. Mainly I'm glad you're all right." He grabbed a mug and sat with the guys. Buck poured in barely a shot's worth and raised his mug. "Here's to another wrap."

I didn't care how much flour I had on my hands, I lifted my mug along with Phil. Abe raised his water bottle.

"I got to thank you, Robbie," Buck began. "For your bravery and guts, nabbing Pat like you did."

"To Robbie," Phil said.

"Well, it was self-preservation, but thank you." I sipped, letting the bourbon warm me all the way down. "I didn't so much nab her as escape from her. Oscar said someone was assigned to tail Pat, but she got away from them."

"She did, at that." Buck took the tiniest of drinks.

"So, did she kill Vi?" I asked.

"No, but she knew all about it," Buck said. "She's an accomplice to Nanette Russo, the poor thing."

So it had been Nanette all along.

"You're pitying a murderer?" Abe tilted his head, his question less a challenge than a curious inquiry.

"The lady's dying of cancer," Buck replied. "Of course she's a criminal, O'Neill, on a couple few fronts, and misguided. I can still feel sorry for her in my heart."

He was not alone in feeling sorry for her. I was right there with him. I gazed at Buck fondly. He did have a big heart, and it seemed our friendship was intact, too. "Pat said they were half-sisters. Quinton didn't seem to know Nanette was his aunt."

"Maybe she never told him," Phil said. "They might have found each other as adults, like Danna and her brother."

I nodded.

"Do they look alike?" Abe asked.

I thought. "Not really, other than being on the tall side, and lean. But you don't look much like your brother, either, and you're not even half-siblings."

Abe laughed. "True enough."

"I surely didn't have no idea about them two being kin," Buck said.

"Buck," I began, "you said Nanette was a criminal on a couple of fronts. Was the notebook helpful to you?"

"It surely was, hon. They was cheating folks from way back."

Which Quinton had also confirmed.

"Did Vi know about it?" Abe asked.

"It seems she did." Buck took another tiny sip. "But she'd asked to get out of the scam 'long about a decade ago. As you know, she stole that folder from Nanette's room. My pop told me she was upset that the gambling was still going. She planned on going public about it, confront Nanette in the dining room or some such."

"How did you learn for sure the murderer was Nanette?" I asked.

Buck stretched out his legs. "After I heared about Pat being apprehended, I took myself over to Jupiter Springs and asked Nanette. She fessed up to stabbing poor old Vi with one of them turkey needles you told us about."

I blew out a breath. "And your dad heard her and picked up on her scent."

"Yup. Nanette said she only has a month or two to live and didn't care," he continued. "She seems to be going downhill fast."

"May her transition be an easy one," Phil murmured.

Amen. Even if it happened with a prison guard outside her room.

"Did you ever speak with Melissa?" I asked Buck.

"I stopped by, but she was doing an activity, and then I got busy."

"And now you won't need to question her, I hope," I said.

Buck shook his head. "We can leave the girl be. Don't want to be upsetting her any more than she will be when her grandma goes away for a good long spell."

"I'm glad you won't have to."

"Did you or Oscar ever figure out who sent Robbie the threatening text?" Abe asked.

"Appears to have been Pat Blake," Buck said. "Nanette and her were onto Robbie's investigation pretty early."

"It wasn't much of an investigation." I dusted off my hands and went to Buck's side. I laid my hand on his shoulder. "Did Nanette also kill your mom?"

He gazed at the table for a moment, then looked up. "Nope. That would be Pat Blake herself. In Mom's case, Nanette was the accomplice."

"But why?" I asked. "Why would she kill Yolande? I thought they were all friends, wives and mothers."

"My grandma Simone said Mom didn't approve of their gambling business. She'd only figured it out on that Floyds Knobs jaunt of theirs and was about to go to the police about it." He shook his head. "Quite a pair, them two. Nanette and Pat."

The two cheaters who could trust each other. I wrinkled my nose. "One of the first times I met Nanette, she said something about getting rid of her husband. I assumed she meant divorce. Did she kill him, too?"

"I do believe old Oscar is looking into that. At this point, nothing much would surprise me." Buck stood. "I thank you kindly for the drink. My sainted wife is eager to see me again, as you might imagine."

"I should think so." I also rose. "Thanks for filling in the gaps, Buck."

"We've still got the odd few loose threads to tie up, but the case is basically solved, as of tonight."

"That's a relief." Abe squeezed my hand.

And it was. Abe had never tried to stop me from investigating, but I knew he worried—rightly so—when I did.

"Please bring Mrs. Bird in to eat one day," I told Buck. "I'd love to meet her."

"I might, at that," Buck said. "That's a distinct possibility. I know you two would get along better than gravy on biscuits."

He said good night to Abe and Phil, and I walked him to the door.

"How's your Adele doing off in wherever the heck she is?" Buck asked, hat in hand.

"She's fine. Samuel was a bit sick, but he's recovered. They'll both be home tomorrow."

"Glad to hear it. It don't seem right, old folks gallivanting all over the world like they do."

I laughed. "They love it. Travel's a good thing, Buck. Widens your horizons."

"We'll see about that. Me, I'm content to glue myself as close to home as the front gate." He pulled open the screen door and trotted down the steps.

I stepped out onto the porch after him into a lovely twilight. I was happy to be at home, too. For the moment, the humidity was mostly gone and the oppressive heat along with it. And with any luck, murder was also vanquished. At least for now.

RECIPES

Yankerdoodles

Robbie serves these delicious cookies at the Fourth of July get-together before the book opens, and then Phil brings in another batch.

This recipe was adapted with permission from the author's Hoosier sister, Barbara Bergendorf, who sells her popular snickerdoodle cookies in the greater Lafayette area. (Please contact Maddie via her website if you want to find out where to purchase these treats.)

Ingredients
1½ sticks butter at room temperature
1 cup brown sugar
½ cup white sugar
2 eggs
1 teaspoon vanilla
1 teaspoon baking soda
1 teaspoon salt
3½ cups unbleached white flour
Cinnamon and sugar
Red and blue sprinkles

Directions
Preheat oven to 350°F. Line two baking sheets with parchment paper. Cream butter and sugars. Add eggs and vanilla. Mix well. Mix soda and salt into flour, then add the flour mixture at a low speed until blended. Chill dough for thirty to sixty minutes. Form spoonfuls into one-inch-diameter balls and roll in cinnamon and sugar mix. Flatten with a fork and add blue and red sprinkles. Bake at 350° about 10 minutes or until just barely tan.

Spanish Gazpacho

This no-cook cold soup is perfect for a refreshing summer meal, but please wait for local tomatoes to be available. Robbie and the gang serve bottles of hot sauce on the tables for Hoosiers with more adventurous palates.

Ingredients

2 pounds ripe local Roma-style tomatoes, halved and cored (remove seeds and any white core)

1 small cucumber, peeled, seeded, and roughly chopped

1 medium green bell pepper, cored and roughly chopped

2 small garlic cloves (or 1 large clove), peeled and roughly chopped

3 tablespoons olive oil

2 tablespoons sherry vinegar

1 teaspoon fine sea salt

$\frac{1}{2}$ teaspoon freshly ground black pepper

$\frac{1}{2}$ teaspoon ground cumin

1 thick slice of good bread, soaked in water for three seconds, then wrung out

Optional garnishes: homemade croutons, chopped fresh herbs, a drizzle of olive oil, or any leftover chopped gazpacho ingredients

Directions

Combine all ingredients in a blender or food processor. Purée for 1 minute, or until the soup reaches desired consistency. Taste and season with extra salt, pepper, and/or cumin if needed. Refrigerate in a sealed container for 3 to 4 hours, or until completely chilled.

Serve cold, topped with desired garnishes.

Summer Crêpes

Turner makes these popular thin pancakes rolled around an herbed mushroom, shallot, and Gruyère mix. Diners could also choose to have them with fresh berries and powdered sugar.

Crêpes:
Ingredients
1 cup unbleached white flour
2 eggs
½ cup whole milk
½ cup water
1/4 teaspoon salt
2 tablespoons melted butter
Mild oil or spray

Directions
Whisk together flour and eggs. Gradually beat in milk and water. Add the salt and butter. Beat until smooth. Heat crêpe pan or other flat nonstick or seasoned skillet over medium-high heat. Use a paper towel to wipe pan with a mild oil or spray it with oil.

Pour 1/4 cup of batter in pan and swirl to thinly cover the bottom. Cook for about two minutes until bottom is lightly brown, then flip.

Remove to a plate when done and keep warm. Repeat. Fill immediately before eating.

Note: Crêpes freeze well. Stack cooked and cooled crêpes with a piece of parchment paper between each. Seal well in a ziplock bag or wrap tightly with plastic wrap. To thaw, place in refrigerator overnight or leave at room temperature for two to three hours.

Savory Filling:
Ingredients
2 tablespoons butter
12 ounces mushrooms, cleaned and sliced
1 shallot, peeled and minced
½ teaspoon fresh thyme
½ teaspoon fresh rosemary, minced
Salt and paper to taste
½ pound Gruyère cheese, grated

Directions
   Melt the butter in a skillet and sauté the mushrooms and shallot until tender. Remove from heat. Add herbs and salt and pepper to taste. Spread two tablespoons on a crêpe, sprinkle on cheese, and fold into thirds over filling.

Sweet Filling:
Ingredients
1 cup blueberries
1 cup strawberries, rinsed, hulled, and sliced
1 teaspoon granulated sugar
Powdered sugar

Directions
   Toss fruit with granulated sugar and let sit 15 minutes. Spread two tablespoons on a crêpe and fold into thirds over filling. Sprinkle with powdered sugar.

Cold Corn Salad

Robbie and her team offer this cool salad as a hot-weather lunch special. It's best with freshly picked local produce.

Ingredients

3 ears fresh sweet corn, lightly steamed and cut off the cob
1 cucumber, peeled and diced
1 cup cherry tomatoes
2 tablespoons fresh basil leaves, cut into 1/8-inch ribbons
2 tablespoons olive oil
1 tablespoon fresh lemon juice
Salt and pepper to taste

Directions

Combine all ingredients and lightly toss.

Orzo Salad

Abe makes this easy side dish for a Sunday night dinner.

Ingredients
3 cups cooked orzo, tossed while warm with 1
    tablespoon olive oil
½ cup pitted Kalamata olives, halved
½ cup sliced marinated artichoke hearts
Fresh basil leaves, slivered
2 tablespoons olive oil
1 tablespoon freshly squeezed lemon juice

Instructions
Toss all ingredients and serve at room temperature.
Option: Add other Mediterranean vegetables like halved
cherry tomatoes, diced red sweet pepper, or diced roasted
eggplant.

Blueberry–White Wine Spritzer

Robbie loves a spritzer to cool off with at the end of a steamy July day.

Ingredients
Pinot grigio, well chilled
Fresh blueberries
Mint leaves
Lime seltzer

Instructions
For one drink, muddle a dozen blueberries and three mint leaves with a teaspoon of sugar in bottom of a wide glass. Stir in four ounces white wine. Add ice, top with seltzer, and sprinkle on a dozen more whole blueberries.

Connect with Us

Visit us online at
KensingtonBooks.com
to read more from your favorite authors, see books
by series, view reading group guides, and more.

for sneak peeks, chances to win books and prize packs,
and to share your thoughts with other readers.

facebook.com/kensingtonpublishing
twitter.com/kensingtonbooks

Tell us what you think!

To share your thoughts, submit a review,
or sign up for our eNewsletters, please visit:
KensingtonBooks.com/TellUs.